NIGHTWOLF

A NOVEL
BY WILLIE DAVIS

7.13 BOOKS
BROOKLYN, NY

"Even among *Nightwolf*'s vivid landscape of smart-assed car thieves, bruised oracles, and horribly-named bar bands, Willie Davis's tender, witty voice utterly steals this show. Every page of this brilliant, tough-willed novel is so alive with laughter, vulgarity, insight, wonder, wisdom, and heartbreak, often within the same impossible breath. What a book."
—Mike Scalise, author of *The Brand New Catastrophe*

"Davis, a master of wit, one-liners and dead on observations, has done everything right. *Nightwolf*, often funny and always smart, is told through the eyes of Milo, a devastatingly funny and keen social critic. And through him, this story of Kentucky and youth and angst and self-discovery gleams."
—Natashia Deón, author of *Grace*

"This is a story of profound loss—missing mothers, brothers, babies, hearts—populated by trash-talking, drug-addled, thieving, violent, wickedly funny, elegiac, fail and fail better prophets and preachers. Part Elmore Leonard, part Padgett Powell, part Eugene Ionesco if he'd trained his eye on the seediest corner of Lexington, Kentucky, Davis is a wildfire talent who understands there is no end to seeking, only endless reckoning with desire and mystery."
—Maud Casey, author of *The Man Who Walked Away*

"*Nightwolf* is by turns hilarious and tragic, acerbic and tender, despairing and triumphant—and brilliant withal. Willie Davis's kick-ass debut novel heralds the arrival of a major new talent."
—Ed McClanahan, author of *The Natural Man*

"The reader needs to tread carefully or he (or she as the case may be) will wind up as a character in *Nightwolf* and never be seen alive again. Happened to me. *Nightwolf* is delightful, compelling, utterly original, funny as hell, such a bright new light on the literary landscape it makes the turn of the century seem like ancient history. Linguists are applying for NEA grants in such numbers to study *Nightwolf* they have had to resort to handwriting because of declining access to digits."
—Gurney Norman, author of *Divine Right's Trip*, Poet Laureate of Kentucky

"Like a shotgun blast at the moon, Willie Davis's debut novel enters the world. At its heart is Milo Byers, wayward son of Prospect Hill, a derelict Kentucky neighborhood where violence is arbitrary and opportunity nil. Haunted by the memory of a brother who disappeared and caught up in a power struggle between petty criminals, Milo must navigate the injustices of growing up poor in a forgotten place. And yet this isn't your standard coming-of-age fare...Sure, teeth are broken and scars are formed, but Milo manages to laugh at the ridiculousness of it all. He's literary kin to the protagonist in Denis Johnson's *Jesus's Son*—a princely fuck-up and a worthy companion. Tragic, comic, and brilliantly perverse, *Nightwolf* is a bighearted novel heralds the arrival of a gifted storyteller. Read this book."
—Jesse Donaldson, author of *The More They Disappear*

Printed and distributed by 7.13 Books. First paperback edition, first printing: July 2018

Cover design: Matthew Revert
Author photo: Joshua Simpson

ISBN-10:0-9984092-8-6
ISBN-13: 978-0-9984092-8-3

Library of Congress Control Number: 2018944580

For information about permission to reproduce selections from this book, contact the publisher at https://713books.com/

For Jenny. O'Neill. When I was a boy, you named the world to me, animal by animal and vegetable by vegetable. In your voice, it sounded enormous.

PART ONE:
THE EGAN RABBIT

2000 A.D.
LEXINGTON, KENTUCKY

1.

It started with a miracle. It was a useless miracle, but it still counted as a jaw-dropper, a total malfunction of reason and time. That was the year of miracles. We believed the millennium would come baring knives and fangs, ready to carve up our comfort and give us the kick in the ass we needed to embrace the apocalypse. Instead, the year 2000 came as quietly as a twelve-year old sharing a hotel room with his parents, and we had to spend our death wishes elsewhere. People sounded disappointed—almost betrayed—that these next thousand years could resemble the last thousand. No one, not even the believers, called it a miracle.

I can burn my own bushes, so I have no patience for miracles. They are to heavenly grace what writing BOOBS on an upside down calculator is to trigonometry. The long-burning Jew oil and the loaves and fishes felt like a means to prove God can be replaced by a coupon from the Sunday paper. For every leper with his dick reattached, we get four instances of Jesus Christ, supersaver, saying "You bring the water, and we'll throw in the wine for free!"

And still, there's the inexplicable, the slight bending of time and sense. Recounting it, I sound like a child at a magic show, reciting what I saw, knowing it can't be true. In the end, when we somehow survive, we're too busy tallying up the losses to remember we've accomplished something monumental. It takes a lot of delusion to keep up with those fantasies, but, then again, I'm the sort of dumb motherfucker who believes in miracles.

Meander Casey leaned against the side of The Egan Rabbit, a downtown warehouse converted into a space for small shows and hard liquor. He handed out flyers for his brother's band. "Only give them to girls," his brother Corey Casey demanded. "You think I play bass for a bunch of fraternity mouth-breathers?"

"I think you play bass because you can't play guitar," Meander said.

"Guys will come no matter what," Corey said. "Just give them to girls."

Meander knew it didn't matter. People don't notice flyers when their own missing daughter hands them one with her face on it. Anyway, Corey sang for a gutter punk band called The Violators whose amphetamine speed and feedback-from-the-amplifier melodies would treat his lyrics the way an alarm clock treats a dream. Technically, the band's proper name was Senor Low-Penis and The Violators, but when Corey—who had unironic dreams of stardom—joined, he referred to his new running mates only as The Violators to make them sound like respectable punks.

The flyers themselves were pretty things. They had a black-and-white picture of Corey staring directly into the camera with his eyes blacked out. Unlike Meander, Corey got his hair from the white side of their family, and he had it teased into a perfectly coiled cowlick just right of the center of his forehead. The text under his neck read, "Corey Casey is A Violator."

On the previous night, Meander swiped his brother's computer and changed the text to read, "Corey Casey is a Violator of Megan's Law." These were the ones he handed out in front of The Egan Rabbit when I saw him on the night of the show. They still looked to be on the upper end of punk rock flyers, but he'd also written that The Egan Rabbit was "The Rockingest Joint Not Within 200 Yards of a Middle School."

The Rabbit hired Meander because they couldn't make him leave. He was seventeen, not old enough to be a customer, but no matter how many times they shoved him out the door, he'd show up an hour later, sporting the same fake ID, but now with a showy Irish accent. Finally, the owner, Egan Hopper, decided to keep the kid in the back, hand him a mop, and let him work for the half-dozen free drinks a night it took him to pass out. They hired me because I was Meander's friend, but also because I was bigger and looked older. That meant I could work the door or the register. Later, Hallahan, the bouncer, could tell me the make and model car belonging to whichever patron was too drunk to notice. While Meander kept watch, I'd jimmy the door and grab what I could from the glove box and under the seat. This was my audition, and the men at the Rabbit were my judges.

Meander Casey wanted his brother to bring him on as The Violators second drummer. "Each set has something like four or five different drums and the average drummer has two arms," he told me that evening.

Just then, Corey stomped up to us and grabbed his brother by the lapel. "Hey asshole, show me one of your hilarious flyers."

"I'm sorry," Meander said. "I can only give them to girls."

Corey grabbed his brother's nose between his fingers

and bent his head backwards. "This is my *livelihood*."

"Livelihood?" Meander spit at his chest. "I'd rather people think I blew Cub Scouts than play bass for my livelihood."

I wanted to delay their slapfight to when it wouldn't hurt business. The bosses were already in a pissy mood because Nightwolf tagged the side of the bar in big, purple letters. He'd only written his name three times, none of the aphorisms or loose advice he'd scrawled on the downtown businesses.

"Mark it down, Milo," Meander said to me. "Today, October first, my brother hits the zenith of his artistic powers, playing the thirtieth coolest music-joint in Lexington, Kentucky on a Wednesday. As the opening act."

Corey winced. The Violators were opening for Surrender Dorothy, a more successful band. Corey desperately wanted to join the higher profile act, but they needed a bass-player the way most bands needed a second drummer.

The Rabbit only had one rule they enforced. They pinned it to the back room, so it'd be the last thing we saw before we interacted with the public. *Not In Front of The World.* People came into The Rabbit for drink and darkness and anything auxiliary was waste or threat. Fighting out front was a direct violation of this rule, and so were Meander's fake flyers. If we got too out of hand, Hallahan would drag us to the wooded part of Orman Park and trample the bejeezus out of us. Sometimes, Egan would tag me as his bruiser, but he knew I'd go easy on Meander. Anyway, I punched like a flyswatter next to Hallahan, who loved meting out Old Testament-style punishment on our spines.

"You going to Prophet's tonight?" I asked Corey. "Shipment's in."

"That man's a pervert," he said. "A tumor on a herpes

sore on this city that you have to cut out."

"Is that bad?" Meander said "If you have to have herpes, wouldn't you want them on your tumor. Two birds with one—I'm thinking out loud."

"The man is killing you both, and you're too stupid to do anything about it but say thanks." Corey turned to take in the view of a purple-haired girl riding by on her bike. "You go up Prospect Hill, not all of you comes back down."

Corey grabbed his brother by the scruff of his neck and shoved him into the locked side door like he wanted to stamp his face on the metal. He would have done more except I grabbed his right hand and pinned it behind his shoulder blade.

"What's the least number of unbroken fingers you need to play bass?" I said. "I know it's not five."

Corey turned around to smack me in the ear, but Hallahan stepped around the corner, trying to light a Camel. We went silent. Hallahan whistled. When he wanted our attention for his business, he yelled; when he wanted us for Egan's business, he whistled. It was time to get ready for the show.

The crowd was thicker than normal. Egan scoured the customers for moles from the ABC Board. He knew a reckoning was coming, but he didn't care. I admired the attitude, even if it was nestled between drunken madness and drunken stupidity.

Meander and I had to keep eyes on everyone: strangers, friends of the band, each other, and ourselves. It had happened before where the singer's girlfriend puked on stage or the drummer walked out of the bathroom with a gram of coke in his beard. New people were good for when they drank too hard and let the cash and cards slip from their pockets. Old people were good for shielding us from the new people.

The Violators played exclusively to the strangers.

Even if there was only one fresh face in the crowd, Corey made the same jokes before his songs—each time pausing, shrugging, and chuckling like he surprised himself. A veteran of his practiced spontaneity, I could see the wires and trapdoors where the magic should be. He'd hammer the guitar like this music was as inevitable and over- whelming as gravity. The lyrics were dishonest, but not in a useful way.

In the middle of the set, Hallahan smacked me in the back of the head. "Can you watch the door, dummy? Keep your hands in your pockets and look stupid like you've been practicing."

"Where're you going?"

"On a run," he said, meaning he'd shoot down the street to the darkened parking lot to look for overstuffed cars. At this point, he wouldn't take anything. He was out to spy, to see if he could match the cars to the patrons or see if anyone left a purse in plain view. There were four different lots we grabbed from—ours, the one Jerry Marimow's Pub shared with a Christian coffee house, the one by a defunct hotel, and the small one to the side of Orman Park.

When Hallahan went on his runs, I stood by the door, mostly to make sure nobody got a drink spilled on them and ran to the parking lot. Hallahan only carried his phone half the time, so it was a pointless job, but such was life at The Rabbit.

The Violators finished their song, and the guitarist fiddled with a few high notes for the next one. Corey didn't play right away, but instead scanned the crowd with his hand on his forehead. He stepped to the micro- phone but instead of singing, he put up his palm to stop the music. The band, confused, kept playing. This wasn't part of the act.

The drummer stopped, leaving only the guitarist furiously plucking away. "Ladies and gentlemen, if you'll indulge me for a song or two," Corey said. "I'd like to bring my little brother here to help on the drums."

Meander was carrying a tub of glasses backstage when he heard. Almost immediately, he handed the tub to a girl with a homemade leopard print shirt, who had no choice but to take it from him. Meander, who always looked like three parts goat and one part zombie, smiled so large that the strangers in the crowd beside him smiled as well. I ran to the foot of the stage, praying no one would take that moment to wander to the parking lot.

Meander waved to the crowd despite no applause. I heard him ask for the song as he leaned over and reached for one of the spare drumsticks.

"Song's called 'Guitar Heart,'" Corey said into the microphone. "Goes like this." He swung his bass by the neck and slammed it into his brother's chest, sending him sprawling off the stage. Meander fell onto his side and skidded into the leopard-print girl's shins, causing her to drop the tub of glasses on top of him.

For a second, there was no sound except the high notes of the guitar. In an instant, someone would scream, then the crowd would go rabid, half of them tossing bottles and half headed to their cars. If I couldn't control the door, then Hallahan would flog me until my ass was more welt than skin. I'd heard rumors that Heath Rosenbaum, who worked part time at The Rabbit before me, left after Hallahan broke his arm just above the elbow. Hallahan half-liked Heath, and he hated me.

The guitarist was helping. So long as the high notes kept coming, people could believe it was part of the show. I heard myself clapping before I knew why. I tried to get the audience to follow along, but they weren't having it.

I walked on stage. Corey Casey wiped the sweat off his face with his t-shirt. The drummer started hitting the high hat to go along with the guitar. It didn't sound like a song yet. Corey bit his lip and spit on the ground at my toes. I didn't know what to say, so I closed my eyes and put both hands behind my head. The music kept going and I started to hear the pattern—the looping, the hook, and then the chorus. I wanted to hear it one more time, but then he hit me.

I reckoned it would hurt like a cleat to the chest, more of a push than a punch. But Corey must have cocked back and treated my spine like an uncoordinated kid treats a tee-ball stand. It knocked me from the stage, sending me sliding across the floor on top of the leopard girl's spilled glasses. This time people laughed. I rose to my knees. The Violators had started playing a song. They were already on the chorus—I must've lost time. For a moment, the bass stopped, and I heard a loud thump. Someone fell on my ankles. It was Lemon the Soundman, except he was smart about it and landed carefully so as not to cut his hands. He hopped back to his feet, quick as a calico, then lifted me up. There was a small line formed to the side of the stage now, people waiting for Corey to pound the devil out of their chests with his bass.

Lemon yanked me out of the way, just before the drummer for Surrender Dorothy tumbled on top of us. Corey knew better than to hit him like he hit me. Now that it was an act, the crowd bought into it. They were here to see Surrender Dorothy or to get drunk. So long as this was a dance and not a fight, they'd stick to their plans.

I rubbed my eyes. In the line for the stage, I saw Meander, still clutching his chest from the last time. That was his sense of humor and his sense of life—loud and uncomplicated. He laughed at busted noses, a bowl of soup to the face, people being where they shouldn't and falling down when they should stand. Lemon grabbed me by the chin. "The door, numbnuts, the door."

By the time I made it to the doorjamb, my chest was pounding. The pain was shooting from the middle of my breastbone, pushing out to my ears and kneecaps. I pitched forward and spit out a mouthful of blood.

Hallahan walked across the parking lot. A group of three smokers came up to me. "You okay, man?" One of the strangers put a hand on the curve of my neck. He smelled like cherries and menthols.

"He's going to puke," someone said.

"No he's not," said the man holding onto me. "I think he's been—I don't know. Are you okay, buddy?"

Hallahan put a hand on each side of my ribcage and stood me up straight. He couldn't have known he was doing it, but each of his thumbs pressed against the edges of my bruise. "Someone fuck with you, my man?" He spoke delicately, like an unformed word was as unappealing as an uncooked quiche. "Let's get you to the mattress," he said, clapping me on the back of my neck and shoving me to the side of The Rabbit. The mattress was an un-sheeted bed in the side room backstage. On weekends, the mattress went to whichever worker drank himself helpless first, but occasionally Egan used it to temporarily store a sick customer.

When we got around the corner, out of the sightline of the smokers, Hallahan squeezed my neck and hugged me close. "You got it, honey," he said. "Slow and steady." He looked like a side of bacon had grown a moustache, but he had tremendous gentleness in his hands. If he'd been born weak, we might've been friends.

An hour later, I woke up on the mattress alone. There was a slight pain in my side, more of a distraction from the overall throb in the middle of my chest. From the main room, Surrender Dorothy sounded like they were winding up for a big finish. My mind was a shining blank. As I blinked myself into awareness, I saw a boxy blue shape blocking the doorway.

"Rise up, Lemur, and get your kill." It was Egan Hopper, holding a cup of tea, the steam rising and fogging his glasses. He sometimes called me Lemur because he'd read that lemurs were the most vicious and lazy of all the big cats.

"Who's got the bar?" I said.

"What's wrong with you," he said. "What is going on in your head?"

"I got hit," I said. "Senor Low-Penis and the Unfulfilled Ambitions brained me."

"Make sure you get your breathing patterns back." He gave me the teacup, and I brought it to the side of my face, like it was my head and not my chest that ached.

"Is fucking Corey still out there?" I asked. "Ninety percent of anything that's gone wrong here signs his name with a Casey at the end of it. I'm going to tie that man's balls to a race car."

"Listen to your revenge-minded self." Egan had the thick glasses and wholesome smile of a cartoon on the side of an ice cream truck, but he pulsed with the anger of a man who practiced never raising his voice. "Talking your killer talk. Revenge can't be parceled out, dollar for dollar and penny for penny."

I took a sip of the tea, and it warmed my bruise on the way down. "I saved that fucking show. I did good."

"My God, listen to you," he said. "Just listen to you."

"You're good at saying, 'Listen to you,' but I'm not convinced you know what it means."

"You sound just like him, you know?"

"Stop."

"It's true," he said. "Out there, when you act tough, you sound like a kid. But here, when you're genuinely mad-dog angry, I know you're Aaron's brother."

"When you knew him, he was a kid."

Egan kicked the door closed behind him. "You like Meander because you think you're the same. And you hate Hallahan because he can hurt you. But Meander is much closer to being Hallahan than he is to being you. Those two don't think."

"Which is what you say about me when you talk to them."

"Would they listen?" Egan said. He was in his late twenties, but he had a spattering of pimples under his right temple that made him look younger. He wiped off his coke-bottle glasses with the bottom of his shirt and then repositioned them on his face. "Do I lie to you? Have I sold you on us all being family? You want family? Get yourself born from a better snatch than the one God put you in. This is business, and business eats and bleeds loyalty. Do you know how to foster loyalty from an employee?"

"Talk about his mother's vagina?"

"It's honesty." His grin hung on the corner of his face like it was weighing down his lips. "I'll always speak to you honest as I can. Hallahan is useful because he's big and he's loyal. He does what I ask, and he likes doing it, which means he's thorough. Meander's useful, but not as much. He's good company, and he's desperate for friendship, which can make him valuable in a pinch. Best thing about him is he brings you on board. Meander's more skull than brain, but you're different."

I still had blood in my mouth. I tasted it as I rolled my tongue around on the back of my teeth.

"Right now, you're on the drunkard's mattress," he said. "This ain't where anybody wants to be, but it's where you are. Where're you going from here?"

"Enough with this," I said. "You want to talk to me, talk to me. Stop making it a game of mother-may-I? Tell me where I'm going because you obviously know."

"That's the way you ask a favor?" The smile left his eyes. "Okay, hotshot, since you're in a hurry to resume your life as a cum-rag for this bed, let me get to the point. You know how we make our money. And it's not whiskey shooters and bottles of Bud. And it's not tickets to see eyeliner rockabilly like Surrender Goddamn Dorothy. You've been in people's cars, and you know what Lemon's slinging."

The song came crashing to an end with a smattering of slowly rolling drums.

"Nickel and dime stuff is fine, and maybe that's what you want." He grabbed the tea, finished it in one swallow, and dropped the mug on the mattress. "Next step for you is cars. I've got a shop in Lawrenceberg that can't be traced back here. It's a real bump in salary, and you can get paid whichever way you want. Cash, dope, or goodwill. But no one ever chooses goodwill."

"You got Hallahan on this too?" I said.

"Think about it," he said. "Take your time, and sift through what I told you. In the meantime, watch the company you keep."

"You mean Meander?"

"Not only Meander," he said. "You're young, and this is the time to max out, the only time you'll have. You got a girl?"

I shook my head.

"Get one," he said. "Get two. Don't piss your nights away talking power chords and precious lyrics with the Casey boys."

"You said it's not Meander."

"Not just him," Egan said. "It's you that matters, not your wastrels." No matter the situation, Egan never spoke with his hands, instead draping them at his sides like he was holding two basketballs in the crook of each elbow, but he punctuated these sentences by moving his chin from side to side. "Get you a girl before you get old. It's better when you're older, but it's not the same. You miss out now, you can't make it up again. What's the name of that redhead you hang around?"

"Let me clarify," I said. "It's not that I don't know what girls are, nor am I boycotting them. What I'm saying is I don't right now have a girlfriend, and what you're saying is anything to avoid my question, which is, who are you talking about?"

"You going up the hill tonight?"

Thomas the Prophet, I thought. Thomas and Egan hated each other, and they both had points. I was determined not to take sides, because while I liked Thomas better, he was twice as useless. Anyway, it amused me how they each thought the other cornered the market on degeneracy.

"Kick a tire or two on what I just said." He opened the door. "We'll take care of you no matter what you do."

"Let me ask you something," I said. "Why you call yourself Rabbit?"

"Hopper," he said. "Egan Jackson Hopper. I kept waiting for someone to nickname me Rabbit, but I got bored and named myself."

"You're middle name's Jackson? Why not call this place The Jack Rabbit?"

"Can't do that." His smile was back. "That's what they expect you to do."

This was the year Nightwolf popped up around the city. He began in the suburbs and the bus stations, but gradually moved downtown, and now he was tagging the bars near campus. At first, we thought he was a crank, spraypainting his name in deep purple on anything big enough to take nine block letters. Sometimes he wrote sayings like *"Let's Be Friends!—Your ole buddy, Nightwolf"* or *"If you can read this, thank a teacher. If you can't read this, thank a teacher sarcastically—Nightwolf."*

It was harmless, and I liked that someone was giving Lexington a personality. Except then our local CBS reported that a perpetrator wearing a garbage bag on his head attacked a man and two women. The man was fighting with his girlfriend and her sister, the three of them screaming at each other on the street, when the garbage-bag man attacked. "Stop in the name of The

Nightwolf," he yelled, again and again. The girlfriend said Nightwolf was trying to help, that he thought her boyfriend was beating them. The upshot was that the man and two women kicked the ever-loving shit out of Nightwolf and held him almost until the cops came. Except Nightwolf elbowed the girlfriend in the neck and escaped.

That changed his reputation. Now he was a vigilante and not a good one. The news didn't have a picture, but they showed the police sketch, of a man with a bag over his head, with one gigantic eyehole and a diagonal slit over the mouth. It felt unnecessary—I know what a bag looks like.

After that, his graffiti turned cryptic, almost threatening. "*'You might as well appeal against a thunderstorm as against these terrible times of war'—General Sherman/Nightwolf.*" Egan figured if we caught him, we could parlay it into good business for The Rabbit, so he offered a bounty if we could capture him in an entertaining way. "Don't just call the cops," he told us. "That's fine. It'll get you three hundred. But shoot him in the ass with a Taser dart like a real wolf, that's a thousand." Nightwolf was still a joke, but we didn't know which side of the angels he was fighting on.

Theorizing about Nightwolf became a sort of parlor game. Meander thought the tagger was someone like him—a bored suburban kid, giddy at swallowing too much freedom at once. When you're on your own for the first time, the world looks immaculate and almost impossible not to destroy. Thomas the Prophet thought it was a citywide conspiracy orchestrated by the police so we wouldn't focus on the real crimes because he's addicted to having people tell him to shut the fuck up. Most people figured Nightwolf came from one of Father Compost's homeless kids. Lexington had more than its fair share of runaways, and some of them had formed a sort of religious following, communing about the beauty of living outdoors with no money. "What good is a rainbow," I asked one of them when he came up to Thomas the Prophet's for some unholy intervention, "if the first thing you want to do is eat it?" I could never keep it straight if Father Compost was a man or a metaphor, but they were friendlier than the average non-religious homeless person and the average Christian with a house.

Here's the thing: I think my brother is The Nightwolf. My older brother Aaron Byers ran away when he was fifteen, and we never looked for him. I was only seven, but he loved comic books and even went a whole month where he made Mom call him Aquaman. He didn't read me his comics, but he summed them up, mentioning Bruce Wayne and The Penguin like they were his fraternity brothers. Plus, he wrote on my toys and on the walls of our room. Both he and Nightwolf had the same G's where they looked like eights.

Those days, the only bonafide adults we had vying for our attention were Egan Hopper and Thomas the Prophet, who described himself as "a philosophy dealer." The rest of Lexington described him as an "inexpensive dealer" and that kept his house full. After most shows at the Rabbit, the band, the staff, a few of the regulars would trek up Prospect Hill and park at Thomas the Prophet's house, take whatever drug he offered and drink from his endless supply of booze.

Thomas was only a decade older than us, but he was aging in dog years. He had a swallow of success, working for an advertising firm. One of his ads for a gum-flavored soda went national, and for about twenty minutes he was a warm commodity. It didn't last, but he held onto his money, and when he moved back to Kentucky, he wrote occasional ads for local business and small-time political candidates. He looked like a five-year-old's drawing of a handsome man—he had the ingredients for attractiveness, but the proportions were off. Thanks to a snakebite in his youth, his left hand hung off the side of his wrist, turning his arm into an oblong checkmark. To some, that hand served as an extension of the man: unneeded, unnerving, and not quite finished.

He lived at the peak of Prospect Hill in a hulking shell of a house originally meant to be a duplex. He started tearing down the dividing wall, but abandoned it halfway through. Instead, he hung paintings of his friends on the drywall, and when he ran out of canvasses, he finger-painted directly on the wall itself. The house was a teardown, too big for one person, so he routinely housed anyone who needed a bed. It was rare the morning sun would find the house empty of stragglers from the night before.

Prospect Hill itself was a neighborhood on the rise twenty-five years earlier. The houses around Thomas's looked every bit as dingy, but much smaller. Frequently I'd see the neighborhood children playing with Thomas's power drill or covered in his green house paint after a block-wide paint fight.

I hitched a ride up the hill with Meander, the back of his car smelling like week-old banana pudding and pizza crusts. "If he shows up tonight, I'll kill him," Meander said. He shook his head and rolled his unlit cigarette from one side of his mouth to the other. "If you think I'm joking, fuck you too."

"I believe you," I said. "You talking about Corey?"

"No, not Corey. Stop fucking around, okay?"

"Who then?" I said. "Who do you want to kill?"

"Little fucker." He looked at me, temporarily ignoring the road. "You are not a serious person. People say that about me, but it's because I hang around you."

"I still don't know who you're talking about."

"Jesus, Milo." He lifted up his shirt. "Does that help at all?"

"I'm not trying to be a hard-on, but what am I looking at?"

He looked down at his own chest and then back on the road. "It's bruised," he said. "Tomorrow you'll be able to see it better, but that's a nasty bruise."

"Hallahan?"

"He burned me," Meander said. "I was down already, begging him to stop, but he kept going. Then he put his cigarette out on me."

"What's the world coming to?" I said. "Meander Casey reaching his threshold for pain before he hits the wheelchair."

"He wouldn't stop," Meander said. "I asked him nice, then I asked him mean, I yelled, and I even threatened him."

"Okay, of those, only asking nice will work. The rest are counterproductive."

He smacked the steering wheel. "They're going to fire me, man."

"Egan tell you that?"

"Hallahan did," he said. "Laughing at me while my chin's bouncing off the concrete. Says every bit of trouble in the joint comes signed with a Casey at the end."

Egan ordered this as my payback. Was that what he thought I wanted? I looked at the side of his chin where Hallahan's boot had been. Nothing showed, but when he stopped talking, I heard a hitch in his breathing, making me wonder if he'd cracked a rib.

"If he comes up Prospect tonight, trying to be my buddy, you know what I'm going to do?" He slit his throat with his thumbnail. "*Pow.* No joke. Murder."

"Did that knife go 'Pow?'"

We passed Leckett's Ark, home of Thomas's down-street neighbors, Roxy and Monroe Leckett. Roxy and Monroe were my age, but their parents were out of the picture. We called their house The Ark because every afternoon, Roxy laid out whatever food she didn't want for the feral neighborhood animals. On any given night, you could come across raccoons and squirrels and cats and dogs and opossums all scouring the yard for supper. Once I saw a deer. Inevitably the animals turned on each other, and because the Lecketts rarely cleaned the carcasses, they became food for the next night's grazers. It helped that Roxy and Monroe were twins. Even the people were lining up two by two.

Occasionally, Meander liked to drive off the road and into the yard to scare the assembled animals. He claimed he'd once hit a hedgehog, but I didn't believe him. The dogs were howling, and he was staring out the side window into the Ark.

"Don't do it," I said. "Just keep going."

"You don't think I can?" Meander pulled to the side of the road and stopped the car. "You don't think I will?"

"What's the point?" I said. "It's a bad idea."

"Not to hit them. Just scare them a little and make them scatter. That way, I'd give Thomas a little peace from that racket."

I reached under the seat and took out his emergency bottle of rum. Meander drank sweet liquor—once I'd even seen him dumping sugar and cream into his bourbon and coke. "Take a sip of this," I said. "It'll be good for that bruise."

"I can't lose my job," he said. "It's my main motivation for drinking."

"Egan likes you," I said. "Well, he doesn't, but he doesn't like anyone. And the temp agency ain't sending anyone to replace you. And Hallahan—"

Meander stiffened. "You think I'm joking, right?"

I reached over and honked his horn three times. My hope was to send the animals away from the yard and into safety, but just as many scurried into the road by our car. It didn't matter. The honking worked like an alarm for

Meander, waking him up and knocking the smoldering pity from his eyes. He took the rum bottle from my lap, took a long swig, and sloshed it around his cheeks like mouthwash. Then, without a word, he drove us up the hill to Thomas the Prophet's house.

Just inside the door, I saw Harmony Dulles, a crabapple-cheeked girl from school, smearing finger paint onto one of Thomas's bed sheets. "They're upstairs," she said, not looking up. She put a glob of yellow on the side of her hand and chopped at the sheet until it turned into a checkered smudge.

I knelt down to her level. "How does he seem tonight? Mood-wise?"

She flitted her hand back and forth to mean fifty-fifty. "Some of the Rabbit people are up there, so I came down here."

Meander looked at me and mouthed "Hallahan?"

I shook my head like I knew something.

He sprinted toward the staircase. Harmony didn't seem to notice, and when I looked at her again, I saw her eyes were blank and pink as a hamster's. I hesitated for a moment, and then sprinted after Meander.

I was just in time to grab at the ankle of Meander's blue jeans, but not enough to slow him down. As he kicked away from me, I banged my elbow into the bannister. I heard his footsteps thumping up the stairs and growing softer, then some scattered voices shouting greeting and recognition at Meander. The bump on my elbow redoubled the pain in my chest.

A loud thunk and a peal of gratified laughter came from above. Not yet, I thought. I bolted upstairs. The first person I saw was Corey sitting splay-legged in front of a doorway, passing a hash pipe to the girl with the leopard print shirt.

From the room behind him, I heard the thunk again. I opened the door, expecting some version of a fight. Instead, it was a crowd of people, some hunched over in hysterics, some passed out asleep. In the middle of it all, was Petey Peyote, usually pale but tonight almost translucent. He collected bottles and cleaned up at The Rabbit, and sometimes after a good night, Egan would send him home with an extra twenty dollars in his pocket. When he came up on Prospect Hill looking to score, some people tried to take it off him. His real name was Pierre Graniaux, but he let people call him whatever they wanted so long as they bought him the occasional beer or bottle of Ale-8-One to help the meth kick in. Now, he rolled around the center of the floor, breathing heavy.

The lights were off and it took a second for my eyes to adjust to the dark. Thomas the Prophet sat Indian-style in front of his own closet, hunched over with his chin hanging above his knees. Shea Stanford, my oldest friend, sat beside him, slowly massaging the back of his head, her fingers running through his long stringy hair. Meander stood in the opposite corner, glowering, but laughing his unhinged hyena howl—his telltale sign he didn't understand the joke. Lina Darby, lead guitarist for Surrender Dorothy, said, "Come on, Petey, do it again."

At that, Petey hopped up, moving from flat on his back to crouching in a two-point position almost instantly, without even using his hands to balance. Then Lina flicked one of her cigarettes so it sailed end over end just above his head. Right as it started its descent, Petey jumped from a flat-footed position backward, biting at the cigarette and collapsing on the floor.

"They give him a bump each time he gets it in his mouth," Shea told me. "What? It's Lina's thing, not mine."

The joke must've been wearing thin. This was the third thunk since I'd come in, and the laughs sounded patchier each time.

I didn't much like Petey, but I had no desire to watch him break his jaw. I wanted to leave, but I saw Meander surveying the back corner. He cracked his neck back and forth and kept his hands in front of his chest like a toy boxer. He wanted to fight.

Lina stepped out of the way, and I saw Hallahan standing behind her, fiddling with the sprigs of his moustache. His chin was lined with a ring of smoke from his thin black cigar. I shook my head, but Meander wouldn't look at me. If he took a swing, they'd kill him. It was a matter of seconds. I felt a light strain in my knee and let it buckle, howling in pain and collapsing on the floor.

It was enough for a moment's distraction. "He kicked me," I said, moaning and pointing behind me to a sleeping Thomas the Prophet. "He got me right in the knee."

Shea Stanford raised an eyebrow. Of all the people in the room, she alone knew I was lying, but she bit her tongue.

"He didn't mean to," I said. "But he got me real good." The room was standing over me now, and I knew that if Meander ever did want to swing at Hallahan, now was his best chance.

"You got your ass kicked by an unconscious man," Lina Darby said. "That's like getting raped by a sex doll."

"Don't take that shit, man," Hallahan said. He threw his zippo across the room and it landed straight between Thomas's eyes. This prompted others to empty their pockets and throw their keys and loose change at Thomas, though no one else had Hallahan's aim.

"It wasn't his fault," I said. I tried to smack away the debris, but it was a lost cause. Even Shea Stanford had slipped away from behind him so as not to get hit. When I tried to interfere, I got smacked in the head by a contact case and a barrage of nickels. All the while, Thomas never stirred, not even when someone hit him in the side of the mouth with a battery.

I cocked back and smacked him across the cheek with the back of my hand. "Wake up," I said. For a moment, I thought I'd have to hit him again, but just then I saw two hands poke out from under his armpits. It was Meander, trying to lift Thomas the Prophet's upper body. I stood and grabbed him by the ankles, and together we carried him across the hall and dumped him onto his bed. I rolled him on his belly.

It struck me for the first time how similar his bedroom looked to the floproom in the back of The Rabbit. They really were almost the same, Egan and Thomas. The hatred had long roots. In time, it would spill real blood. I sensed that even then, but it didn't feel urgent. That's just the nature of blood and time.

"Look at this guy," Meander said. "He's tore up worse than Christmas wrapping. Who gets fucked up this bad?"

"You do," I said. "I do. We're in his house, using his junk."

"But this?" Meander waved a hand over Thomas. "He looks dead. You don't believe Egan, do you? The pervert stuff?"

"Those are rumors," I said. "He lies about everyone. Yesterday, he told me you tried to drink a bucket of paint thinner because you thought that was how you huff it."

"What?" He laughed, and immediately, I knew it was true. I turned from him so he wouldn't catch the recognition in my face. From behind, I heard a choked wheeze. He's about to confess, I thought. Don't admit it, just laugh it away. When he didn't speak, I turned around and saw Meander hunched over the bed, strangling Thomas the Prophet.

The choking sound. Which one of them did it come from? He was killing him. But he couldn't kill him, not if he's already dead.

All the while, I couldn't find my feet. Instructions were building in my thoughts, distant and unwelcome as a siren four cars behind. Do something, I told myself, and I felt myself moving. But I wasn't.

Then the bed broke. Meander slid off and collapsed

laughing. Thomas gave a burbling noise and rolled onto his side. "The fuck?" I said, too stunned to yell. "The fuck are you doing?"

"You see that?" Meander said, gurgling on his own laughter. "He's all—that man's stone dead knocked out. I never seen someone so gone."

I put my fingers on Thomas's throat. He was still breathing. "Were you really choking him?" I said. "What's wrong with you?"

He shook his head, with every motion, his laughter lightened until it ran out. "I can't lose my job, man," he said. "Not for some gropey shit-sack like him."

Thomas the Prophet was still alive, and I had the proof of that drumming through my fingertips. Part of me wondered if the pressure was actually moving down, from my fingers to his pulse and not the other way around. What if I was the one killing him?

I did nothing. I felt myself rooted to my sneakers, barely noticing as Meander loped out of the room.

I expected to see Hallahan on Thomas's stoop, but instead I saw the girls—Harmony, Lina, and Shea—huddled in an awkward triangular hug. They didn't make natural allies, but they fit as snugly as dishes in a dishwasher loaded back to front.

When I got closer, I saw Lina weeping.

"What's the matter?" I asked.

I expected a scowl when Lina turned to face me. She protected the circumference around her friends more fiercely than most people protected their assholes, but she smiled, looking sweet and dizzy. She never wore makeup except the nights she played, and then she smeared it all over like a child making a mud pie on her eyes. Now it was wet and it made her face look like a 3-D picture, the actual shape buried deep beneath a cascade of colors. "It was my fault," Lina said. "I was just messing around."

"Peyote dove for one of Lina's smokes and cracked

out a tooth," Shea said. "He only uses his teeth to scare children."

"But he was bleeding so bad," Lina said. "It was just a joke. Tell them."

"So this was a permanent tooth, right?" I said. "Not a baby tooth or nothing like that?"

They stared at me and then at each other. "Are you serious, Milo?" Shea asked. "He's, like, thirty."

I wish I could create an invisible box around their sadness, extending upward, so it couldn't escape and drift into the rest of the night. All my mistakes felt beautiful enough to withstand their judgment, but only when I kept them close, in this house, away from the infinity of stars. If I push back against the rest of the world, against the endless nighttime, then I could hold onto our sadness, our injuries, everything that makes us part of one another. People say all things old can become new again, but they don't mean it. It's only new now, in the instant before we name it.

A glint of streetlight curled under Shea Stanford's ear, lighting up her cheek. She smiled openly now, the shared guilt drying off her face. She was getting better, the body moving faster than the mind.

We were thieves, all of us. My chest was cracked, my nose was leaking, and my friends stood in front of me, crying and recovering. Upstairs, Thomas the Prophet must be moving away from his nightmare of being lost underwater, his scarf caught on the hull of the boat, tightening around his neck. Tomorrow, he'd wake up and face the world, but now, all he knew was he'd escaped the ocean. We didn't have to improve, only recover. I could face myself, take the medicine of the mirror, but only if I held us all together and didn't let our pain seep away.

The dogs at the Ark at end of the street screamed toward space and a wave of crickets answered them. When I was young, the world was green and full of ungrateful animals.

2.

Thomas the Prophet declared war on the rest of the world, and he thought it was a fair fight. We called him Thomas the Prophet because of his endless pronouncements, spoken with the cocksure fury of a Pentecostal, elbow deep in snake. He declared himself an unsleeping enemy of anonymity, of dying before you made this world take notice. Fighting was his religion. What offended the righteous was righteous.

Recently, he'd volunteered to lead the local chapter of the Jews for Jesus. Kentucky was a border state, neutral in the Civil War, so it seemed right to him that our Jews couldn't decide if they wanted to be on the side of Judaism. He stood in front of local churches and synagogues with fliers that read, "Jews For Jesus: We Killed Him For Your Sins."

A Christian woman smacked him with her purse, two squarebeards shoved him into a lamppost, but Thomas loved it. "Imagine the day your holy service leads into your local brawl," he said. "Couldn't you believe the world's gone crazy?" I didn't see how it profited a man to instigate war between the uncircumcised and the aerodynamic, but Thomas wasn't interested in profit, only blood.

Every weekday, from eleven-thirty until they kicked him off the property, Thomas planted himself in front of a different local business and worked as a human version of the inflatable advertising man. He wore a sign around his neck, stood by their door, and waved his arms like he was being shot through with helium.

Once, he wrote to the CIA. Everyone knows it's a crime to say you want to kill the president, he said, but is it illegal to say you want to flash the president? He followed that with a letter to the governor of Kentucky, saying "Don't worry, I checked with the CIA re: your question about flashing the president. I'll let you know what they say." He signed both these letters "Milo Byers, Esquire." That's me.

"You said you wanted to be involved," he told me.

"When did I say I wanted to be involved?" I understood his confusion. When the sun was down, his house teemed with people, but his drugs couldn't buy him a nod hello from those same kids the next day. Even Father Compost's runaways pretended they stayed the night doing whip-its behind the JIF factory rather than admit they climbed Prospect Hill. Still, I half-liked Thomas the Prophet, even if I was a minority of one-half. So by not protesting too much, I became his friend.

This was the autumn I learned how to steal cars. Ollie Hallahan tutored me, pinching my cheeks when I did well and cracking my skull when I fumbled with the locks. Egan told me to follow Hallahan, ape his every move. If I made a mistake or showed up late, Hallahan treated my spine like a kid treats a sheet of bubblewrap. Everything about him was enormous, even his dimples, and he tried to keep his face blank as a way of fooling you into thinking he wasn't paying attention. If a doorframe became sentient, and turned out to be an asshole, you couldn't tell it apart from Hallahan.

He pocketed my keychain. "Start with your own car," he said. "Jump it or walk."

"Those have my house keys on it," I said. "It's mom's car. Those are her keys."

"And if she needs them, tell her they're right here." He patted his front pocket. "Shit, if she needs them, tell her to give me a half-hour warning, so I can be the fuck off the road. I wouldn't trust that bitch behind the wheel of a tricycle."

"All right," I said.

"Outside ambos and paddy wagons, she ain't been in a car since she made you."

"All right, already." Technically, Mom didn't drive and didn't lock the front door. In fact, apart from her spells, she barely went outside. Still, it felt wrong that a man could take your keys and rob you of nothing. So I swung for Hallahan's jaw, just below the ear. He leaned back fast, and I hit the wall. Before the pain could spread throughout my knuckles, he clamped down on my hand and bent it backward toward my wrist. He didn't stop until I was on my knees.

"I ain't your friend, and I ain't your daddy," he said. "You want to cry, I won't stop you. Sounds *fucking* gorgeous to me."

It taught me, I suppose. Hallahan believed in knowledge through desperation. The whole game was speed. After two weeks under Hallahan, my thinking became simple—what slowed me was wrong.

"Walk away," Hallahan told me. "If it ain't, it ain't. Force it, you fuck yourself."

Once I mastered my mom's car, he moved me to my friends. I'd take their cars for a couple laps around the block, and then park on the other side of the street to see if they notice. The idea was our friends wouldn't rat us out. On top of that, Hallahan liked to study people, to see if they paid attention. Most didn't notice their cars were spun around or that the air freshener was missing. The thief's biggest trump card was that the mark blamed himself.

He had me move Shea Stanford's hatchback in front of her next-door neighbor's house. He took a Coke bottle from the passenger side cupholder with the label half-peeled off. "This you, man?" I always peeled the labels. People said it was sexual frustration, and I had no counterargument. "What you doing in this car, my man?"

"Drinking Coke, apparently."

"You fucking Shea Stanford?" he said.

"Then I'm drinking a Coke right after, so I don't get pregnant?"

"No," he said. "I mean, you fuck a girl, and now you lift her car. That's—not ironic, it's, you know, it's what?"

"It's a Coke," I said. "In my friend's car, where I sometimes drink Coke."

"She catches you, she call the cops?" He put his hand on the back of my neck. "Say 'Officer, officer, arrest that evil man?'"

"Maybe," I said. "She'd definitely do that to you, and you'd do it to me."

He slammed my head against the steering wheel, busting my lip. "Buckle up for safety," he said. "Police see no belt, they pull you over just to say hi. This is a girl's car, so they running your plates. You don't look like no Shea Stanford to me, and you won't have a chance to talk yourself clean."

"You're the one drinking." His breath smelled like a rancid combination of vodka, cinnamon, and Mott's Apple Juice.

"Our thing is a house of cards." He licked the underside of his moustache. "You think you're just fucking yourself, but you fucking me, The Rabbit, the whole operation."

"A minute ago, you said I was fucking Shea Stanford.

This sounds like a demotion."

That night, when I went home, I called for Mom, but she didn't answer. She still had a pot of egg noodles boiling on the stove, but the water had evaporated. For the last month, she'd left the same supper out for me every night—noodles and a can of tuna for me to make my own casserole. Normally, she'd stop at one pot of noodles, but sometimes she'd forget or think she had company coming and çook two or three.

We had four rooms in our apartment, so it didn't take long to search our house. I checked her room, and then my room, and then I spotted her out the window by the dumpsters by the side of our complex.

It was cold outside when I went to collect her, worse for her without her coat. She was circling the dumpsters, and I thought for a second, she was putting lye around them to keep the raccoons away.

I put a jacket around her shoulders, but she didn't flinch. Even as she brought her hands up to her mouth to blow on them, she didn't meet my eyes. "Fuck's wrong with you?" I said. "If I stayed out tonight, you'd be green and frozen as a bag of peas?"

"Listen to the way you talk to me, like you're some-body big." She spat on her shoes. "If I'm late one more time, you know what they'll do to me?."

"Late?" I said. "Do you know if I want—if I so much as take a small walk and forget my keys for an hour—you'd be dead as an alley rat, remembered by nobody?"

She put the fat of her arm around the back of my neck, close to where Hallahan had grabbed me, except her touch was soft and cold. "You used to love me," she said.

"That's right."

She opened the jacket as if to invite me in. I put my hand on her shoulder, and we walked upstairs to the apartment. All the noodles had burnt because I'd forgotten to turn the stove off. This time, the house would've burned down, and it'd have been my fault. We ate cold tuna in front of the television.

Here were the five most talked about rumors concerning Thomas the Prophet:
1. One night soon, he'd lace his drugs with laundry detergent to create his own Jamestown Massacre.
2. He had a tattoo of a penis on his penis.
3. He was filming us for his next commercial and would sell the footage to the CIA.
4. He was faking his inability to use his left hand, so he could collect for disability.
5. He had sexually assaulted two neighborhood boys who came to his parties.

Of these, only the fifth took root. At first, the whispers were that Thomas had exposed himself to Avery Comstock, a thirteen-year-old built like a bowling ball. Nobody believed that because Avery would bite Thomas's dick off at the first sign of danger. The story then changed to Avery's friend Otto Larkin, a bushy-headed boy with a smile like an alligator, who lived two blocks away.

Otto was eleven and mostly stayed outside during Thomas's parties, flying a red and blue box kite. When I was his age, I fell in love with kites and model airplanes even after my buddies had moved onto cigarettes, and so I enjoyed standing on the porch and watching him. When he put the kite away, we'd place orders with him, and he'd ride his bike to the convenient store to pick us up Mr. Pibb or Big League Chew or cigarillos. Otto had grown up on Prospect, had a father who treated him like a second cousin, and was probably a long shot for working at NASA. Amongst Prospect Hill kids, this made him somewhat less uncommon than a three-nutted horse. I thought of him as a glorified vending machine, but when he was with his kite, I understood how the kid saw himself. Otto never accused him, at least not directly. He stopped coming to the parties. In real time, no one noticed. Then the rumor started that Thomas, blue-blind drunk and stoned as a heathen, stumbled into a room when Otto was sleeping on the couch, unzipped his pants and fondled him.

The gossip crested and fell but never disappeared. We showed up to Thomas's one night to find two of his living room windows busted out, which led to whispers that Otto's mother had shot them with a BB gun. No one believed all of it, and no one believed none of it.

"He's a fondler?" I said at my next shift at The Rabbit. I had to paint over Nightwolf's purple tag, and Hallahan was below me holding the ladder. "Of all the stories to make up about a one-handed man, they went with fondling? What sort of pedo-ninja can unzip the pants of a sleeping boy without the kid noticing?"

"He unzips his own pants, don't he?" Hallahan said. The smoke from his cigarette rose and gathered around my face. "Buttons his own shirt, ties his own shoes? Boys Otto's age wear pants two sizes too big, so they grow into them. Easy to unzip."

"You remember Avery Comstock?" I said. "This was his story. Now it's someone else. Maybe something happened, but not this."

"Listen to you," Egan Hopper said. He lay on a lawn chair with his shirt unbuttoned. "What's this something that happened? So it's not him jacking off an eleven-year-old, it's just something that could be mistaken for that? Start with the fact the boy shouldn't have been there and work backwards."

"You don't understand," I said. "That's Prospect. Everybody comes."

"I ought to yank this ladder out from under you," Hallahan said. "You wouldn't be talking this way if you had kids."

"You don't have kids," I said. "None of us do."

"I know," he said. "It's what they say on the news."

I climbed down the ladder, the job half-finished. "Look," I said to Egan. "Sorry to do this, but I have to cut out early."

"Maybe I ought to start paying you, so I can fire you."

"My mom's birthday's on Saturday," I said. "I have to buy her something."

"Your mom?" Egan sat up and inched his sunglasses down the bridge of his nose. "She doing any better?"

I shook my head.

"And you're not shining me on? Like, you aren't actually going up to Prospect?"

"I'm going to the mall," I said. "For Mom."

Egan told Hallahan to finish the painting job and signaled for me to lean in close. "The trials in our life can serve as a good moment to take stock of your surroundings," he whispered. "Take your life seriously now—not later." He reached into his shirt pocket and handed me a fifty-dollar bill. "Get her something unique, something with edges. Our memories are tied to texture, so get her something she can feel."

I hotwired my own car and fought the traffic on Nicholasville Road until I made it to the mall. There, as planned, I met Thomas the Prophet in the parking lot. "You're late," he said. "You need to get dressed."

His plan was for me to dress in fatigues and a Santa beard. Thomas had chicken blood splattered down the front of his white t-shirt, and a necklace full of fake ears. Together, we set up a card table in the mall parking lot and posed as recruitment officers for The Salvation Army. "This is stupid," I told him. I reminded him he has a day job, one that relies on public relations. Who would want to hire the neighborhood crank to make their commercials. Thomas was unmoved. This was his legacy. All that mattered was the memory we left the world.

When a child with freckles so thick they looked put on with magic marker approached us, Thomas rang the bell slowly, trying to make it sound intimidating. "You think we let any scrubbed up cocksucker ring that bell," he said. "Do you know what it means to collect change for us?"

The boy nodded. "You ring the bell?"

Thomas had me mostly silent, the heavy. He gave me a long paring knife that I used to trim my nails. On top of my Santa hat and beard, I wore wraparound sunglasses, and suspenders with no shirt.

"You see shit over there, man, shit you can't unsee," Thomas told the kid. The boy was anywhere from nine to twelve, wearing oblong glasses and a giveaway t-shirt from a bank. His mom was a hundred feet away, loading up the car and lighting one cigarette with the end of another. "Once you see a teddy bear with its eyes ripped out of its head, there's no amount of acid in the world that can make you sane again."

I tapped my knife on the table three times. That was our prearranged sign for him to lay off. Of course, he didn't listen. At that point, he was in the third month of what he called "strategic coking." The world was war, he told me, and you either fought or became a bloody smudge on the American terrain. He threw his blip of influence in with the underdogs. That means he sided with the rebels in the Middle East, the bullied in school, the bullies in every depiction of school on TV, and the bankers in the war on poverty, because, as he put it, 'Who likes bankers?' On a more practical level, he decided to take the drugs' side in the drug war.

"I did not watch my buddies get their tongues cut out by those cunts in the Toys For Tots, so we can have this— this," Thomas said, signaling at the boy. "Keep walking, kid. You're not bell and nickel material."

The boy stood still, looking to his left and right. For an agonizing moment, I thought he might cry, but instead he signed his name on our paper and walked away.

The sun was shining, and I had nothing else to do, so why argue? In a few hours, Thomas would be a sweaty, sentimental mess. For now, we had the sunlight, we had the slight gasoline smell of the suburb, we had our charring skin, and we had time.

In the downtime, we talked about everything. I asked when the new shipment would come in and what new prank he was cooking up. He asked about my mother's birthday. This is friendship, I thought—though I only thought it and never felt it. I told him my theory about my brother being Nightwolf. We even made a half-assed plan to make a map of his targets and track him down.

Thomas was a believer, a zealot, and he cared about what he said, but only in the rare moments when he would relax and wait for the world to come to him. That's when he felt free. These were the good times, the fragile times, and I could feel that even as they grazed over me and receded into the past.

Are you evil? I tried to ask.

3.

Mom's in love again, this time with a glasses model who says he's a commercial fisherman in Alaska. It's the same picture she fell in love with eight months earlier, when he claimed to be a bounty hunter in Lincoln, Nebraska. I explained it was a scam, but she didn't believe people could lie over the computer. A year ago, I would've fought it.

Spiritual or vengeful people might call this karma. Back before her memories had the same shelf life of an open carton of buttermilk, she was one of the internet's first grifters, working as a professional girlfriend. To be fair, all she did was send pictures of herself to lonely men and occasionally ask them for money to get her car fixed. A man in Billings, Montana set up the business and handled the cash. It brought in a pretty penny, but as her mind faded, it left her vulnerable to these scams in her own life. She didn't know which side of the game she was playing anymore.

She spent her time surrounded by her old pictures and yellowing magazines, staring at the computer and waiting to fall in love. Every couple of months, she'd get an email from a series of 1's and 0's masquerading as a blandly handsome suitor. I'd hidden her Visa, so that eventually the emails would stop, but the cycle would start again. Better this way, I thought, with the constant seesaw between love and loss. Every day she'd have to tear off the Band-Aid and stare at her wound, remember the pain and the cure, and there'd be no room for stillness, no room for death. It would have to catch her with her back turned. Then again, I prefaced most of the thoughts about my mother by saying *Better this way*.

She wanted to sell the apartment, to move to Alaska with her new man. When I told her it was impossible, she interpreted me as saying she no longer looked pretty enough to snag a husband. She couldn't sell her property, but it wouldn't surprise me if one day she lit out for the far west. She'd think she was going to the Great North but she'd almost surely wind up wearing a "Jane Doe" toe tag before she crossed the state line. I had to revitalize her day-to-day life in a way she didn't expect. To keep her here with me, and to preserve whatever strains of sanity she had left, I had to find Aaron.

Nightwolf was in the news again, this time for trying to stop a vandal. He had a gigantic wooden spike, sharpened to a point, and he came charging from down the street and pierced the man in the stomach. While the man was down, Nightwolf took the vandal's phone and called the police. "Nightwolf has struck again," he said. "I am a hero, but a dark one. It's okay for people to be split on me. Be sure to write that."

"Sir, I don't write the articles," the 911 operator said.

When the police came, they saw no one. Still, they traced the vandal's cell phone and found him crouched in a bus station, blood soaked through his shirt. He admitted to tagging the building, and they found a diamond necklace in his pocket that they assumed he stole. The public felt sorry for the vandal—stabbed for writing on a wall?

The paper ran the same sketch as before, a pencil drawing of a wrinkled garbage bag. This time, however, they drew a long wooden spike behind his head. The caption read "Artist's Rendering."

"It's Aaron," I said to Meander. "Every time I think about it, I get more positive. I wish they'd print something about his voice."

"How old is Aaron now?" Meander asked. "If he's alive."

"Twenty-five."

"Then how do you know what his voice sounds like? You're imagining him as a thirteen year old?"

"Fifteen."

"I'll tell you what Nightwolf's voice sounds like," Meander said. "Like a dickhead impersonating Batman."

"I know my brother."

"One time, when I was six, waiting on the bus, Aaron snuck behind me and shoved me into the street. A car had to swerve to miss me. I ran back to the sidewalk and he pushed me in the street again."

"What's your point?"

"Nightwolf sounds like a real asshole," he said. "But that alone doesn't prove he's your brother."

In the time before my imagination and memory split, my father existed as a human. I remember him as a stubbly shadow who smelled like Doritos Cool Ranch dust and coconut rum. Later, when I was sturdier in the world around me, he existed only as a series of letters and bimonthly checks.

My mother made up for the loss by teaching us what he'd wanted us to know. She slipped into our room most nights and whispered stories to scare us awake.

Aaron laughed and clapped at each of the devils in my mother's tales. When he was scared, his accent sounded clipped and spit-out, like a cartoon Brooklyn gangster, but he laughed slow and astounded, mimicking a dime-store cowboy. I shook under the covers, my hands clasped between my knees, listening to my brother's voice as a signal of how to feel.

My mother prized justice above all virtues. She thought of herself the high sheriff of our imaginations, keeping the community safe from prowlers and bad influences. In reality, she was a former second place beauty queen in a C-Level circuit that ran out of hotels in Lexington's endless suburbs. But in her stories, where she controlled the law and the lawless, all transgressions were punished. She believed the dead demanded vengeance. The selfish were left to rot in the cold, and the ungrateful were fed to packs of roving coyotes. She had a season's worth of success in Arizona, so coyotes were her favorite henchmen, the sharp-toothed guardian of a better land. No matter what animal policed her story, the disobedient child always died in the cold. It taught me to fight my nerves, to pretend it was only the story and not the chill making me shiver.

Not long after, my brother disappeared. We let him go, my mother and me, and didn't talk about it. Aside from that, things kept steady. My mother continued telling her stories, peopled with the same animals and corpses, but quieter now, not just at night, and more often to herself. Dad's checks kept coming, but Mom didn't always cash them, so I signed them over to myself. I still hear traces of fear and sloppy Southern accents in most people's laughter.

Later, when her sickness came, I slept most nights at Thomas the Prophet's. All Mom knew was that I was in Irishtown, what they used to call Prospect Hill when it was all white. I like to think she stayed posted in our room, muttering about the coyotes and the cold. To her, I was as real as her other son.

After Aaron disappeared, I swore I'd never tell her another thing about me. In case I wanted to run as well, I could leave and she wouldn't find me. But she never asked. Secrets are no longer secrets if nobody wants to hear them.

On the night before Mom's birthday, we hit Thomas the Prophet's car again, a powder blue Studebaker with frayed wires. The order came directly from Egan, or else I'd have refused. It was the third time we moved his car that week. "How is this not stupid?" I asked Hallahan as we were driving away, him adjusting Thomas's passenger side seat. "He'll call the cops."

"We want him to," Hallahan said. "Get a cruiser in front of that house, have him make a statement, see them hangers-on scatter like roaches in a spotlight. Let him lose all them friends for good. I'm out of patience with that child-licker."

I kept my eyes on the road. The first weeks when we started boosting cars, I'd slam the brakes if a dry leaf blew onto my windshield. Hallahan fattened my right ear after I swerved to miss a shoebox. Slowly, I was learning patience.

Hallahan offered me some of his apple and vodka drink. He wasn't used to acting friendly, and he wore it like a kid wearing his father's overlong necktie. "Over there." Hallahan pointed to a light pole in front of a chain-link fence. "Pull up in front of that."

Behind the fence was an abandoned factory that separated Prospect Hill from Hawkins Woods, where I lived. When we got out, Hallahan motioned me to stand back. He launched his vodka glass against his windshield. It bounced off harmlessly, but the drink spilled down the side. Suddenly, Hallahan jumped on the car and kicked the front bumper. I know from being on the wrong end of his toe, Hallahan kicks like a kangaroo.

Before he finished, I turned and started climbing the fence. I could feel Hallahan shaking the fence under me as he climbed. When I dropped on the other side, I landed on my heel and collapsed in a pile.

I started to shout in pain, but Hallahan landed next to me and clamped his gigantic hand on my mouth. With his free hand, he put his finger in front of his lips. Then he lifted me up and started dragging me across the lawn, until I found my feet and could walk on my own.

We were past the factory and off the property when he slowed down and put hands on his thighs to catch his breath. The birds rattled the branches above us. I had to squint to see his breath riding above his hair. "What do you think when you see a car like that? Way we left it."

I shrugged.

"Looks like a drunk drove it, maybe into that pole," he said. "It's bent a little. Vodka everywhere."

"Vodka's on the front of the window," I said. "How inexperienced of a drunk driver are you?"

"Psychological warfare," Hallahan said. "You know where we left his car?"

"Over there?" He hit me before for answering rhetorical questions, so I flinched.

"Stand at his back bumper and look to your left. Two houses down is the residence of Otto Larkin. Tomorrow morning, his mom's going to see his car, drunk and beat up." He saw me start to speak, but waved me away with a flick of the wrist. "We're taking Prospect from him. Once people hate him here, he got nowhere else."

"But the kid."

"He's a bad man," he said. "An awful man. You know what happens to kids who get fucked over like that? You think they hit the reset button?"

"You got it wrong," I said, not believing myself as I spoke—my voice arguing against my words. "It gotten blown out of perspective."

"Put it in perspective, motherfucker," Hallahan said.

But the neighborhood? I thought. Surely, we can leave him his neighborhood. When Otto Larkin's mother saw the car, maybe she'd scream and march up to Thomas's stoop, raising high hell and alerting the neighbors. But what if she reacted smaller? If she cradled Otto's skinny head against her side to try and keep him safe? She must've imagined seeing Thomas's car in the side of her eye every time she looked out the kitchen window. We were adding flesh to her nightmare.

I invited a handful of friends to my mother's birthday party. Mom liked noise, and seeing me happy. My friends were polite in other people's homes. At one point, I knew my mother's age, but I'd forgotten, and she wouldn't say. I offered to take her out, but she said she was scared of the rain. "It's going to be dry," I said.

"So now he knows the weather too." She clucked and shook her head. "Believe it or not, I'm not stupid. Rain is unhealthy."

"People go out in the rain," I said. "You might be confusing it with fire."

"Umbrellas are inefficient. That's been proven." Her sweater was caked with crumbs and tuna oil, and she hadn't changed in almost a week. "You used to beg me to stay home when it rained. You weren't always so smart as now."

I could kill you, I thought. I could rob you and leave you in the gutter, and there'd be nothing you can do about it but die quicker. I could shake you until your skull tears through your paper skin. My ankle hurt again. One day, maybe, I'd live up to my boasts.

I told my friends to bring wrapped boxes with open tops. They'd give them to me, and I'd stick some trinket from the apartment. She loved tearing the paper and yanking the ribbon, but she'd forget the present wrapped inside.

For the first hour, I didn't think anyone would come. Mom didn't notice because she barely knew it was her birthday. But then Meander showed up, reeking of whiskey and Camels. His left eye was rimmed red, certain to be a bruise in a day or two. Hallahan swore he stopped beating him, but he has a liberal definition what it means to beat someone. Shea Stanford showed up shortly thereafter, balancing four wrapped boxes on top of each other like she was a trained seal. Twenty minutes later, Corey Casey came in with his arm around Lina Darby. They weren't dating, but he's possessive about other people's space, and she can meld into other people's rhythms. Corey handed me a roll of duct tape, saying it was for my mother.

"I said boxes, wrapping, shit like that."

He ruffled my hair. "This is better. Trust me."

Mom wasn't supposed to drink on her medication, but she didn't take it often, so I figured she was all right. I gave her Chardonnay in a wine glass while the rest of us drank from plastic cups. When she got confused, we told her we were drinking juice. That calmed her, but it made her too casual. Once she thought she was alone and began taking off her skirt and humming to herself.

I bought her a pair of earrings and a plastic bracelet, thinking she'd appreciate the jangling. We had five more boxes, but nothing else in them. I ran into my room and put a dirty coffee cup in one of the boxes, and a square of Corey's duct tape in another. Lina volunteered her necklace if I promised to swipe it back for her.

When I came back out, I saw Mom asleep in her chair, and the rest of the room empty except for Lina. I nodded in my mother's direction. "Is she——?"

"She's in and out," Lina said. "Too much juice."

"Where's everybody?"

"Shea's making a call. The boys are in the boys' room." She brought her hand to her mouth like she was hitting a joint. "We're going in shifts, keeping an eye on her."

I went to the bathroom. Meander was sitting on the sink and Corey was on the lip of the bathtub, his face ringed with smoke. "Go spell Lina," I said to Corey.

"You do it," he said, puffing out smoke as he spoke. "She's your fucking mom."

"It's my house," I said. "And you gave her tape."

"It was a gesture." He walked past me, leaving me alone with Meander.

He waited until the door closed to offer me the joint. "Your mom," he said, when he was sure we were alone. "She's, I don't even know what to say. She's, you know... fucked."

"You stole that from a Hallmark card, right?" I took a toke and closed my eyes. "That smell, man. It's there all the time." I exhaled and sniffed at the smoke, rising above my face. "It stays with me no matter where I go. At The Rabbit, on Prospect, even school. It's brutal."

"Smell?" Meander said. "We're in a bathroom."

"Not that." I gestured above my head, trying to mean everything. "That cream, the tuna, the mayo, the mushroom soup." At school, the nurses thought I was asthmatic, but I was trying to keep my breaths short, to take in as many strange scents as possible.

Meander left the bathroom but before the door closed, Thomas the Prophet walked inside and sat next to me on the edge the bathtub. The smoke went up my nose, making me cough.

"Shea told me," he said.

About the car? I wanted to deny it, but the smoke was choking out my voice.

"I brought your mom a bag, all wrapped up." He reached out and snatched the joint from my hand. "Shea said we didn't have to put anything in it, but I gave her a candle that's only been burned once and a napkin holder." He looked at me, then looked at the joint, then looked at me again. "Seriously, what the fuck is your problem? You going to say hello?"

I ran it back in my head and snapped my fingers. Told me about the birthday is what he meant. "Sorry, man," I said. "I'm pretty stoned."

He took a drag. "I've seen you stoned. This's something else."

"Tired then," I said. "Just call it tired and leave it alone."

"Your mom called me Aaron when I came in," he said. "Shea warned me that might happen because we're the same height."

It wasn't the height, but the hand. Aaron cracked the knuckles on his left hand in a car door as a kid. While it didn't do him any permanent damage, it left him petrified. As a result, he almost never used his left hand and it hung from his wrist like a dishrag.

"I had an idea for the two of us, but believe it or not, I got some proper work in Louisville." He tried to hand me the joint but I didn't take it. "I've got to impersonate a reasonable human for a few days until the check clears."

"The dream is over? This better be some hell of a commercial."

He shook his head. "Some docudrama bullshit about ghost-chasers."

"That does sound respectable."

"It's a couple of weeks, then editing," he said. "I may need somebody to keep an eye on the house if you're interested. You can even run the parties if you want. It won't make you a rich man, but there's money in it."

"Yeah, I have a job."

"You don't need a party to come by my house." I could smell him. I thought it was a familiar cologne, but as I blew his scent out my mouth I knew it was from his car. "The parties are fun, but they're for Margo, Peyote, people like that. I don't invite anyone. It gets away from me. Now you, Shea, Meander, you all can come, party or no."

He was my friend. I didn't want him to be, but he knew me, and he fit into the folds of my house. Go away, I wanted to say to him. Friend or not, I hated him a little.

"All this shit that's eating you," he said, shaking his head. "Talk to me about it. Own up, and let it take you."

I snapped my head toward him. Own up, and let it take you was a phrase that Aaron always said. Unless it wasn't. Thomas sat on the lip of the bathtub, his legs spread wide, his bad hand resting on his knee. Didn't Aaron used to sit that way? I thought. But I was wrong, and I knew that even as the thoughts formed. I was passing my imagination off as memory, grafting one man onto another.

"Egan and them, I know they talk about me. But it's bullshit. Egan I've known forever, and he's forever been a sanctimonious bitch. The other guys, who cares? But seeing you clam up around me? That's too much."

"Really?" I smiled at him. "You really don't know why they talk about you?"

"I've learned to let the shit people talk behind my back stay behind my back. "I'll answer what's asked of me, but I don't shadowbox." He stood and nodded to the door. "Come on, slick, let's check on your mom."

"Won't do any good," I said.

"So we'll lay off healing her." He pushed past me and into the living room. "But let's say our hellos while we still can."

I wanted to follow, but I held back. If I could find peace anywhere, it had to be out of my head. It had to come from other people.

When I left the bathroom, I saw Corey next to my

mother, holding her head by the bun in her hair, trying to keep her upright. He nodded to the joint in my hand. "You suck that whole thing up or what?"

"Is there a better way you can do that?"

"You got any ideas?"

It felt like a useless vision of the future. It wouldn't be long that I'd gather my friends to watch this same scene. My mother, hardly paler than now, slumped to the side. The drugs would help us pretend that she was still judging us, willing us to do better.

"Let's get a drink somewhere," I said. "Like somewhere not here."

"We can go to my house," Thomas said.

"I meant out-out," I said. "Like, I've got this weird energy, and I don't want to be in a living room."

"You're seventeen," Thomas said.

We looked at each other. Corey finally said, "Rabbit serves everyone."

When Thomas parked in The Rabbit's lot, he made a move to lock the door, but stopped at the last second. In the same way I could sense him in his car, he could smell me in the recycled air, and feel me in the lower back of his seat. So why lock the door?

When no band played at The Rabbit, it turned into a calculatedly drab party. Whereas the scene at Thomas's was fluorescent and hyperactive, like a junkie's aerobics class, this one was dark and quiet. Not dark like most bars, but dark like a basement, where you had to squint to make out your friends' reactions. Even our crew, high and slurry and familiar with one another, dried up when we stepped foot in the door.

Egan, behind the bar, didn't move when he recognized us. It wasn't unusual in itself, but even as we approached the bar, one by one, he didn't move to get us our drinks.

Instead, he bobbed his head as though listening to his own separate song. Finally, when I approached, he leaned forward. "Otto," he whispered to me. "Remember Otto." Then he walked into the recovery room, leaving me to go behind the bar and grab the drinks.

"What's that about?" Shea said when I returned to the table.

"Work stuff," I said. "I didn't call in tonight and he's pissed."

I have night terrors about losing memories—not all at once, but one by one. Each would make muffled popping sound as it flew from my brain. I imagine your thoughts could be plucked from your face as easily as your beard or your eyes and leave you smooth as stone. I fear it like I fear sleeping without dreaming. There's only so much reality you can draw from when you're awake, that you can rearrange in your sleep. Dreaming is a constant act of forgetting. But you know it happened, for at least a flash. You haven't run out of imagination yet.

For a long time, dreams, even nightmares, comforted me. I wanted to leave them slowly, second by second. When Aaron left, he woke me by taking my breath. He put one hand over my mouth and, with the other, pinched my nose. My eyes shot open and I tried squirming away from him, but he tightened his grip. I bucked against the bed, but it wouldn't give. The sides of the pillow felt hot around my ears. Then he started laughing.

"Hey kiddo," he said. "Got to guard yourself better than that. If I wanted it, you'd be a speed bump now."

I sat up on my elbows.

"I'm stepping down one, all right?" he said. "You be okay?"

I leaned over and started coughing. He put his hand over my mouth again, but this time only to silence me.

"You got the right idea," he said. "Be quiet, and nothing will happen."

He put on his favorite hat, a pinstriped throwback Houston Astros cap. Then he put one finger up to his goofy grin and sidestepped out the door.

I wasn't dreaming. The next morning, it was just my mother and me at breakfast. The next weekend, when she asked with practiced calm, "You haven't heard from your brother, have you?" Then on into the next Thanksgiving when neither of us ate the extra portion of food, I knew it wasn't a dream. Maybe for the last time, I was positive of the dividing line between reality and the dreamscape.

Now when I sleep, I look for pictures in my head. When they don't come, I wait for someone, stranger or kin, to snatch my breath away.

Thomas leaned into me and whispered, "You want me to go?"

I shook my head. "He's got this idea about—well, you know. Can't we just have our beers and not talk about anything?" They stared at me. "Look, you all were there. She's dead. My mother's pretty much a ghost right now, and it won't get better."

"I'm confused," Meander said. "I thought you were talking about Thomas and all that kid-fucking stuff."

"This isn't news." I took a gulp of beer and smacked the glass on the table. "Don't ask me for news about her—we're beyond news at this point. You," I said, pointing to Meander. "You wear glasses. Not all the time, but you need them to see. Anybody ever ask you if your vision recovered? Did you get over being nearsighted? That river only flows one way."

Meander put his hand to the side of his eyes, where his glasses rim would be. "All right, but what's that have to do with Thomas fucking a kid?"

Shea put two fingers to her lips, asking me to step outside and smoke. I didn't want to, but in my pause, I heard the rattle in the silence where I'd been speaking. This wasn't a conversation anymore. I stood and pushed my way to the door.

Outside, my fingers felt like they were frozen through, and I couldn't light my cigarette. I took a deep breath and tried a second time, but Shea Stanford plucked the lighter from my hands and flicked it on.

"Tell me something," she said. "Is it as simple as it looks?" She waved her hand, pushing her smoke in my face. "This whole thing. You make it sound so simple."

"Please," I said. "If you do nothing else, please don't confuse me." My nose was running now and my cheeks were so cold I didn't know if I'd started crying. "For just one time, say what you mean."

"I am," she said. "I'm saying you make it sound so simple. You don't call it by any other name, just as it is. I don't think I'd want that if I were you. Or if I were her."

"My mother?" I said. "Otto's mother? Who?"

"You think it means something to just say what's in front of you?" She shook her head. "All you're saying is what we know. Repeat it and repeat it like we can't understand. I think it's sad."

"Of course it's sad," I said. "She's—"

"Dying." Shea flicked her ash at my knee. "Dead. I know already. Thomas knows, Meander knows, everyone. Corey probably."

I took a drag off the cigarette. The smoke hung around my nostrils.

"It's such a goddamn pull on your life to just be honest all the time. What if we could only be what we wanted to be?" She slurred the last three words together. Jesus, she was nearly as wasted as I was. But even with her defenses wearied, she aimed for connection, hoping to make sense of what she sensed. "Wouldn't that be the worst? If we could only be what we wanted to be, never anything else? So that a tiger would always be a tiger, a cancer a cancer, and never see themselves as anything but that."

"I don't get it."

"Meander told me about Nightwolf," she said. "Your theory. It's the one slice of your life you're willing to take on faith. Everything else, you say the obvious like you're making a point, but when it comes to Aaron, you think maybe the world isn't exactly what it seems."

I could feel the blood flood my cheeks. "It was just a thought I had."

"No, I love it," she said. "It makes as much sense as him dematerializing, or whatever the prevailing theory is. I'm saying when you think like this—when you have theories and guesses and can play with the unknown—I recognize you again. With your mom, you just restate the obvious like it's profound."

The smoke in my lungs felt like a fishhook, the only thing leading me through a river of ice.

"It comes from guilt, you know?" she said. "People feel guilty, so they start listing what they know for sure rather than speculate and uncover what's wrong. Easier to say, 'My mom's dying' than 'I wish my mom would die.'"

I laughed at that, big and raspy, and suddenly I could feel the tips of my fingers again. "You really think I wish Mom was dead. Shit, I guess I do, but then I also wish your mom was dead, so we could have something to talk about."

"It's okay." She put her hand on my chest. "There's nothing here you can say that'll change that. It's okay. You're just a kid who's been left alone, same as all of us. We're just making noise here." She took out a fresh pack of cigarettes and smacked the bottom of it.

"There's really nothing I can say to disappoint you?" It hurt to smile—even my teeth were frozen. "Those words just don't exist?"

Somewhere that night, on the other side of town, Otto Larkin comforted himself against his memories. Maybe they were benign memories, but he'd have to protect himself against the people in his mind. That's the human condition.

Somewhere, even if it's only a moment in time instead of in space, my brother Aaron skulked around the outskirts of town. For him, there was no past. He could unpeel his memory like a potato, but when he forgot something, it was lost forever. Our mother predicted it somehow. Forgetting the world was her last defense, her last comfort.

The coyotes did not eat the boy because there were no coyotes. They did not lick his skin away because they had no tongues. The boy did not shiver himself to death because he did not have nerves. His heart did not rattle against his ribcage because he did not have a heart, and he did not have bones for that heart to batter. He did not get lost in the forest because there was no forest, and he could not get confused because he had no expectation of order. The forest did not exist. The boy did not exist.

The boy does not exist because the story does not exist because the storyteller does not exist. The useful part of her brain has evaporated, and the rest will follow. Even my brother, the listener, has disappeared. What good is our story without us?

I can't roam in the somewhere, sometime. I'm like the rest of us, forced to live in my own forehead. Our lives are the answers to our mothers' stories. Maybe we can't defeat them, but we can answer them, protesting that we are the ones who matter. And here we are, and here I am, swearing against all instinct, that I am real, that my pain is your pain, that I can outlive the sound of my own voice.

4.

As a child, Roxy-Jane Leckett preached to the chickens in the garbage heap that separated her property line from her neighbor's yard. Her mother was a constant runaway, and her father loved chasing, so Roxy and her twin brother, Monroe, were raised by the neighborhood. The family called themselves back-to-the-landers, though impatient ones. When the natural world squeezed too tightly, they flipped on a light or sparked a Zippo, and simply left town, one of them fleeing, one of them chasing.

The family never threw anything away. It added to the sadness of the world, they said, all the refuse, how quickly we say goodbye. On a practical level, it meant piles of garbage—coffee grounds, turkey necks, old toys, rotted wood—cluttering up their house and enormous yard. When their mother tried her hand at homesteading, instead of planting a proper garden, she spread the seed haphazardly around the backyard. Some of the seeds sprouted, though it was hard to tell when the garden started and the weeds stopped. The chickens were a left-over from a season the parents decided to raise their own eggs. The neighborhood children loved feeding them, so when a fox or stray cat would turn the coop into a mosaic of blood and feathers, some kindly neighbor would bring a replacement White Leghorn hen to make their own kids happy. The cats kept coming for the chickens and the dogs came for the cats and rats would come for the garbage and us kids would come for the show. Roxy, at age eleven, stood in front her house, with ribbons whipping haphazardly from her hair, holding a Bible she never opened, and spoke the good word to all of us.

Roxy was a natural preacher, passing judgment before she was old enough for pimples. We gathered to watch her bless the chickens, each sentence sounding high and light as a song. "Ain't no shame in sinning," she said to a brown guinea hen. "The shame comes in living a life unexamined." Monroe never spoke, but clapped his hands and laughed. "Let the spirit move you," Roxy told her brother when he interrupted her.

When we were young, not all of us were allowed at the Leckett House. Through the unending game of telephone that kids play with their families, some of the chipmunks or opossums sniffing the trash in their yard turned into wolves or cottonmouths. Meander Casey swore to heaven and back that he found himself face to face with an AIDS-monkey on their porch. Nobody believed him, but a few of us boys carried sharpened sticks to protect ourselves and show off for Roxy and the neighborhood girls.

Every summer, the Leckett twins went to a religious camp in Knott County. "Spiritual stamping grounds," Roxy called it. She made it sound fun—more canoeing and campfires and pickup basketball than fire and brimstone and blowing your priest—but Mom wouldn't let me tag along. For one, it wasn't Christianity exactly, but a hippie Christian offshoot. The longhaired preachers insisted we were already dead, and currently occupying heaven. We spent our lives seeking salvation when we'd already achieved it. "What do we know of heaven?" Roxy asked the animals, her brother, and me one morning. "All we know is that we got rewarded with life forever. But we living now, ain't we? We have our heaven without the pain of dying. I've won, and you've won, and we've all won, my friends—now we need to stop playing."

The other reason I couldn't go with the Leckett twins to Knott County was that, starting from the age of twelve, when they came home, they brought back enough industrial strength acid to keep the neighborhood tripping until All Saints Day. They called it eyeglasses for the spirit, a chance for the soul to step out of the skin. Monroe quickly sold his portion, and even at a dime on the dollar to what it's worth, he made a handsome day's pay with the high school kids who hung around the edges of Prospect Hill. Roxy held onto hers, using it sparingly, sharing it only with a select number of friends. For her, acid was a key to the kingdom, a decoder ring to see the invisible ink God had spilled before us.

We got older.

Before long, the Leckett twins drove themselves to Knott County. Monroe stopped selling his acid after one client got sick and tried to name him as the dealer in the hospital. The client, still high, said Monroe was his last name, causing confusion among the police officers and a narrow escape for Monroe.

Roxy began taking Lina Darby to her yearly retreat. Lina loved Roxy and the trips out east, not for the drugs or the heaven-speak, but for the time away from the city, away from her family. When the rest of us called Roxy "Kentucky Fried Christian" or "Mary Magda-hen," Lina swore she'd crack our skulls if we kept teasing her friend.

"It takes no mind to be scared," Lina told us. "The best part about the good news is that it has you whether you want it or not." These lines came straight from the funny farm, but Lina said them proudly. Before long, it was hard not to catch the believer bug. We were friends after all, and we owed each other our faith.

Monroe gave up acid and focused on becoming an aggressive and self-righteous alcoholic. He wore a powder blue baseball cap backwards, and kept a toothpick in his mouth. He was wonderstruck by his sister's sermonizing. Even us vandals—the most destructive, tear-it-down cynical among her friends—couldn't smartass our way out of Roxy's charm. I counted myself among the devoted animals, lining the edges of the Leckett yard.

Meander asked for time off from The Rabbit. His father was sick to where each deep breath sounded like his throat was trying to start a lawnmower.

"Time off?" said Egan Hopper. "You don't work here. You show up and collect empty bottles. You asking for time off is like a serial rapist threatening to go on strike."

Meander drained the bottom end of a beer he was bussing. "Not exactly."

"That's your argument?" Egan said. "It's not exactly like a rapist strike."

Egan could piss on Meander because I'd been his gold-star employee for the last couple months. At that point, they trusted me with cars. I knew how to get in, what streets to avoid, even how to sidestep the chop man's bullshit. The only downside was they were taking all the shit to Meander they could no longer dole out on me.

"Did you know your dad?" Meander asked me when we were alone.

"Not much," I said.

"That's the way to do it," he said. "If you don't know him at all, it gets in your head that he's this great guy. You grow up in the same goddamn house, and you can't get away from him. Best is to know him some. You did it right."

"I had very little to do with it."

"Dads are bullies," he said. "They shove their way into your mom, shove you around, and now they won't even die quietly."

In truth, Meander's dad was a solidly mediocre presence. He walked with a hunch and favored t-shirts that almost covered his belly and was dedicated to his own jokes. When he married Meander's mom, he expected blowback as he was a white man, marrying into a black family. But no one was outraged, and no one seemed eager to congratulate him on his open-mindedness. I found him a little uncomfortable to be around, like a man who was wearing a goofy tie and waiting for you to laugh at it.

"And my brother too," Meander said. "My family tree is probably that one kind that smells like semen." He was fidgeting, withdrawing from God-knows-what "You hear the news on Prospect? One of the Lecketts' camp friends replenished the supplies at The Ark." The Ark was what we called the Leckett house in tribute to the collection of animals in the yard. "I bet they'll be at Prophet's tonight."

Hallahan walked in, and Meander stiffened. He looked to me like he wanted to apologize, like his talk of bullies had brought one into existence. But I was no longer his ally. There was a quick, bright pleading in his glance. Please, he was saying. Let him hit you one more time. Join me one last time. But it was too late. Friendships don't have to die, but they can never remain equal.

The band at The Rabbit cancelled that night, so the bar was near empty. I was on the clock until ten, at which point, he sent me on the prowl. For the first time, Egan was getting specific. "Clay wants an Escalade," he whispered to me behind his hand. Clay was either the head of the chop shop or the middleman. They didn't tell me, and I don't even think Egan knew. "You know what an Escalade is, right?"

"Those stairs that go up automatically."

"I bet it was your mom who told you you were funny," he said. "Should've known she was nuts then."

"Why the Escalade?" I asked. "For his records and stuff?"

Egan cuffed me on the back of the ear. "You think I keep records about stolen cars? If you keep so much as a dream diary, I'll break your knuckles."

Egan wasn't good at being intimidating. He was almost big enough, and I didn't doubt his follow-through, but I'd known him too long. Beneath his bluster, he wanted to be my friend. You can't be a villain with one eye on the mirror.

Egan told me about a wedding party he wanted me to check half a mile down the road. It didn't make sense to me—by the time I got there, the wedding guests would be filing out, but he wasn't looking for an editorial.

I'd gotten high with a customer in the back of The Rabbit. Egan had forbidden me from doing that, especially on the nights I chased cars, but I was mad at him for joking on my mom. Anyway, I just had a few puffs, which gave me the confidence to take a few more. I tried to drink myself out of it, which was an imperfect strategy.

I made my way to the wedding, half certain I'd blow it off and head to Prospect. After three blocks, I heard someone call my name. I turned to see Corey walking to me. "You seen my brother?" He licked the crust at the side of his lips. Jesus, I thought, he was crying. I was used to seeing him perform on stage, near tears from the power of the music. Now that it was real, it looked fake.

"Pop's blood pressure dropped," he said. "Doctor says it's a matter of time."

"How much?"

"Don't know," he said. "Days, weeks, tomorrow, I don't know." He wiped the tears off his cheeks with the back of his hands. "We know what he's going to die from, where he's going to die, how he's going to die. 'When' is the last question left."

"Didn't you know all that yesterday?"

Corey put his hands over his eyes. "What's wrong with you? I have one last chance to get the family together," Corey said. "There's no tomorrow on this."

"I've got to do something for Egan," I said.

"Just tell him if you see him," he said. "Pop's on the clock."

I walked to Marimow's, a fake Irish Pub whose owner tried to antagonize his clientele. They had a dark parking lot and a deck in the back, so the smokers went there. That made it a decent spot for taking cars. Tonight, I noticed they were fancier than normal. Maybe this was the wedding, I thought, the after-party. Guests swam in a pack, which meant I likely had time. But if one saw me, they'd swarm, breaking me worse than anything Hallahan could do.

Escalade, I thought, sidling up to the nearest fancy car, unsure, as I was still half-a-mile away from sobriety, what kind it was. It had what looked like three lines and two layers of bumper stickers. Probably belonged to a kid, maybe a rich one. Some were hotheads, but rich kids made good marks.

I slid my slim jim from my boot and tested the edge of the passenger door. Hallahan said a surprising number of drivers only lock their door. The passenger door was locked, but I popped it easy enough. I stood up and looked around. This was the only time to slow down. Once you stand upright, dust yourself off and look confused. Most people give the bewildered a little space for fear they'll be asked a question.

I removed the cover and connected the wires. It was an older car, so I didn't have to work around the alarms. The lot was still empty when I peeled off, and I had gone four blocks before it even occurred to me to check the rearview.

This was definitely a teenager's car. The seat was tucked in tight by the steering wheel, which was how teens drove.

They think it gives them more control. Plus, the driver left the air and the radio on, which kids do, forgetting how that drains the batteries. I'd gone half a mile before realizing I was heading the wrong way. My drop-off was on the north end, but I was heading south toward the highway. The most direct route back was to retrace my steps, but I didn't want to drive back by Marimow's. I curved down Market Street, forgetting that it T'ed off into Orman Park. When I hit the cul-de-sac, the engine hiccupped and the radio whined, making me think the car would die. But it smoothed out, and I switched off the radio.

I threw it in reverse and backed down the street. Suddenly, I heard a siren screaming. I slammed the brake, stopping in the middle of the road, my heart popping out of my chest like a bubble of olive oil snapping in a skillet. The police car passed me, and I heard the siren growing dim. Right when I needed quiet, all I could hear was a husband and wife talking about insurance premiums. I hit the radio to turn it off again, but for some reason, I still heard static. I hit a different button, but nothing happened, so I hit it again and again, waiting for the hissing to stop. Then I spun around. On the ground, between the back and front seat, sat a small basket, with a baby wrapped in yellow. What I thought was radio static was the baby crying quietly.

I hit the gas to hide under the trees of Orman Park, but my car, still in reverse, shot backward and slammed into the bumper of a pickup truck. I reached back and let my hand hover over the baby's face, and then put the car in drive. As we started to roll, I felt him grab my ring finger with two hands.

The cops would be all over this and soon. Who leaves a kid in a car? Were they part of the wedding, maybe a bridesmaid dropping off her friend before calling it a night? Maybe that's what people did with babies. Could you leave them for fifteen minutes when they can't walk away? People were coming for me—I couldn't hear them, but they had no choice but to come. I scooped up the baby and ran into Orman Park.

At first, I figured I could leave him somewhere and then call the police. I ran to the slide, but I stopped. It would take ten minutes at the quickest for me to find a phone booth and another ten for the cops to come. The baby would survive in this weather, but it might crawl off the edge and fall on the rocks. That pretty much eliminated any apparatus higher than a bench. They had a kiddy swing where I could lock the kid down, but it had rained that afternoon. If the kid caught a cold on top of the jostle from the car wreck, he may be done for. Even if I left him on a dry spot at the ground, I couldn't feel safe. Wild dogs roam Orman Park at night. I opened my coat, tucked the kid inside close to my chest, and zipped him up.

Hold his head. I remember Roxy Leckett yelling that to her brother when he was cradling one of the neighborhood babies. So I secured his head outside of my coat. My chest shook from the cold, and I worried it would hurt his neck.

There were schools around here and churches. But this was a Saturday, so both would be empty. Whatever happened, I wouldn't let the kid starve. If it died, it'd die quick. The kid grabbed at the buttons on my shirt, and I could feel it brush up against the hairs on my chest. It thinks I'm his father, I thought. It was a girl's car—it had strawberry air freshener—so maybe it didn't have a dad. This was the first chest hair the kid had felt. I spread my fingers across my coat, around the impression of its head.

They'd kill me. The Rabbit wouldn't save me, Mom wouldn't save me, and I was too dumb to save myself. I broke through the edge of Orman Park. The city felt empty. I took the kid out of my coat to give it some fresh air.

There was a firehouse. They'd take it, but I couldn't

leave without them grabbing and holding onto me. But I could run. I'm fast, so I have an even chance.

On the street, away from the park, my thoughts came in, slow and steady and one at a time. I wanted to name him. It wouldn't have to stick, and even if this was a baby bound for the dumpster, his mother would have already named him. I didn't know why I was so sure this was a boy. He was dressed in yellow, and it's not like he had a moustache. But I thought from the way it tugged and wrestled with my chest that these were boy hands.

I turned the corner on the street with the firehouse. I'd started to hear the birds holler back and forth, which meant I was calming down. Right now, right here, I'm just a boy with a baby. I am no one to fear.

There was an alleyway next to the firehouse. I could slide in and try to pry open the side door with my slim jim. Most likely that would set off the alarm. Maybe the firefighters find the baby, giving me enough time to run away. Except as soon as I peeked into the side alley, I saw two firefighters smoking. One was yelling something inside to someone else.

"What about Chloe?" he said. There was an answer, but I couldn't hear it. "No, Chloe." He took off his visor and straightened his hair.

They still hadn't noticed me, even as I approached. The second fireman stubbed his cigarette out on his shoe, and I remembered myself. I almost ran—I tried to run—but my body could only reorient itself and walk away.

On Grayson Avenue, between Third and Fourth, homeless people had busted out every streetlight. It had started as some limp dick rebellion from a pack of roving anarchist teens, but after they left town, some of the religious runaways kept it up. They said Father Compost believed darkness revealed true light. God divided the night from the day, they said, and they rejected man's effort to merge the two. I had at least a pool of darkness to sit and gather my thoughts. Thomas the Prophet said it was dangerous there, but every time I saw it, it was abandoned. A lot of people confuse danger and emptiness.

When I got there, I sat on a bench, unzipped my jacket and examined the child. He was asleep but stirring. Maybe I just bite the bullet and call the police, I thought. My fingerprints were all over his everything, and it wouldn't take much to link me to the car.

It felt easier in the pool of darkness, like I'd signaled the moon for a timeout. Except then the baby started crying. I knew it was coming, but there was no warning—the kid went from dead silent to one long piercing shriek. "Hush, hush, hush, hush." I said it quickly like hail on a tin drum. I thought if I kept it up, he'd stop, or at least match up his noise with mine, but he kept screaming. I thought about singing a lullaby, but every lyric I knew vanished from my head. Instead, I made my voice low and imitated a bassoon playing a tuneless version of "O Come All Ye Faithful." Two men approached. They were loping, one moving to my right and one moving to my left.

"What you doing, man?" the man to my left asked. He was obese with a nose the size and shape of a toddler's fist. He had blue stars and spiderwebs tattooed across his neck. "You singing jazz or some shit like that?"

"I couldn't remember the words." I leaned back, and the kid inched up my chest.

"Naw, shit," said the man to my right. He swayed like a weed in a windstorm, and somebody had already worked him over, leaving him a fat upper lip and a badly broken nose. As a result, it looked like he had a half-moustache. In spite of the cold, he wore only a teal-striped tank top. This guy was high—they both were. "What you got a baby for?" He turned to his friend and jerked his thumb my way. "You see he's got a baby?"

The obese man with the neck tattoos laughed, then smacked his lips so it sounded like wet popcorn popping.

"Maybe you don't hear so hot. He asked you a question."

In the crook of an arm, I cradled the baby and, with my free hand, reached for my slim jim in my back pocket.

"Naw," said the half-moustached man. "I asked you a question, but it wasn't like a real question type question."

I couldn't take them both, but if I hit the half-moustache—the one who'd already been hit—his friend would linger over him, and I could get to the light.

"Why don't you tell me that kid's name?" the obese man said.

I grabbed the jack and went to swing it, but it slipped out the side of my hands and clattered at my feet. The noise made me jump, and I landed funny, twisting my ankle and making me fall back. The two men had their hands on me, but instead of rifling my pockets, they had scooped up the baby. I rubbed my eyes and saw the half-moustache, holding him at arm's length, making faces to make the kid smile. The obese man yanked at my hand. He kept pulling at me like he thought my elbow was something apart from the rest of my body.

"Shit, boss, you dropped your pryer," the obese man said. "You got to be carefuller than that with a girl."

"It's a boy," I said. "He's not mine. I saved him."

The two men looked at each other. All the sudden, the boy was toxic to them, something incriminating. "Saved him from what?" said the half-moustache. "He used to come home drunk and whoop his woman 'til you told him about Jesus?"

I shook my head. "No, no, a bad man tried leaving it in a car to die. This is the only way I could have saved him."

"If he ain't yours, why do we give him back to you?" the obese man said.

"Here," I said. "Take him to the firehouse on Third." I reached in my pocket and grabbed the cash I'd gotten from The Rabbit. I had a hundred, a fifty, and a twenty.

"This is for you all," I said, giving the hundred to the obese man. "The rest belongs to the kid."

"This is some bullshit," said the half-moustache. "We take him anywhere, we're going to say you gave him to us."

"Do," I said. "Tell them everything." I went in my pocket again and found two twenties. "This doesn't belong to me. None of this belongs to me. Just take him to the firemen and tell them you rescued him."

"They ain't pinning shit on us. We telling them about your crazy-ass."

"Talk about me," I said. "I don't care. Say you got him from The Nightwolf."

"Night what?" said the half-moustache. He took out a boxcutter, but didn't bare the blade. "Man, you fuck us and I'll put your balls where your eyes used to be."

"No scam, honest," I said. "The boy was in trouble, and Nightwolf saved him."

I ran. The men said they'd give me a two-minute head start before going to the firehouse. They were honest men—at least I thought they were—but all I believed in at that moment was speed. I didn't want to slow down. My stomach clamped down and I could feel myself doubling over, but I didn't stop.

Behind me, I heard a car horn honk. If this was it, then there was no escaping. Someone was calling my name—a woman. I stopped and put both hands over my head.

"Milo?" she said. "Wherever you're going, it'll wait for you."

I looked up. "Roxy?"

"What's the hurry for?"

I could tell from how she looked at me that I was crying. She smiled, big and questioning.

She rapped on the outside of her car door with her

ringed fingers. "If you're going up Prospect, I can give you a ride. You going to Prophet's?"

I shrugged.

"Get in," she said. "I can get you there faster than you can get yourself."

Her car was warm and dirty, which was exactly what I wanted at that point. She was muttering something. It reminded me of the boy's crying. It was like she was chanting a mantra, repeating the same line again and again. "Hold me, Father, don't let me escape Your creation. Hold me, Father, don't let me escape Your creation." Whatever meaning the phrase held for her at first, it was now a nursery rhyme, existing now as a rhythm on her tongue.

"Say, Roxy, I don't mean to be rude, but can I ask you something?"

She answered by sticking her tongue out at me, showing a tab of acid on it. "Don't panic," she said. "I drive better like this."

"Okay, for a second, I worried you were one of those chumps who drive worse on hallucinogens."

She went back to repeating her prayer, and it became stuck in my head as well. I tried my own. *I saved the life of the child I almost killed*, I thought. I tried repeating that to myself, but it didn't feel right. Instead, I repeated the phrase, I've earned this pain. It felt better. After all, that's what people do—exchange pain for pleasure, back and forth. I'd been on the good side of fortune for too long now.

And the kid? He wouldn't remember me unless I came back to him as a recurring shape in his dreams. For him, the cold would feel like the space between my fingers where I couldn't cover his head. Fear would taste like my chest hair.

There was a full crowd at Thomas the Prophet's

House. When the neighborhood was flush with Christian acid, the people weren't centralized in any one place. The boys stayed at Thomas's while the girls drifted from the Leckett Ark to up and down the street. The party swarmed around the bulk of the block, picking up neighbors in its wake.

Roxy stayed with me on Thomas's porch. From inside, I heard someone plucking a guitar and another playing a scratchy un-tuned fiddle, while everyone tried singing. Thomas loved sing-alongs, and kept his house stocked with instruments for his guests.

Roxy put both hands around my right forearm. "Do you want to come inside?" she said. "Your friends are in there."

I shook my head.

"Come on," she said. "If you don't talk to someone, it'll never get better."

"Things always get better because we forget about them."

"I can help," she said, almost whispering. "You're not the first boy I've seen who thinks the world's ending because he's bluer than a blue jay."

"And you're not the first girl who offers insight because she's higher than a blue jay," I said. "I don't need the Lord right now. Not even the suggestion of the Lord."

From inside, I heard a crash and people yelling. The door opened and Meander shot out, moving backwards. I thought he'd take a header off the porch, but he righted himself at the railing. "What do you say, Milo?" He bobbed like an inflatable clown.

Dirk Henson flew through the door, carrying a bow for a fiddle. "These are expensive, asshole."

"Relax," Meander said. "I was seeing what she sounded like."

Dirk Henson had moved to town a few months ago from San Antonio. He fit in well with the rest of us except for his unrelenting sincerity. It was an open secret that he loved almost every woman in front of him—not like a womanizer but an honest romantic. That scratchy fiddle sound was most likely that of Lina Darby, who was learning her instrument and hadn't found the proper notes as of yet. That must have meant that tonight, Dirk loved Lina, and he was out here defending her honor.

Thomas the Prophet came outside and grabbed Dirk by the shirttail to hold him back. "It's okay. We're all friends here. No one got hurt."

Meander started to walk to the door. "Is Monroe in there?" he said. "It's your brother," he said, pointing to Roxy. "He's got my stuff."

"You don't need any more," Thomas said.

"Not that," Meander said. "My phone. My wallet."

I could see his wallet half-sticking out of his front pocket, but I didn't want to contradict him. Instead, I lit two cigarettes and gave Meander one.

"Fuckers," Meander said. "That's right, I'm talking to you."

Thomas and I looked at each other, unsure which of us he meant to insult.

"You heard me," Thomas said. "You, your brother, all you fucking Christians with your Bible junkie shit. Jesus was a shitty carpenter who talked like a pretentious teenage poet, and His only talent was God raped His mom."

Roxy didn't move. She'd heard worse, so she knew not to feed the heretics.

"Hey, listen to me," Meander said, snapping his fingers in front of Roxy's face. "You mumbo-spewing maniac, I'm talking to you."

The music started up again, and the sound immediately pacified Meander. His pose slackened and he smiled. "I—I'm sorry. You know I'm joking, right?" He stepped forward with his arms out like he wanted Roxy to hug him, but Thomas stood in his way. "I'm trying to apologize, okay?" He reached over Thomas's shoulder like Frankenstein.

"Take it easy," I said. "I'll get your wallet." His face snapped back to anger at the word 'wallet' but he buried it in Thomas's shoulder. Thomas kept murmuring into his ear, like Meander was his dog, and he was trying to get him to swallow a pill.

In the front hall, next to the circle of musicians, Dirk had his arm around Lina's shoulder. She still hadn't let her violin bow out of her hand. Dirk saw me, but Lina wouldn't open her eyes. It looked like she was in the middle of being kissed.

"Meander," Dirk said as means of explanation. "He swiped Lina's bow and sawed it on her forehead. He said he wanted to play her to see how she sounded. That bastard played his shoe, the fireplace. He played some stray basset hound in the kitchen. Even tried playing Monroe Leckett's dick, but Monroe hit him in the chin."

From the musical circle, I heard a fiddle take the lead, except it was especially scratchy. It was Monroe, playing the instrument with a wooden soupspoon. He was a preternaturally gifted guitarist and a mediocre dobro player, but this sounded unbearable.

"He's using my fiddle," Lina said, "but I wouldn't give him my bow. He said he could make it work."

One by one, the other musicians put down their instruments. Soon, it was only Monroe and a skinny Spanish stranger tapping on a steel drum with his fingers. Then, in a sudden burst of melody, a cell phone at Monroe's feet went off.

"This ain't mine," he said, meaning the cell phone, but holding up the ladle. "Oh, yeah," he said, kicking the phone away, toward me. "This belongs to your dick-grabbing friend? Keep that prick away, or I'll throw it in the laundry."

I took Meander's phone, and saw he had twenty-seven

missed calls. Over half were from Corey, four were from his mother, one was from me, which I didn't remember, and the rest I didn't recognize.

I checked his texts. Fourteen read, "Where Are You?" from his brother. Twenty others, also from his brother, simply had one, two, or three question marks and exclamation marks. Three more were from "Mom." They read, "DAD DYING. COME QUICK", "Dad dead", and "Please come, let me know u are safe."

When I came outside, I saw Thomas, Meander, and Roxy, all talking at a maniac's pace. None of the three were looking at any of the other's faces.

"Jesus," I said, "what's going on here?"

"It's a summit," Thomas said. "It's a convention. We need a fourth."

"I got your phone off Monroe," I said. "You have missed calls."

"Calls," Meander yelled as if in surprise. "Missed calls, found calls. Mr. Popularity is my middle name."

"Your middle name can't be Mr.," Roxy said. "Mr. Popularity is your last name."

"Check your messages." I looked around at the others, holding back laughter. "What's going on here? Did I miss something?"

Thomas tapped his left nostril twice. "Just a line or two apiece. I thought they needed sobering up."

"Do you have any left?"

Thomas shook his head.

"Did I fuck today's girlfriend?" I said. "What's it got against me? And Meander, you need to look at your phone."

"Excuse me, sir," Meander said, hunching over and pacing the porch. "Have you seen my calls? I seem to have misplaced them."

That did it. I looked at his phone and dialed his mother's number. That shut him up, though it didn't quite kill his coke-fueled smirk.

A man answered the phone. "Lee? Where are you?" I'd forgotten that his family still called him Lee.

I offered Meander the phone, but he shook his head. Though he still smiled, he looked scared.

"Goddamn it, Lee, where are you?"

"Hello," I said. "I'm calling about—"

"I know why you're calling, Lee. Are you—I mean, we're all—are you okay?"

"Is it done?"

There was some deep breathing on the other end of the line. "No," he said. "Not yet. We thought so, but he came back. I don't know how long, but—Goddamnit, Lee!"

"Can I talk to him?" I said.

"He can't talk. He can't see. This is the end, kid. His last tomorrow happened yesterday." He laughed. "Remember when he said that about Granny? You thought he was crazy, and I—"

"No," I said. "I'm coming over."

I was the one who hadn't done coke, so I had to drive. Thomas was the one who could calm Meander down, so he had to come as well. Roxy decided she was coming too, and we figured, why not? We wanted to take Thomas's car, but three separate cars blocked him in. Roxy couldn't find her keys, and we didn't have time to root around the porch to look for them. I knew my cue.

I took out my slim jim and opened her door. Then after a minute's fiddling, I hotwired the car. As soon as the engine purred, and I could feel the gasoline scent moving from my nose to the back of my throat, I looked out the driver's window to see Roxy dangling her keys at me. "They were in my purse," she said.

Thomas and Meander filed in the back, and Roxy

moved in the passenger side. This was a confession, I thought, jumping a car in front of Thomas. But Jesus, after tonight, I'd give anything to only be a car thief again.

"Where am I going?" I asked Meander. "What hospital?"

"He's at home," Meander said. "They took him off the machines and sent him home yesterday."

I hadn't been to Meander's house in a year. It smelled like Comet and generic cat food. Tonight, it would smell like old men and medicine and rubber gloves and powder.

Roxy rolled down the window and stuck her hand outside. Her fingers were open and she rolled her palm up and down. She was the only one in the car who was at peace.

"I ran into Corey," I said. "He told me what's going on with your dad."

"Can we not talk about my father?" Meander's voice was shaky, and he kicked the back of my seat over and over again. "I can't think about him anymore tonight."

"Okay, but to give you a heads-up, where we're going, his name might come up."

I heard Roxy singing a song that was lost on the wind. Not a prayer this time, but a high, looping children's ballad.

"I'll talk about him if I have to talk about him, but I don't want to," Meander said.

"You have to," I said. "Think of it like a game."

"He gave me a gun." His voice remained lodged between tears and laughter. "A Colt that he stole from his uncle's store. I'd turned eight, but it was an everyday I-love-you present, not for my birthday."

"Eight?" Thomas said. "Unbelievable."

"It wasn't for shooting," Thomas said. "It was just to play with. Like to show to the other kids."

"How's that better?"

"He never gave me bullets or nothing." He kept tapping

his foot against the back of my chair. "I called myself Kid Colorblind, and pretended I's this deadeye gunslinger."

"Colorblind?" I asked.

"Dad thought it would be good to be a non-racist cowboy. I liked that too, because, historically, the Indians were more fun. We named the gun 'The Equalizer' because of equal rights." He laughed. "Once, Shane Larkin and I were playing, and Shane's trying to ride this mastiff like a horse. I have the gun trained on the dog, thinking I'm keeping it in line. Then I black out."

I turned down Olive Avenue.

"The mailman had brained me," Meander said. "He thought I was shooting Shane, so he takes his mailbag and knocks the light out of my eyes. When I come to, poor Shane's crying, and the mail-bastard's trying to comfort him."

The porch light flipped on, and I could see shadows in the windows. It was a matter of time. Meander couldn't stay lost on his story for much longer.

"The mailman hadn't taken my gun," Meander said. "He'd hit me, then gone to Shane. So I rise up and point and aim and fire. Nothing happened at first, and I waited for him to fall, but he didn't. So I shot him again, this time in the back of the head."

Roxy put her head out the window. This was all about to come crashing down.

"I forgot it was unloaded," Meander said. "All I knew was I wanted him dead, and I really tried to kill him. I guess that's not a story about my father, but, you know, kind of." The tremor had returned to his voice. "Normally, when I tell that story, it's funny. It didn't sound funny just then. Oh, and when my mother found out—"

"Meander," Thomas said. "It's time."

"Right, but just one thing."

"They're coming for you," he said.

Meander's mother and a man I didn't recognize were

on the porch, their faces bisected by the porchlight. "Pay your respects," I said.

Meander swallowed and shook his head.

"Tell him the story you just told us," Thomas said. "Tell it like you told it just now. Everyone will like it."

"He won't."

"You're not talking to him anymore," Thomas said. "You're talking to yourself, but it's a good talk to have."

Roxy shook her head. She had been listening. Maybe she wasn't as high as I thought. It was hard to tell with Roxy because so much of her life was a sermon.

"Wait for me," Meander said. "At least for a little, please don't go." His face corkscrewed into a strained smile as he left the car. I'd seen this look on him before, in the seconds prior to his beatings at The Rabbit. His mother guided him inside.

Thomas the Prophet sat on the hood of Roxy's car and took out three cigarettes. He gave one to me, one to Roxy and kept one dangling out of the center of his mouth.

"He's a troubled soul," Roxy said. "I've seen him sad before, but, God, he's scared to be around death."

"Troubled soul because death scares him?" Thomas said. "Shit, what else is there to be scared about?"

The smoke from the cigarette went in my nose, making me cough. I wanted to join their conversation, but I felt the buttons on my chest brush against my chest hair, and I thought of my boy. What if his mom leaving him in the car was a minute's fury, no more than Meander Casey trying to murder the mailman? At that point, what's the difference between a baby and a dog? A bark is as expressive as a human cry.

"I saw The Nightwolf tonight," I said. "Outside of the Firehouse on Third."

"It's just Nightwolf," Roxy said. "It's not The Nightwolf."

"Honestly?" Thomas said. "Was he—was he who you

thought he was?"

"I don't know," I said. "He had a kid in his arms, and he was running."

"Why do you say it was him?" Thomas said.

"He had a—I don't know, a uniform." I was stammering. "Not a mask, but he had his face painted. Or not painted, but, you know."

"Tattooed?" Thomas said.

"Not tattooed," I said. "Just in the way he ran. It was him."

"Aaron?" Thomas mouthed.

The cherry of my cigarette burned my fingers. I took out another and jumped it from my first. "He had a kid in his arms, a baby boy," I said. "I don't know if he stole it or he was rescuing it or what."

"How do you know it was a boy?" Roxy said.

"From his hands," I said.

"The baby's hands or the wolf's hands?" Thomas said. "I don't understand."

"His hands, I don't know." I smacked my leg. "What's with the fucking questions? You, Roxy, everyone, you all talk gibberish every hour you're awake, and you pass it off as philosophy. I say one thing that doesn't make sense, and suddenly my bullshit gets peer-reviewed." I took a deep breath. "I thought this is how breakthroughs happen. You say shit and sound sure of it. It works for everybody else, but I can't even have a proper breakdown."

"Breakdown or breakthrough?" Thomas said. "Again, I'm lost."

The front door slammed. Meander stood on his front steps, rocking back and forth, his arms folded across his chest. It looked like he was about to fall, but he stepped back at the last second to right himself. After he found his feet, he brushed his chest off, as though he was covered in crumbs, and stumbled his way to us.

"Did he—?" I waved my fingers in front of my face,

though I'm not sure why that was my nonverbal euphe-
mism for dying. "Is it over?"

"They told me I could go," Meander said.

"Who?"

"I fell down," Meander said. "It wasn't fainting, but
I fell down, and no one laughed." He swallowed and
looked at the three of us, one by one. "They wasn't mad
or anything. It was just it's time for me to go."

"Lee," Thomas said. He'd never called him Lee
before, but he knew what he was doing. "Is he gone?
Dead."

"Man, I don't know," he said. "More or less. He'd,
you know, he did what he came to do."

"Lee, you don't have to leave," Thomas said. "Maybe
don't go back inside, but you don't have to leave."

"It's okay," Roxy said. "You don't have to worry
anymore."

No religion, I thought. Please, no religion, no fighting.
Because if she slips in one word of her here-is-heaven
philosophy, then Thomas would turn on her, and we'd
lose our harmony, the last thing we had to offer.

Meander looked to the house. "I want to go back
inside," he said. "But not yet. Until it's a hundred percent
finished, we just wait here."

"It's cold," I said.

"Fuck the cold." Thomas covered his eyes to try to
look inside the house. "We can wait until whenever."

"There is no outside, and there is no inside," Roxy
said.

In the shadows between the side of the house and
the bushes, I saw the boy, rolling around on his back.
I wanted him to crawl, but he was too young for that,
barely old enough to lift his head. He was safe here, rolling
around in the yard, ignored by the family. I wanted to
picture him asleep in the firehouse as the firefighters
scrambled through the city to pin down the mother. No

longer hungry, no longer cold. What else did he know at that age? There was hunger and there was the nipple and there was the time when the world went away. *I did no more damage tonight than on most nights.* That sounded good—not right exactly, but it felt comfortable like a loose pair of pants—so I said it again. I repeated it to myself, muttering it. I didn't think anyone could hear, but when I focused, Roxy and Thomas were looking at me.

"You OK?" Thomas said.

"Of course not."

Thomas put his hand between my shoulder blades. He meant it as a comfort, but it occurred to me that this is what Otto Larkin must've felt.

"There was a kid," I said. "A boy. He almost died."

"Right, the Nightwolf," Thomas said. "You told us."

"No, it was me," I said. "I almost killed someone today."

Thomas looked at me and then Meander, who was staring at his front door, rattling his knuckles on the hood of the car. He thought I was confusing my story with Meander's. I almost killed someone. He pictured me with my father's gun, closing an eye and taking aim at the mailman. Shade by shade, we were blending into each other.

"You didn't kill anyone," Roxy said.

"Almost."

"No," she said. "You don't have that sort of power. You never did."

We're already dead. I'd heard her spiel before, but right now, at least, it made sense. Each of us had our flirtations with death, but we outdanced it, moving just a little quicker. And each night we're rewarded with life, and the expectation that life will wait for us in the morning. Oh, why not? It was as good as any other.

A light in the front hall flipped off. They were going to bed. So the father was gone, already slipping through the night. I'd like to believe in the quick soul, one that could push its way from body to body, but we move no faster than we do on earth. Slower, if anything. We'd have time then.

Couldn't this be a subdivision of heaven? Maybe there was wisdom in the mountain hippie and acid camp that existed beyond the barriers of my understanding. That's a bitter pill to swallow, the world outside of my imagination. Roxy kept something of the ocean in her voice when she preached. It made the life she promised sound mysterious and real, pulsing with an endless beat.

This is the time, I thought. If we were ever to change, it would have to be now. We were worn down and opened up and ready to accept whatever the wind blew at us. In the cold air, with reason surrounding us and receding from our grip, it was easy to believe we could stay that way forever.

But soon Meander stretched out in the back of the car and fell asleep. Not long after, Roxy used Meander's blacked-out body as a mattress and fell asleep on top of him.

Thomas and I stayed up. He put his hand on my back again, and this time, it felt good. After a while, we were both ready for bed, but I stayed outside for a quick cigarette. Halfway through my smoke, Thomas passed out as well, leaning over the stick shift. Sunrise was coming, but with no urgency. I tossed the cigarette, then hotwired Roxy's car, and drove them back to Prospect Hill.

5.

The police thought they collared Nightwolf. The newspapers kept cagey about it, saying the cops booked a person of interest in a "prolonged vandalism case." Prolonged vandalism—like the tagger had writers block and agonized for weeks, and then returned to the scene of the crime to erase a comma.

It was a game, I figured. Say you have Nightwolf to send the real Nightwolf into a tizzy. That way, the criminal could go on a graffiti binge, making a careless mistake along the way.

That was a losing strategy. Nightwolf relished a game of chicken with the cops, seeing who would flinch first. If anything would tie his dick in a bow, it was how the papers implied he was nothing but a tagman. He saw himself as a freedom fighter. The tags were the leaves of his tree, not the acorn.

But I was wrong. After about four days, the paper reported that the cops released a drifter named Delaney Moore who they had kept on charges of possession and making threatening statements. I wouldn't have noticed it at all except they printed the man's mug shot in the top corner of the article. He looked redder than I remembered, but it was the obese man with the neck tattoos. The papers didn't mention the child.

I imagine Delaney Moore told the firefighters he was The Nightwolf, or at least that's what they heard in his Nyquil accent. By the time the law got involved, they'd see this demented hobo with someone else's kid, muttering vigilante haiku, and they'd pin him as their guy.

The day after they returned Delaney Moore to his world of stew and tire fires, the paper ran a new sketch of Nightwolf. Now you could see his face. The lips were too thin and the eyes too close together, but it was a drawing of me.

Thomas the Prophet must have bought every spare paper in town. He cut out dozens of the sketches of Nightwolf with an Exacto knife and pasted them all on the kitchen wall above his sink. Not everyone saw the resemblance, and those who did took it as just that—a funny accident, no different than if the Unabomber and I wore the same sunglasses. But to Thomas, my mug in the paper had one concrete consequence: the unambiguous cleaving between me and The Egan Rabbit.

"You got about as much freedom as the cops want to give you," Thomas said. "Most times you can't wake up a Kentucky cop unless you need someone to beat a striking miner, but they want this guy badder than they want to fuck around on their jobs. They get half a lead, and it brings them back to the Rabbit. You're good as booked."

"For what?"

Thomas shrugged. "If they can't nail you as The Flying Trashbag, they'll settle for kidnapping. They are determined to fuck someone, and you are a gaping vagina."

"Metaphorically?"

"You really need to learn what a metaphor is."

According to Thomas, Egan only understood pain—a good day was when he caused more than he caught. That sort of work took all the intellect of a cue ball, and it was beneath me. It was a childish outline of us both. No one understands just one emotion, especially not Egan. He tried to mentor us, and he wanted to show us the three dimensions of the world. Pain was the salt of his life, not the meat. But Thomas was right about The Rabbit. I told myself I'd drop out at the first sign of trouble. Having my face in the paper was too big to ignore.

The next day, I showed up to my shift early with the intention of shaking hands and filing a no-fault divorce from the place. Egan had run off to a concert in Cincinnati, leaving me to resign to his flunkies. Lemon the Soundman was behind the bar that night, but he told me, "Don't know, don't give a shit." Instead, I had to wait for Hallahan to check in, so I could talk to him instead.

Hallahan took me outside. "You quitting because a drawing in the paper?" He spat on the ground. "That ain't up to you."

"I didn't think you were going to miss me so much."

"There's a way out if you want it, but you don't want it," he said. "He gives the word, I have to beat you out."

"That sounds similar to 'beat you off,' but I doubt it means the same thing."

"I don't want to, but that's the job," he said. "You can leave, but first I turn you into a grease spot."

"That's big talk. You think you can handle it?"

Quicker than a camera's flash, he grabbed my face and slammed my head against the brick. I took a step toward him, but he blasted me with a forearm to the ribs. I bounced back to the wall and took another step forward. This time, I tripped over his shoes and fell face first on the cement.

"That was with my left hand." He squatted down, so he could whisper to me. "Don't make me use two."

And then it was over. I'd been away from school for so long that I barely knew how to get there. Mom's apartment was an unwaking nightmare. So I holed up on Prospect Hill in Thomas the Prophet's guest room. If Egan found out, he'd kill me. But by night three, that fear felt ridiculous. There was no "if"—Egan knew my mind before I did. Anyway, the parties kept happening. Sometimes at night, right before I slept, I felt the baby's hands against my ribcage, his mouth clamping onto my chest hair.

I might have stayed on Prospect Hill for keeps, but on day four, Thomas evicted me. Time to check in back home, he said. Nightwolf had hit my neighborhood Kroger though his heart wasn't in it. He'd just written "NIGHetc..." on the side of the building in capital purple letters. Directly under it, a second tagger had drawn a masturbating owl with a monocle and a cigar. I wondered if this was a new thing—an answer to Nightwolf, saying, "This is what a real nighttime animal thinks of your signature."

I walked home. Someone had drawn rainbows on the street in erasable paint. Whoever did this didn't care about posterity. Jesus, I thought, maybe the whole city had a tag now. Everybody wants to claim their share of Lexington, but no one has anything to say other than their name and spirit animal.

The markings continued down Sunset Avenue and the final stretch before my apartment complex. The rainbow tagger first ran out of blue, then green, then orange, so after a while there were only two parallel lines—one yellow and one red. The yellow line turned patchy and the red had lightened to pink. That was a temporary setback because fifty feet later, all the colors came back, bold as in the beginning. This time the lines crisscrossed and blended together to where they looked like a blob, somewhere between brown and purple. They straightened into lines again and then connected into one gigantic X at the building catty-corner to my complex. Above the X, in the familiar big-block letters, it read, "*DON'T BE FOOLED BY CHEAP IMITATIONS, THERE'S ONLY ONE NIGHT-WOLF.*" Below it, in smaller print, it read, "For best Nightwolf, add lentils to two cups of boiling water. Mix in three teaspoons of Parkay margarine to…" The print became illegible, but I'm pretty sure it was the beginning of Mom's pilaf recipe.

This was Aaron. He'd seen my picture in the paper, and he thought I was stealing from him. If he was anything like I remembered, he wouldn't stop.

My mother was sitting on the couch, squeezing her head between two pillows. The phone rang, and she squeezed tighter. She didn't look at me when I slammed the door. I started to walk past her to the phone, but she grabbed my wrist.

"Don't answer," she said. "It's them."

"Them?"

"Yes," she said. "It's you."

"I'm me," I said. "The phone is something else."

"Your friends are calling," she said. "Your Chinese friend."

"I don't have a Chinese friend."

"Not a Chinese-Chinese friend," she said. "The other type."

"Chinese acquaintance?"

The phone stopped ringing. She took the pillows from the side of her head and stared at the receiver. Five seconds later, it rang again.

"A man came for you," she said. "Are you in trouble? The man said he wanted you at work. To protect you."

I put my hands over my eyes. "He's not Chinese, Mom.

He's from Cleveland, and his name's Ollie Hallahan. That sound Asian?"

"I don't like it. I do not like it." She spoke like she spoke to me when I was a boy—slow and pointed, with her mouth puckered like she was whistling.

"I think I saw Aaron outside." I heard myself say it without knowing why. "I didn't talk to him, but I'm pretty positive."

She walked past me and answered the phone. She didn't even say "hello" but stayed with the receiver cradled by her ear. A touch of wind blew open her bathrobe.

"Who's there?" I said. "Don't blink at the fucking thing. It's a phone."

She nodded her head and opened her mouth to speak, but said nothing. Finally, she put the receiver on her shoulder but kept working her jaw like she was trying to keep up her end of the conversation.

I grabbed the phone off of her chest and jerked it up to my ear. "Hello." I was speaking to the wrong end, so I flipped it. "Who is this?" I heard a noise—slow wet breath first, then a hum. "Talk to me, motherfucker."

"Please," Mom said. "That language."

She knew, I thought. It's Aaron trying to talk to us. Surely, one of the last thoughts to barnacle the hull of her mind would be her firstborn's voice.

"I don't want ugliness," Mom said. "This is my house, so respect my wishes."

"You think you can't be found?" I said into the phone. "I'm not seven anymore."

I heard a smoky cough and then a laugh. "Oh shit, he's back. You hard to get ahold of, ain't you?" It was Hallahan. I could practically smell the weed through the receiver. "Jesus, man, where you been at?"

On the phone I heard a muffling and then a different voice. "Milo, I'm scared for you." It was Egan. "We need to make sure we're on the same page."

"I don't want to work anymore."

"This isn't about the job; it's about you," he said. "We want you to be safe."

"I'm safe," I said. "I'm home now."

"And we're glad," Egan said. "A woman in your mother's condition can't take on additional worry."

"What do you know about it?"

He laughed, and for the first time, I could actually believe he wanted to comfort me. This felt uncalculated. "Take some time to settle in. Order a pizza, eat it with your mom. We're not particular on this side of the sun."

Mom was running her hands up and down the front of her robe like she was trying to give herself a rash.

"What you do over the next two hours and forty-seven minutes is entirely up to you," Egan said. "I've made my suggestion, but as God said to His buddy, the problem is I'm giving you free will."

"His buddy?"

"Come seven o'clock," he said, "you lose free will. At that point, you'll be outside of your building meeting Peyote. You'll get in his car and come to The Rabbit."

"I don't want to work."

"It's customary to give two weeks notice for your employer to find a suitable replacement." I could hear the humor creeping back in his voice, hanging off the edges of tone like a wart. "Our relationship was atypical, so I'm willing to overlook that stipulation provided you give an exit interview."

I tried looking at my mom again. It was like seeing myself in the reflection of a twisted piece of aluminum foil.

"You dodge us, we'll wait for you until you come outside," he said. "You think you can outwait us, but you're wrong. Anytime from now until when the river runs in reverse, we'll be there across the street, waiting for you."

"This is supposed to scare me?" I said. "It's not torture

for me to go to a bar."

"Here's the thing to remember," he said. "We'll wait until doomsday, but we'll never go inside. Do you know what I'm saying?"

He knew me too well—his threats cut so deep, blade bruising bone. If I stayed here, I'd turn into my mother. Nothing on the outside—not Hallahan, not Nightwolf, not even shaking myself to death in the snow—could scare me as much as that.

At 7:00, Petey Peyote pulled up beside me in his Outback. Petey stayed nice to me, and it made me confident, but I'd worked for Egan long enough to distrust my own smile. There was always a game beneath the game, and believing you'd won was the first sign you didn't know the rules.

When we pulled into The Rabbit's parking lot, Hallahan was perched on a ladder trying to cover up the newest coat of Nightwolf graffiti. This is what they wanted me to see—Hallahan the strongman, cleaning up a mess. They wanted to rub it in his face, so he'd be double primed to bite a hole in my ass as soon as they gave him the thumbs up.

The Rabbit was empty, save for a tourist in a cowboy hat dry-humping a teenager in the corner, and two college students whispering to one another from across the jukebox. Both couples had an unopened six-pack of Bud on the tables closest to them—Egan's foolproof way of saying "Drink what you want, but don't bother me."

I stood by the bar. Egan leaned against the wall, reading the paper and refusing to look up. I plucked an olive and a maraschino cherry and popped them both in my mouth, a defiant move I wished I'd thought through better.

Finally, a woman with tightly curled dark hair came

out from the back. She moved unevenly, like an infant on a skateboard. "You're Milo," she said. "The two of us met before. In different times."

"A lot of times were different times," I said. "Maybe even most."

"So after all this, you're going to be a smart aleck to me."

"I'm sorry," I said. "I don't know who you are."

"That's what it took," she said. "You don't know how long I spent wondering what it was going to take for you to say 'I'm sorry' to me."

I looked to Petey for help, but he shook his head. Egan lowered his newspaper. "I'm sorry," I said. "I could keep saying it, but I have a feeling you'd get fed up."

"You really don't know me?" she said. "Maybe it wasn't a big deal to you." •

"Look, I'm not trying to be a dick," I said. "I meet a lot of people, and I drink. Plus, my mother has this memory thing, and I'm sure it's just lurking in me."

Petey sidled in beside me, lit a cigarette, and then put it in the woman's mouth. "Come on, Becks," he said to her. "This ain't about him."

"Of course," I said, snapping my fingers. "You're Becky, right?"

"My name is Bonnie Boudreaux Larkin," she said. "I never told you my name when we first met, but you should remember anyway. My son remembers you."

"So I know your son," I said. "This still leaves me with a lot of questions about you. Or rather, it should, but it doesn't. Maybe it's not because you're so fucking mysterious. Maybe, Bonnie Boudreaux, it's because you've given me no reason to care."

She tilted her drink forward like she was about to splash me, but changed her mind. "Okay, this is the boy I heard so much about. It's precisely that attitude that made you so successful and well-liked."

In that sentence, I heard my mother's battery acid love. Was this one of her distant friends—a modeling buddy gone to seed? But then she looked to Egan Hopper, and crinkled up her mouth to the side. Otto Larkin did that on Prospect Hill when he concentrated on his Box Kite.

"Otto's mom," I said.

"He remembers." She let her glass tumble from her hand and smash on the floor.

"What'd you do that for?" Egan said. "It's Petey's got to clean it."

"You wanted me here," she said. "You bring me here, and you keep saying to trust you, and goddamn, how long do I have to wait?"

"Well, I have some bad news for you." Egan walked close to us and put his arm around Bonnie Larkin. "You see, Milo here found himself in some trouble the other night. I don't know what's got into him, but he's turning in his card, leaving the business. Now I'm typically all for giving a man his privacy, but this—"

"This's fucking obnoxious," I said. "We're not on a talk show. If you want to talk to me, talk to me."

"Now I'm all for giving a man his privacy, but this—" He stopped and ran his finger around the rim of his glass. "Did you think that's how I end my sentences, or were you being an inconsiderate shitbird?"

I looked back and forth, but neither of them moved.

"See, that was a question," Egan said. "A sentence that, when finished, necessitates a reply. I asked if you were being a shitbird, and you gave me the rare non-answer that provides an answer. You seem to have lost a manner or two in the last few days, and I'm not clueless as to where it went." He tapped one of his nostrils.

"Listen," I said. "Things are confusing right now. Now, I know—"

He smacked me in the jaw. Before I even felt it, he had

his hand re-cocked at his hip. "Tell me what you know," he said.

The man in the cowboy hat and his date stood up.

Egan put his hands up. "It's his birthday," he said, nodding toward me. "One to grow on. Take another round."

Petey Peyote brought a soggy six-pack to the back and plopped it on one of the back tables. It seemed to satisfy everyone.

Egan leaned close. "We're not here to negotiate. We're talking about your debt."

Behind him, Bonnie Larkin was crying. It could have been the violence or her memories. It could have been from the joy of seeing me get hurt.

"You made me out a liar," he said. "When I vouch for you, you have an obligation. Now you plan to walk away and leave me with my dick in my hand."

"That's not the worst place for it to be."

"I can't keep hitting you, Milo," he said. "Business isn't good enough to give away more beer, so you need to listen. Part of what I paid you for was your loyalty. You running away is a violation of our contract."

"I never signed a contract."

"I asked you for something specific," he said. "To pick up a car and deliver it to Clay. Did you do that?"

"I tried," I said. "There was a curveball."

"A *curveball* put you in some junkie predator's house?"

I wanted to run. They'd make me wash with a cheese-grater once they caught me, but it would be worth it just to be away from this conversation.

"A business like ours depends on reputation. Because I'm sweeter than is healthy when it comes to you, and because I sometimes have the brain of a drunken fetus, I attach your name to mine. 'Don't worry, Clay,' I say. 'My Lemur's on the hunt,' I say." He opened a bottle of club soda and poured it into a coffee cup. "All right, we both misjudged, but as we share profit, so we share blame."

"Eighty-twenty?"

"Stop pulling numbers out of your ballbag." He faced Bonnie, who was still crying, and then spun back to me. "In terms of future earnings, there's no telling what your MIA act cost me, but I'll be generous to myself and say fifteen thousand."

"Come on?" I said. "Bullshit."

"Relax," he said. "You don't have two percent of what you owe. I'm not looking for your blood. I want a proper severance."

"Just let me go, and we'll forget this."

"Forgive and forget," he said. "Your crowd talks about them like they're the same. Forgetting happens. Forgiveness is an act of will. Okay, I get it, you're young, and these are the forgiving years."

A bottle shattered behind me. Egan grabbed my chin and twisted it until I was staring straight at him. "What I'm asking of you is a series of loyalties. Were you ever bullied in school?"

"What?"

"Bullies," he said. "Everybody in high school is either bullied or a bully. Which side of that coin did you land on?"

"Neither," I said. "Okay, in seventh grade, I made fun of an autistic kid, but that was a long time ago."

"So you know how it works," he said. "The bully's not the one with power. The bully's just a plain vanilla cunt, regular as an egg in a carton. It's his toadies that are the problem. They laugh at the bully's jokes, make him feel important. The victim doesn't expect anything from the bully, but when the toady laughs, the victim feels alone. I saw it happen with Aaron."

"Please don't."

"Boys shoved him, flicked him in the ear. A girl sat next to him in English and put a clothespin on her nose.

Aaron didn't care about them, but when the rest of the class laughed, his lips would tremble. I think a lot about that, how I wish I'd stood up for him."

I put my hand around a beer but didn't drink. "Did you laugh?"

"You're not a bully," he said. "But when you're up on that hill, having good times with a bully, you're a toady. We can't just have you helping this animal bully small kids. I let Aaron down, and I'm not doing it anymore. You want to quit, you'll have to withstand some things."

"Like listening to you talk?"

"Listening to her talk," he said, nodding to Bonnie. She wasn't crying anymore, and she didn't look angry as much as determined. "You and your friends get a little hazy up on Prospect and forget the parts of your life that should be highlighted. If no one challenges you, you'll keep living in your head. To pay me back, you'll need to get out of your imagination, live down here with the rest of us."

"But here?" I looked over my shoulders at the strangers.

"Fuck it," he said. "She didn't do anything wrong. Why keep it a secret?"

I looked to Otto's mom.

"The balls on this kid," Egan said. "Asking us to protect Thomas's reputation? Maybe I should've let Hallahan loose, no matter who your brother is."

"No, not for Thomas." I leaned forward and whispered. "For Otto."

"No," Bonnie said, her voice as pointed as a hornet's buzz. "Don't say his name."

"Say it," Egan said. "You got no problem with it happening, but you get whispery when it comes time to name names. Otto Larkin did nothing to be ashamed of."

Please, I mouthed to Bonnie and then again to Egan. Surely, Thomas and Egan must have been friends once—

how else could they hate each other so completely?—but now they thought of themselves as the knife between the other's ribs.

Bonnie told me her story. The Larkins met Thomas when he was a volunteer lifeguard at the pool in Prospect Park. Otto swam with a wad of watermelon gum in his mouth because he liked the way the taste of sugar mixed with chlorine. Except he kept losing it in the water, then putting it in his mouth again. This happened three or four times before people complained to Thomas, who had a laminated sheet of the rules. "No Running, No Rough-housing, No Diving in the Shallow End." "Look," he kept saying, waggling the rules in front of the people. 'Find me where it says you can't chew gum, and I'll make him stop."

Otto was ten at that point. It was more than a year before the party, but Bonnie was watching and took note. She saw it as a graceful way to handle the situation, to spare the boy some embarrassment.

Bullshit, I thought. I reached across the bar and poured myself a swallow of whiskey. The people at the pool weren't mad at Otto; they were mad at you. You're the mother who watched and did nothing.

"Thomas called Otto over, gave him five dollars, and told him to buy some food," Bonnie said. "Otto runs to me with a lemonade ice pop and this story about the nice lifeguard. Thomas knew what he was doing. Otto's eating, so he spits out his gum."

"Ms. Bonnie, you don't know what happened," I said. "You weren't there. I don't mean to sound rude, but honestly, you're just guessing right now."

Both Egan and Bonnie reached for my face at the same time, but pulled back at the last second. From a distance, I'm sure it looked like an awkward dance move, but in the moment I could tell how they meant it. Egan was reaching out to brain me—nothing that would double my vision, but a reminder to let my thoughts run a lap or two around my head before I made them public. Bonnie reached out to hold me or at least to glide her fingers down my cheek. It was a move she did to her son.

"I was raised that same way you were," she said. "Full of being certain at all times. Sweetheart parents, slow to judge." One of her front teeth was as twisted and brown as a leaf in November. "Boys explore. He comes home from Thomas's the next day, shaking like a wind chime. Kid's so pale he's about to come out the other side and get colored. Not like black-colored, but blue, dark night-blue, like an eggplant."

"Purple?" I said. "It's easier if you just said purple to begin with."

"Except his eyes," she said. "They were pink, not like he'd been crying, not even like he was tired. But like he was a mole, a badger, some species that never sees the light. I say to him, 'What's wrong, Pellet?' Pellet's what his uncle De'Shawn calls him when he was first born and looked like something squirted out of a test tube. It made him smile. Before this, he was okay with being small."

"But Ms. Bonnie," I said. "None of it happened. None of it ha—I don't know what happened, but neither do you, and neither does anyone. Some stories don't end. You have to be okay with not knowing, because it's a story that will never end."

"Shaking," she said. "It's a boy, and he can't sit still. Shaking."

I took a sip of my beer, but it tasted skunked. "What did he say? Did he mention Thomas by name?"

"Jesus Christ," Egan said. "How do you not see this?"

"See what?"

"Your friends got a boy high, then kept him in a room with a junkie dealer all night," Egan said. "The next morning he's in trauma, shaking to where he can't talk. Tell me the story that makes that right."

"I just—" I looked back and forth at the both of them, waiting for one to give me the signal to stop talking. "Prospect is wild, and he shouldn't have been there. But I don't know what happened. This feels like a bunch of us guilty people feeling guilty."

"You say he shouldn't have been there and you're right," Egan said. "Who lets an eleven-year-old into their party?"

Bonnie looked at the floor. Egan didn't realize he insulted her.

"Maybe it's not as bad as you think," I said. "Those nights get wild, but it's always maintained. The boy was drunk maybe. I was drunk definitely. Who's to say?"

"Maybe it's a problem of definition," Egan said. "Tell me exactly what you can forgive. Walk me right up to the line, and explain why what's on this side is okay and what's on that side is an abomination."

"He touched Otto, okay," I said. "Maybe. I'm not defending him, but if it's that, just touching, then..." I raised both my hands. "What's it mean to touch someone?"

"We don't know what happened," Bonnie said. "No, kid, all we know is your friend let my eleven year old son into his house during a party with strangers. I trusted your friend, and so did Otto, and we know he got him high and let him sleep over. We know something happened bad enough to scare him to where he couldn't speak a word for a day and a half, and another day past that, save to ask for his supper. We know he came back with his belt buckle broken. We know that before that night, he never had a bad word to say about Thomas. He called him The Lifeguard and he said it the way my momma said God. Except now he asks to live with his father in Hamburg." She was crying again though it barely even crinkled her face and had no bearing on her voice. "His father has him living like a goddamn fleabag, but even still, he's scared to visit. And you react by saying 'We don't know anything.'"

"We want to bring Otto home," Egan said. "Obviously, we can't do that now."

"This is my son," Bonnie said. "I know what it sounds like before you have kids, like mothers lecturing you like you don't know how to love. And that's not true because you probably have love in your life."

You don't know me at all, I thought. Love comes naturally for most people, especially the one-sided mother-to-child love. What if I had a child and that affection never came? Isn't that what sociopaths feel?

"This is what's going down," Egan said. "Prospect Hill is about to get turned into a plateau. I highly recommend you stay at home for the next month or two. Take care of your mom. My cousin's a nurse, and if you play ball, I'll have him look after her. And there's Leander, who's dumb as a stump, but he listens to you. There's your redhead. There's Lina from that shitty band. You talk to them, and I won't have to. But one way or another, I need that house empty."

"Thomas works in Louisville some weeks," I said. "It's empty then."

"You misunderstand me," Egan said. "I'm not burning his house down. Thomas will leave because he'll understand it's right to leave. That's never going to happen if he keeps his friends around. What do you think you are to him?"

"A friend, I guess."

"You're white noise," he said. "You're the people he deals with so he doesn't deal with himself. That's why he pays you for your company."

"He doesn't pay."

"Fuck you he doesn't pay," Egan said. "Remind me to never buy stock in his drug-dealing business because he doesn't seem to make money. Sure looks like he's paying you. Tell your friends if they need a fix, they can come here."

"There's more people there then just my friends."

"They'll leave, and it'll get quiet," Egan said. "In that quiet, he'll only have me to listen to, and his black mind, and he'll see it our way. It'll be a matter of good and evil."

"Come on," I said.

"Otto will come home," Egan said. "You're going to pay what you owe me by cash or by bone. Tell me you understand, and you can leave."

"I don't want to be in the middle."

"Nobody does," Egan said. "On one side, you have a predator, on one side you have a child. You don't want to be in the middle because you want to be on the side of the child. Don't meet evil halfway for the sake of fairness."

"Fuck this." I tried to finish my beer in one long gulp, but I gagged before I finished, stepping on my moment. "I'll pay what I owe, and I'll fuck off when you tell me, but no more of this staged drama bullshit. Are we good here?"

"No," he said. "This is the beginning of a long series of payments. It won't stop until you're happy."

"Until I'm happy?"

"You'll be happy when Otto Larkin moves back into his home," he said. "Before that, you won't be happy."

Bonnie had her lips parted, savoring my confusion. I'll be happy when she's happy. One day, she'll forgive me, and she'll stand there watching as I struggle to forgive myself. I'll stammer and stutter and swear I can do better. Even then, with her enemies smoked, she'll never look as happy as she is today. Because that day is in the future, and she'll never move on. Time won't heal her—all she'll feel every progressing day is further away from home. She'll be happy when I'm happy.

6.

Meander wouldn't return my calls. When I chased him down after a week, he was hanging out on the seesaw at Orman Park. He had plopped on one seat with the other high in the air, drunkenly challenging all the kids in the park to competitive teeter-tottering. He slurred that he'd take on all comers, and he'd represented America in the Olympics for seesaw. At one point, he knew he was joking, but he'd forgotten.

The flock of sniffling kids scattered, leaving me with Meander—his hat pulled low on his forehead, pounding his fist against the top of his head. One of his eyes was purple and his top lip was fat to where it didn't latch onto his lower one.

"You ought to wear a helmet in these competitive seesaw battles." I reached to touch his cheek, but he turned away, wincing. "Who this time?" I tapped my temple where his bruising was the darkest. "Please tell me it was cops that did that to you?"

"You're hilarious."

"It's not a joke, it's a goldmine," I said. "You don't

need a TV lawyer to get a payday out of the cops knocking the shit from you. But act while your face is still fucked, or else they'll think you're just ugly, and—"

"Milo," he said, his voice almost breaking. "Cops didn't do this to me. Hallahan did. Said that Egan was tired of teaching us lessons. Said to tell you."

"Tell me what?"

"That sounds like a lesson. He said he didn't want to teach me anymore." He put a hand on his forehead. "When I breathe deep, I can smell his ring."

I knew what he meant. Hallahan oiled his ring constantly and had brined fish for every lunch because his dad worked as a wholesale supplier. In most ways, he was a meticulously clean man, but because he kept his ring so polished, he could never get the smell of WD-40 off of his fingers. When the beatings took place between lunch and suppertime, you got a hint of the fish oil on his fingernails too.

"Used to be, I at least knew how I fucked up," he said. "He called me a pervert. Said there were battle lines being drawn. When he's high, he quotes shitty baby boomer music." He took a sip from his flask. "And he said to tell to you, this was your warning."

"My warning?"

"He says you need to stick to the plan." Meander shook his head. "Guy's got his loafer so far up my ass, the penny's pressing the inside of my dick."

It was happening again, I thought. I could quit the Rabbit, but not his laws. My sins will be repaid on Meander's head.

"You going back there?" I asked.

"I don't know, probably. But it'll be a while. You?"

I shook my head. "Staying away. From all of it. Not going up Prospect, not going to The Rabbit. I'm just not playing anymore."

Meander offered me his flask. It tasted horrible, like

a peach soda with whiskey and Sweet and Low. Even the aftertaste loosened my teeth from my gums.

This is how he will look when he gets old. He'll never lose that shadow-skinny frame or that lopsided grin that made him look like he was forever chewing marbles. His brother had angles but was more solidly put together. Corey could grow up in a dozen different ways, but not Meander. I thought about that moment for a long time, long after he grew up outside the parameters of my imagination. That was the first moment I really considered that a friend may not grow up at all.

"Why do this?" I said. "You don't like it. The last advantage we have is we can walk away." I took another small sip from the flask and handed it back. "We're not thieves, not really."

Meander rolled his eyes.

"Not like Hallahan is," I said. "Not like Egan wants us to be. If he's a bomb then we're just the wicks."

"But we are thieves, aren't we?" he said. "We take people's shit. You think we're pretending, conducting a science experiment."

"Egan told me I should go back to school," I said. "To be honest, I don't know what grade I'm in anymore. We're supposed to be seniors, but I never finished social studies. Or anything else."

"You're not going to school, you dumb dick," he said. "Neither am I. We're not smart enough. And don't say what you're going to say next."

"What?"

Meander tipped up the flask. "You're going to say we have options."

"We do," I said. "They hit us because we're in front of them. We leave, they leave us alone."

"Leave?"

"Why not?" I said. "We can go anywhere we want, anywhere you want."

"The road?" Meander said. "Split and start over. That's the flavor of shit you're serving today?"

"Flavor's not the word I'd use in that context."

"It's not real," Meander said. "Do I even have to ask these questions? Where do we go? Why are we there? What do we do? Meanwhile, your mom gnaws off her skin to eat something. My mom rents out my room to her big-dicked personal trainer like I'm the orphan she always wanted. The road will feel good for fifteen miles, and then ten miles after that it'll feel okay. Then you'll picture your mom."

"She won't know I'm gone."

"Which is why you won't go," Meander said. "It already happened to her once, and she barely remembers. You're just the sequel."

From out of nowhere, half a moldy roll flew out of the air and hit Meander in the shin. He didn't react, and I couldn't be certain if he noticed. Another piece of bread sailed from behind the bushes and landed a foot in front of us.

Meander sighed. "Not these fags again."

"What's going on?"

"Latchkey kids," he said. "Twelve-year-old punks with a hard-on for me."

"You see, when you say it like that, I think of a twelve-year-old with a hard-on, and then I hate myself."

One kid peeked out from behind the bush. He looked mousy, his nose sticking out from behind a blue knit hat. I guessed he wasn't the group leader, but the idiot the others could goad into being brave. "What's up, Squirrel?" he said. "That your boyfriend?"

"They call me Squirrel," Meander said. "Or Chipmunk or Duck. They throw bread at me like you feed an animal. It's childish."

"They're children."

Three other kids fanned out behind the first one. An

Asian in a puffy shirt had a loaf of sliced white bread that the others were taking from. The other kids kept calling out "Squirrel" and lobbing wads of bread at him. I gave them the finger, but Meander sat stalk-still. He plucked a jagged rock from the ground and gripped it tight in his hand.

"Don't," I said.

Meander started to rise up, but I gripped his shoulder and tried to keep him still. He wriggled away. "Relax," he said. "The boys just want their seesaw back." He undid his belt, dropped his pants, and peed on the seat. "I intend to give it to them."

I tried being alone, but I didn't have the skill for it. All the voices in my head ganged up on me as I tried to sleep. I took long walks and peered into strange windows, but nothing distracted me. Meander was dying. Those were the exact words I said to Shea Stanford when I showed up at her house, looking to strategize.

Meander was thin, I told her. He was our Angel of Damage, but even he couldn't maintain this level of pain. "He smells like a hobo's ballbag, and his adult teeth are going to last about as long as his baby teeth." I left out that it was my fault, that he was taking those beatings from me.

"That's why you're here?" We were sitting on her porch, me on her porch swing, her on her railing. "Look behind me."

In her front yard, there were her brother's garden gnomes, dressed in Kentucky Wildcat and Cincinnati Bengal Jerseys.

"You want to apologize to me?"

I looked again. Across the street, I saw her hatch-back—the one I'd been in without her blessing—with the bumper twisted and both headlights smashed.

"My car goes missing from the school lot and reappears two days later, looking like that?"

I shook my head.

"So it's not you?" Shea wore fake gold wristbands on each of her wrists and ran them up and down her arms. "Be very clear with me."

"It's not me." This was my reward—to watch Meander and Shea get abused on my behalf.

"Really?" Her hair bobbled as she laughed. "You promise this is all some tireless carjacker who smells like you?"

"It's not me," I said. "I wouldn't."

We smoked a cigarette together and talked it through. I didn't wreck your car, I thought. Whoever did that was a low-rent trespasser, not someone who valued her space.

"So how do we help Meander?" I said. "Everyone else has just written him off as part of God's plan to fill His quota of fuck-ups."

"You know what they say," Shea said. "If you want to make God laugh, show Him your penis."

"Your penis?" I said. "It's plans. If you want to make God laugh, show Him your plans."

"Plans?" she said. "What's funny about your plans?"

We parked outside of Webster Apartments, a plastic box placed on top of a plastic box that passed for cheap living in Lexington's endless suburbs. We'd donned hats and sunglasses and followed Otto Larkin home from school, a surprisingly treacherous task. His school bus didn't travel this far, so he had to transfer to a city bus. It's hard to follow one and maintain anonymity—they stick to the right lane and stop every thousand yards, so everyone else goes around them—but we didn't care. Even if they spotted us, we weren't doing anything illegal. We had a right to follow, same as they had a right to lead.

We spent the first hour drinking can after can of Wild Cherry Pepsi, guessing what Otto Larkin's father looked like. Shea pictured him as a pinched-face contrarian, his mouth curled up in a disgusted "M" like he was chewing on a clove of garlic. I pegged him as the goofball: heavy, dented cheeks, maybe a walrus moustache, and a bald spot he'd always joke about. He'd stare at your ear when he spoke to you, like he was lost in deep, thoroughly uninteresting thought.

"You've seen the mom," Shea said. "What's she look like?"

"Pale," I said. "Dark hair, green eyes. Kind of a high hairline. Would be pretty if she wasn't looking at me like she wished I was having sex with a lawnmower."

"I need more," Shea said. "A lot of women hate you."

"The father's probably a stooge," I said. "Tortoise-shell glasses and a second chin. Just a dumb dick who woke up to find a kid in his house."

In truth, Otto's mother looked like a ghost. She was terrified, almost but not quite woken up from her nightmare. It didn't tell me much about who she loved once upon a time, but it showed me the crisis was real. Otto was living in the plastic boxes in the suburbs because it wasn't safe on Prospect. Once, during happier times, Otto told me his father called into sports radio talk shows twice a week under the name "The Red Marauder," and he stayed up late, jotting down what he would say.

Our plan was extremely simple in that it made no sense. Shea believed the way to exonerate Thomas the Prophet was to find the soft seam in Otto's current relationship with his father. If we found his weakness, then we could strong-arm him into returning the boy to Prospect Hill. That would pacify Bonnie, which in turn would pacify Egan. I didn't understand, but Shea told me my lack of understanding had never stopped any plan thus far in history.

"How'd you get to be such a foot soldier for Thomas?" I said. "His style of asshole doesn't seem to jibe with yours."

"What's that mean?" she said. "You think he hand-jobbed that kid?"

I had a glob of ketchup on the collar of my jacket, and I felt it drip onto my shirt. The car smelled like algae and nicotine gum.

"You think he did it," Shea said. "It's not a question because I know you do. You believe everyone at all times, as soon as they say whatever they're saying. It's got to be exhausting believing that much that hard."

"Maybe he did it," I said. "I hate being this close to a mystery with no solution. Doesn't it kill you? We're likely never going to know if it's true."

"Thomas doesn't know if it's true," Shea said. "Neither does the kid. It's a matter of believing your beliefs and sticking with them."

Otto came out of the house, dragging his box kite behind him. This was good, I thought. He was keeping up with his hobbies. If the night at Thomas's had scarred him beyond repair, he'd have cast aside the kite. We watched him for fifteen minutes, but the wind didn't blow, so he tied the tail of the kite to a bike rack and walked down the road.

"Should we follow him or wait for his dad?" I said.

"We don't know who his dad is," Shea said. Her uncle and older brother worked as private detectives. When she was thirteen, they brought her along on a few low-level jobs, mostly following cheating husbands or deadbeat dads. Nothing dangerous, she told me, but both her uncle and brother carried guns, which they let her hold.

When I asked her about the secrets of the trade, she said something about the art of being unseen. She genuinely loved following people without their consent. Her uncle told her that people didn't care—it's better to be followed than ignored, and those are your only two options. Shea said if you use reflective surfaces to check your mark's face, there's a moment you can see into his soul. Look at him a second before he sees himself and rearranges his face into something more suitable. How quickly he makes himself thinner and happier shows you how much he fears his own soul.

Otto walked three blocks north, his hand covering his eyes from the sunshine. He'd put on weight, and, while that was good, it didn't hang naturally on him. We kept fifty feet distance at all times, but if he had the slightest inclination to turn his head, he would have seen us. He looked determined to get wherever he was going.

"Funniest case I ever heard," Shea told me. "This woman about fifty comes in, worried about her daughter. She thinks the girl's on drugs, doesn't come home half the time. She's worried she's spending time with, what's his name? The head of those Christian junkies?"

"Father Compost," I said. "As of yet, not ordained by the Catholic Church."

"My uncle went there to crack heads and make them talk, and they acted like a pack of raccoons. They spat at him, and one guy smashed a bottle against a brick wall, and threatened him with the shard. It sliced his own hand, but this hobo never even changed the look on his face."

Her uncle ran away, but, having no other leads, came back the next day. Earlier this time, giving them less of a chance to get deep in their high. That next night, they were docile as lambs, happy to talk. Except no one knew the girl in question. Not like she doesn't come around anymore, but like they never heard of her at all.

The uncle thought he understood. Part of their religion involves "presence living," which roughly translates to only acknowledging the present as it exists now. So when someone OD's or hops off a bridge, they pretend that person never existed. Finding a reliable record on runaway overdoses took a legitimate badge and a moderate interest, an unlikely combination in Kentucky. That night, the uncle found the same junkie who threatened him, showed him a fake badge, and shoved him into the back of his car. The uncle took him to Nicholasville, swiped his dope, and threatened to leave him there. The kid wouldn't answer questions, only prayed, so the uncle drove away.

"The moral is your uncle's terrible at his job, and we're impersonating him."

"That's not the worst part," she said. "He found the girl the next day by checking her school. The girl had been staying at her parents' house. The woman who hired him wasn't the mother at all, but her girlfriend. After that, he spent the next three days driving around Nicholasville trying to find the guy he kidnapped, but no luck."

"Did he turn the woman in?"

"Grow up," she said. "But he got her to pay in full. That's more of a win than you might guess."

Otto squatted outside of an ivy-covered house like he was defensive lineman in a three-point stance waiting for the snap count. He held one hand behind him, like he was waving away an invisible friend.

"What's he doing?" Shea said.

"I don't know," I said. But I knew. Right now he was creeping up on the house like an assassin, playing the same game I used to play. "He's playing spy."

"What's that?"

"You peek into stranger's windows, get up in their yards, try to see them before they see you."

"That's not playing spy," Shea said. "That's spying. Did you do that as a kid?" Before she even looked at me, she knew. "Did you do it to me?"

"Just strangers," I said. "In my head, that made it sound better, but hearing it, it sounds worse."

I heard the first chirp of a siren behind us. In our rearview, we saw a hand snake out of a maroon Accord and place a small siren on top of the car. A slender man wearing a windbreaker too light for the weather and a trapper hat and sauntered over to us.

We let his breath fog up the window from the outside before Shea slowly rolled it down. "Can I help you?" the cop asked.

"That depends," I said. "Are you a cop or one of those strippers that dress like cops?" I was cocky because we hadn't been drinking.

"I've received two separate calls about people loitering in the area," he said. "These are private neighborhoods."

"Private how?" Shea said.

"There have been break-ins on this street," the cop said. "Vandalism two blocks over. Are you visiting somebody?"

"Vandalism how?" I said, over Shea's shoulder. "Spray painting?"

The cop looked at me with his head cocked back. For a second, I thought he was going to ask me to step out of the car, but he leaned forward and put his elbows on Shea's window. "Some spray painting. There's damage to cars."

"We know that—" I stopped. I was about to say that we know that kid, meaning Otto, but when I looked to the yard where he had been, I saw he had gone. Spooked by the siren, I figured.

Shea thanked the officer, rolled up the window, and pulled down the street. As she drove out of the suburb, I saw she was sweating from under her bangs. It wasn't like her to look uncomfortable. I lit two cigarettes and put one of them in the side of her mouth. She didn't puff at first, and I had to light it again.

"So we can't even park in Hamburg?" I said. "What's the word for racism when everybody's the same race? Shitty police work, I think it's called."

"He wasn't a cop," Shea said. "No badge, never asked for our ID. He wanted us to think he was a cop, but that's some neighborhood watch busybody."

"He had a siren."

"So do tow trucks." She let her cigarette roll to the center of her mouth. "And you're lucky he's not a cop because he'd have beat us both bloody for your mouth." We reached the edge of Hamburg, and she turned left. "Why are you both like that? Meander and you try to get caught."

"Caught for what?" I said. "Parking on a street?"

"You think everything's a joke," she said. "When you strip away the bullshit, all you only want one thing out of life."

"What's that?"

"Aaron,' she said. "Ever since he left, the world's a joke to you," she said. "You and Meander act like cartoons," she said. "This small-cut suicide is fun enough to watch, but it makes it hard to care about you."

"I'm not Meander," I said. "That guy would find trouble in a padded cell."

"You're the same," she said. "You're bigger, which hides the bruises, but you both live like you want to die."

I pinched the fat of her arm. It felt cold, but then her blood flowed back above her elbow, warming my fingertips. I was telling her to be patient with me, but I couldn't say it out loud because I didn't think myself worthy of patience. When we were young, we could have whole conversations through touches and tensions. Her skin reacting to my touch felt more elemental than language. It's our way of saying, "I'll follow you."

"You treat yourself like a five-year-old treats a toy, like death is a reset button." She shook her head. "Me, I take loss personally. I can't understand a world where people are lost. I see it, of course. It's all I see—I get it's true. But I don't understand it."

"My brother's dead, isn't he?"

"You won't let him die." She hovered her palm over the hair on my forearm. "Maybe that's the one thing we have in common."

When Shea dropped me off at my apartment, she told me to take care of myself, and I said I would try. But trying to keep completely free from trouble was like trying to bottle smoke. Anyway, the world doesn't reward the untroubled. I could take care of Shea, take care of our promise to each other. Together, we can find him, she said.

Once upon a time, I believed her. There were horse farms just outside of town where the grass turned yellow in the summer and brown in the fall, and you could stand on one end and see the horizon before the property line. The horses live with more space and freedom than almost any human. Their world was an open area in front of them, so their world was always changing. They were faster and stronger than us. Not two miles away, Father Compost's Jesus Junkies prowled the night, keeping their world riddled with belief. They lived their purgatory in front of us.

The men at the horse farms drank juleps and watched the sun attack the horizon every night. The Composters drank bourbon from plastic bottles and watched the same sky bleed its way into night. There was a space for my brother between these worlds. Shea and I, working together at full speed, could find him and prove he existed.

One day, many years later, Shea Stanford herself became a missing person. At that point, she had renamed herself Ruby O'Shea, unwilling to take her husband's name and also unwilling to stick with her own. When she left, she had a husband, a daughter, and a baby on the way. Her uncle—working a third shift job in the third shift of his career as a night watchman for Hewlett Packard— came out of retirement as a private dick to track her down. He uncovered some hearsay about her maybe having a boyfriend on the side. It was thin gruel. Not long into his investigation, he disappeared as well, leaving his wife with a mortgage she couldn't pay. The police said there was no evidence of foul play, thereby maintaining the precinct's perfect record when it came to being helpful in my life. The rest of us searched for her, but only in our spare time.

I'll remember her touch long after her words have run together. I'll remember the fresh chill of disappointment when that touch went away, how it hit me like air rushing into my stomach when my car takes a hill too fast and loses contact with the road. She'll be the last figure I see before I die, the pennies on my eyes. Even as memories blanch, the remaining colors will cling to her form for one final blast of comfort. It'll feel as it does every night before sleep, almost real and almost enough.

Thomas is our cynic. He lives his life entirely in the vegetable world. Without faith, he has only feelings. What didn't press back against his fingertips was unreal. Shea is our believer. Dreams were windy reality to her, the difference no more substantial than the difference between soup and stew.

I come from the meantime, the in-between. My friends say I lack conviction, but it's just that I'm doomed to live in no man's land, the middle management of beliefs. My life, now and forever, will remain fully haunted by halfway ghosts.

7.

My neighbor was practicing his magic in front of the window. From my couch, I could see into his living room when he kept his light on. I never learned his name, but he was a trim man of about thirty, with thinning red hair and skin the color of the leftover milk after a bowl of Froot Loops. During the day, he had a job that required a tie, a briefcase, and a thermos, but in the evening, he'd put on his showman clothes and go through his routine twice—first in full motion and later at half speed. In the beginning, he looked like a birthday magician with an ill-fitting suit and a loose red bow tie, like an especially confused member of the Nation of Islam. Later, he switched personas, trading his suit jacket in for a torn t-shirt and tight fitting necklaces.

I believed in magic, but only a little. There's a coldness to it, its way of showing us the other side and then correcting itself with a shrug. The sawed-apart woman gets reattached, and we pretend that's the proper order of the world, as though miracles are mistakes. What if nature worked like that? We see the chicken hatch, and while its feathers are still wet, the egg reseals around it? My neighbor outed himself as a believer, and then retreated into his public skin again.

As he moved to his next trick, my mother bent over to kiss me on the forehead. Recently, the part of her brain that told her how to finish a kiss had stopped firing, so now she showed affection by blowing sour breath on the side of my face. It smelled like the halfway point between me and her—with a dash of cherry Robitussin—and it reminded me I had to leave this house and be out in the cold.

Shea and I went back to Hamburg the next day after she was out of school and then again the day after. We parked in the same spot each time. "It's important to pick up the rhythm of a street," she told me, reciting a line from her uncle. After about a day and a half of waiting, I was ready to declare her uncle full of shit.

"Maybe he's already home," I said. "Gone back to live with his mom while we sit and stare at this chunk of nothing."

"Something wacky's going on," she said. "We've never seen this man step in or out of his own house. Does he never come home or never leave?"

"What are you looking for?"

"Otto's dad may be feeding him the proper portions from the food pyramid and tucking him in every night, but you and I both know that's not happening." She looked at me and smiled. "Ask me, I don't know there's a dad at all."

"How is that possible?"

"Think," she said. "What's the one thing Otto's mom cares about?"

"I don't know."

"Me neither," she said. "But I do know that it is not her kid. Otto was a bit part in her life. Now, she uses him to get revenge. Doesn't it make sense that she sends him to this empty house where she can say the father lives?"

"Why?" I said. "Just to give her a month away from motherhood?"

"Have you seen a shred of proof this man exists?" Shea said. "What are we basing the story on? That there's a sad man who calls himself The Red Marauder?"

I'd been clean for the better part of a week, so I was starting to see my friends in a more medium light. Meander and I felt as similar as a man and his shadow, bobbing and weaving in harmony. That wasn't good news. He was a junkie and I was his apprentice. Hallahan was a bully. I'd known this, of course, but the bullied always thinks his tormentor is half-magic. No, I knew now, just a bully. Shea was as close to a conscience as I had. But what if Shea was crazy? There was a reason detectives went nuts.

Otto scampered into his front yard. He had a mix of dirt and Cheetos dust from the top of his chin to an inch below his collar, and he walked hunched low, like he was trying to hide under the sightline of a spy who didn't have the ability to look down. This was the lonely child's game, all imagination and fly-by-night rules. I remembered it well. He walked down the block and past our car, and Shea and I followed him.

He should have seen us, but Otto, lost in the game in his head, either never noticed or never cared. Like before, he went to the big yellow house. Like before, he disappeared into the back yard.

"Whatever he's doing, he's got it to a pattern," I said. "Kids that age believe in math." Shea looked at me like I flicked her nipple. "Not like equations. Having things happen at a certain time, the same way every day."

"How do you not know what math is?"

"That's how kids create a world," I said. "It's fun for them, falling into a routine, thinking that if they show up at the exact same spot at the exact same time, then they can control the planet. It's magic, religion, all that. It begins by believing the world will change if you mess up."

"When I was a kid, I went with the Lecketts to their Jesus mountain," Shea said. "Monroe took my coming as an invitation to grab my ass every time I went to sleep, but Roxy took it serious as life itself. She promised me if I believed in her, I'd see God's face. I had to check in for breakfast every morning at 7 a.m., go for a hike at 9:30, and then she said, at 11:45, no matter where I am or what I'm doing, spin around as fast as I can and look behind you, and you'll see the face of God."

"I bet God looked like Monroe Leckett about to grab your ass."

"I saw the most of God," she said. "I don't know if it's the routine or the mountain itself, but it's overwhelming. The place really feels like the Garden Of Eden."

"Really?"

"Yeah," she said. "At least there are a lot of snakes." She opened the door and stepped outside. "I'm sick of waiting."

I was struggling with my seatbelt when she disappeared behind the yellow house. By the time I got outside and slammed the door, I heard a loud crashing sound and ran to the yard. I had no clue what story she'd tell the boy, but Shea liked to trap herself underwater and follow her instincts to find air.

She was hunched over, with her back to me, whispering something I couldn't hear. She hit him, I thought, and I was certain we were going to jail. I ran to her, and when I got close, I saw her hunched over a brown beagle with white spots along its forehead. The dog was chained to a stake, and it lay with its bell pressed against the ground, making a steady gurgling noise like a malfunctioning weed eater. I looked back and forth, but the rest of the yard was empty. "Where's the kid?" I asked. "He didn't come out front."

Shea stroked the underside of the dog's chin. It tried to raise its head but couldn't quite sustain the effort. "Someone beat the piss out of this dog." She pinched the dog's face and made it smile at me. It was missing half of an incisor, and when she let go of the dog's face, I saw that part of its upper lip had been carved away. "At least one rib's broken if it's breathing like that."

"No way," I said. "Otto?"

"I don't think so." She stood and the dog tried to follow suit, wriggling and stumbling until it found its wobbly legs. "This beagle's been bleeding from the top of his head, but it's not wet. These are old wounds."

From the street, we heard two distinct banging sounds, like an oak door slamming shut, and then a car backfiring. We were trespassing. Shea bolted to the back fence, climbed over it, and disappeared into the neighbors' locusts before I knew what was happening. I followed. How in God's name, did we lose the kid? I thought. We were terrible detectives.

We looped back around to grab my car. After that, we got lunch at Hopalong Diner on Montavesta, a place almost abandoned of other customers, but flooded with sunlight. The thought of someone—a family of some-ones—swinging a hammer to a chained dog made me want to walk away from all of this. As we ate, Shea drew the puppy's paws over and over again on her cocktail napkin.

Our leading theory was as uncomplicated as a heart attack. Otto heard the dog crying, went to help, and the friendless child saw an ally. Otto must have hugged it and tried to nurse it back to fighting form.

There was a darker reading, of course. Whoever lived in that house didn't notice an uncoordinated kid playing with a yappy dog in their backyard. That meant that they most likely weren't home during Otto's visits. Negligent dog owners weren't going to take home the Congressional Medal of Freedom, but they weren't the bunion on America's moral soul either. If they ignored the dog, then who was beating it? We had no evidence, but only one suspect. Otto took an interest in the beagle, knew when the house was empty, and disappeared when he heard us coming.

Shea said it was good for us if Otto beat the dog. Any child who would bleed an animal would lie about his neighbor just to watch his world crumble. I disagreed. In my mind, boys loved smashing things that could hurt them back. They threw rocks at wasp nests and punched shards of windows. Only a damaged boy would take his aggression out on something like a chained puppy, something that couldn't fight. Plus, if the dog was already disabled, Otto might look at it and only see Thomas's worthless hand. He'd hit it and hit it until he could forget.

I heard someone take a chair from our table. A man in his forties with spiky graying hair and a handsome, privileged face sat down. He didn't speak, just stared at us expectedly. I was positive that I should recognize him but didn't.

He reached across me to grab a container of half-and-half and dumped it in an empty coffee cup. Not to drink, but just to show me I didn't scare him. He picked up Shea's drawing and brought it close to his face. "What's this?" he asked.

"Clearly, not a portrait of an asshole or you'd recognize it," I said.

He shot me a weary smile. "What are you doing here? Before you give me one of your lame joke answers, make sure you're thinking very clearly."

"We can be where we want," Shea said. "There's not a law in America that says we can't sit in a diner and talk. And you can tell that to your commanding officer."

This was the fake officer from the other day. All I remembered of him was his shades, his pitiless smile. With those stripped away, he could have passed as any other combination of skill and skin.

"The 'Free Country' defense." The man pressed his palms together like a class clown impersonating prayer. "I don't care where you talk. What I care very much about is why you are where you are."

"Why we are where we are?" I laughed and made the jerk-off motion because I didn't understand the question but didn't want to admit it.

"Bonnie sent you?"

I did the jerk-off motion again, but this time contemplatively, because I was too confused to stop. "Bonnie Boudreaux Larkin?"

"She thinks I've hoarded money," he said. "But you tell her that the rare coins and the life insurance are all I have. I've paid what I owe." He dipped his head and put his hands over his eyes. "You think I don't wish I could pay PI's to dig through her sheets, looking for nickels?"

"You're Otto's dad?" I said it like a question and then tried to cover it up. "We had you listed as The Red Marauder."

He smiled and tapped his fingers on the tabletop. "When Bonnie and I were dating, she gave me a book by Walt Whitman where he calls his penis The Red Marauder. I thought it was funny to hear people say it over the airwaves, kind of an in-joke between Bonnie and me."

"Good night," I said, balling up my napkin and throwing it at my coffee cup. "You're an eight year old with a pituitary problem. Making dick jokes on the radio."

"It's poetry," he said.

"A poet with a serious deformity," I said. "How's he get Red Marauder?"

"Come on, you can see it," he said. "Like it looks red, but—"

"There's a chance we've been side-tracked," Shea said. "We've heard reports that you've been physically and emotionally abusive both as a parent and as a husband. If this is verified, or even if we have probable cause to continue with an investigation, we have a right to review your custody claims for Otto. To be frank, strong-arming us in a restaurant is confirming some of our fears."

"Custody?" His mouth popped open, and he looked like a‚ toddler trying to whistle. "I never—Bonnie said this?"

He didn't know we were kids. I looked old for my age, and Shea had a smoky, clipped voice of TV grandmother, but the illusion wouldn't last. The only thing saving us right now was that Shea was clearly cribbing lines from her uncle, who, I guessed, had stolen them from TV.

"Sir, Ms. Larkin asked us to remind you about the sensitivities of this case."

His expression slid from surprise to suspicion. "What'd she tell you about me?"

Shea swirled the coffee around in her cup. "Mr. Larkin, when people get in touch with us, they aren't negotiating a tab. We're investigating the welfare of a child who we have cause to believe is unsafe in your house."

"With me?" he said. "What about when he came here? His hair was matted together, and he hadn't eaten anything but Pop Tarts, and two of his teeth were so cavity-ridden they had to be pulled."

"Yeah, but he's a kid," I said.

"Did she tell you what she told me?" He started to stammer and righted himself. "She said she was worried she was going to hurt him. She said she hunched over his bed with a carrot peeler." He looked around the room. "Otto's a refugee staying with me. Do you think it's easy to look after a kid like that when you're already pulling more than full-time hours at a security job?"

"Kid like that?" I said.

"He needs attention," he said. "Not like most kids, who need a father to talk to during commercial breaks. Bonnie is very sick."

"What's your son doing at your neighbor's house?" Shea said. "He's doing something with their dog."

"What?" he said. "How old are you?"

"If what you say is true," I said, ignoring his question. "why does Bonnie want Otto to come home?"

"What?" he said. "I'm giving him back in the New Year when his school starts."

"Otto comes back at the end of the year?" Shea said. "And you don't want him?"

"Of course I want him," he said. "He wants to live with his mom, even though he winds up bruised every time he comes over for the weekend."

Shea and I looked at each other, and both of us were clueless.

"Tell her she can sue me, but she's not getting one dime above what we agreed."

"You're saying he wants to live on Prospect Hill?" I asked.

He shook his head, defeated. "He says his friends live there. There are parties and sleepovers. He's lonely here."

The waitress came over but Shea waved her away. "But Bonnie——"

"Won't have him," he said. "I think——" He looked over his shoulder, leaned in close, and whispered. "It's not Otto she's trying to protect, but herself. She knows what she's capable of those long nights."

"The bruises?" I said. "I haven't seen them."

He shook his head. "You don't see the kid when he takes his shirt off." He pointed to his upper arm and his ribcage. "Right where someone would grab him."

"That could be you," I said. "Does grabbing kids put a little red in your marauder?"

He looked at me like he wanted to kill me. It was an oddly unthreatening pose, and it made me trust him. "If you'd have seen this boy," he said, jabbing his finger at my nose. "If you'd seen this boy when he came to me. Barely able to keep down a cup of chicken soup. If anyone's hurting him, I'll grind their bones to make my tea. And if you don't tell Bonnie that, I might."

Shea reached across the table and wrapped her bony fingers around the man's wrist. She had a light touch when she was trying to calm men down.

"He's sick," the man said, muttering it to himself as much as to us. "I can only be home a couple hours, and I'm trying to do what I can, but he's sick."

This is what it would've looked like. If I'd been older or had parents who cared, this is exactly how the last days before Aaron disappeared would've gone down. We would watch him vanish in degrees and not know how to stop him. You only have the symptoms, I thought, staring at the man. This disease has more blood to draw.

That evening, I stayed outside for as long as my fingers would allow. I walked around Orman Park, sitting on the swing set. The snow fell, sticking to the ground in muddy clumps. Shea said our conversation meant Bonnie was lying, that she didn't care about her son, and that Thomas couldn't have hurt Otto if he missed the parties. All I drew from it was that most families were beyond saving.

About once an hour, when I couldn't stand my own shivers, I walked down the block to Drink Of This Cup, a Christian coffeehouse that gave me free warm beverages because they thought I was homeless. But feeling warm reminded me of Shea Stanford's car, of all I'd never achieve, and it made me want to face the cold again.

In Orman Park, I retraced my steps of the night I held the baby against my chest. I pressed him so tight against me that you could see his head imprinted against my sternum. That night felt balmy next to this one.

Nightwolf had hit the Roto-Spinner, the red and yellow plastic circle that kids stood on either side of, trying to spin the other one off. Apparently after writing "NIGH" he spun it because the rest of it was a sloppy blur. I'd outlasted every chipmunk and rat scuttling around this park. At least for tonight, I was king.

I expected some noise on the street on my way home, but I heard none. My ears could pop on a night like this, the condensation in my eardrums freezing, then cracking, then melting from the side of my head like muddy slush. My dreams were soundless; I never heard background noise. It's how I knew I was dreaming. When I stopped listening, the world stopped listening with me.

Egan once asked me if I missed my brother. An old man misses his youth because he knew it once. A child doesn't miss his olden years even though they're every bit as absent. Aaron as he exists now is not someone I know, nor would he know me. I miss my brother like I miss my ability to fly.

When I got back to the apartment complex, the downstairs door was open. The apartment was closed, but there were scratches under the knob. Until a year ago, Mom kept meticulous about locking the front door. Sometimes she'd latch the chain, and I'd have to pound and bang and wake the neighbors to get her to let me inside. The lights in the apartment were on, but it was empty.

I walked to the kitchen and turned on the stove. The front burner clicked four times and then lit up. It could all disappear so easily. The feeling crept back into my hands, and I bent each finger at the knuckles one by one.

My mother was outside. I had to look for her, but not yet. The fire would feel dangerous any minute now, but I still had time. Complete the circle, I thought. Just lie down on the couch—you didn't have to fall asleep, only close your eyes. I was bone-tired, and my eyes were scratching for relief. The warmth had hold of me.

I walked back outside and took a turn down the alley. Instinctually, I looked at the brick walls, half expecting Nightwolf to draw me a series of arrows leading to my mother. In the alley, I saw a pile of green trash-bags next to the dumpster. One was slit open, with flattened milk jugs and coffee grounds spilling out of the side. I called her name and heard nothing.

I went to Bledsoe's Bakery. Sometimes, the bums lined up there to get throwaway bread. There was no line at Bledsoe's, but the light was on. I walked up to it, hoping one of the late night workers could clue me in. As soon as I stepped in, I saw a shape from the corner of my eye. It was a woman, small and hunched over, facing a brick wall. She looked to be grasping one of the bricks, trying to peel it away from the building.

"Mom," I said.

She sniffled. I touched her, but she continued to scratch at the single brick with her purple hand and jagged fingernails. "You're not," she said out of the side of her mouth. "Don't you look at me. You are not."

"Not what?"

"You're not supposed to be here." She swallowed and spat at my feet. I'd seen her spit as an insult before, but this wasn't that—she was clearing space in her mouth, trying to speak. "You are not here. This isn't for you."

"You don't know who I am, do you?"

She turned to look at me. "I know what I know. You think you're the only person in town who can tell your feet from your you-know-what."

"Do you want to die? Are you—are you trying to leave us?"

"Don't backtalk me," she said. "I told you in Tampa I wouldn't stand for it."

"Tampa?" I said. "Does this feel like Tampa?" I grabbed her by the shoulder and held her tight so she couldn't get away. "You have a son. You remember that?"

She leaned back and her eyes rolled into her head. "I had a son, but he left."

I grabbed a fistful of her hair. Some of it came off in my hand. She looked scared of me, her eyes darting to each side. "Leave me alone."

"There's nothing here," I said. "Do you have a fucking mind to lose anymore?" She spat at me again, and I slapped her. "Where you going to go? There's nowhere for you to be except with me."

She shook in my grasp. "Leave me alone. I won't go with you."

"You know who I am," I said. "Say my name at least, okay? Say my name once, and I'll take you inside. That's the price of admission: say my name."

"Go away."

"You want me to go?" I said. "Really?"

"I'll kill you if you touch me."

"If you can't say my name, this is it for us."

She swallowed again. Then she bit her lip, looked me in the eye, and nodded.

"Okay then." I took out my wallet, fished out my driver's license, and threw it against her chest. "If they find you, tell him this was the man who killed you. That's the address where he lives."

She half-stooped to pick it up but stopped. Even if she could bend down that far, her hands couldn't grip it in this cold. We had the same fingers—hers were curved and knobby, mine were thick and stubby, but not one of the twenty of them worked when the weather dropped below freezing. I turned around and started to walk away. That would be our final connection, the cold of our fingerprints.

As I reached the corner, I waited for her to call me. It didn't even have to be my name, just a sound. That was how it ended. My mother fed to the same wind that took my brother, my father, my friends.

I kept walking. I didn't feel relief or sadness or disbelief. At the corner of Rosemount and Gladiola, I saw that Nightwolf had hit the SLOW: CHILDREN PLAYING sign.

Tomorrow, the cops would come. With luck, they'd call

it mercy. Back when I was very young, I thought hurting your mother was the one irredeemable middle finger to God that would roast my soul. Now it felt natural.

I was almost to my front door when I heard my name. It sounded so soft that it could've been a car with no muffler, but when I heard it again, it sounded closer, clearer. "Milo, Milo, slow down." I knew it wasn't my mother's voice, but I still expected to see her when I turned around. Instead, I saw Thomas the Prophet, his good hand tucked in his jacket pocket, his bad hand hanging at his hip. "You're walking like your ass is on fire."

Then he paused and said, "Are you crying?"

"No," I said. "I'm fine."

"Bullshit, you're crying." He took his good hand from his pocket and pointed to my face, like I didn't know where crying came from. "What's the matter this time?"

I couldn't feel the tears on my face, but I knew they were there. He wasn't perceptive—no way he could guess at my sadness unless it was written in bold. "It's mom. She's—I don't know. She's gone."

"Gone?"

I nodded. "I came home, and she was gone. She's out here, but I don't know."

"What don't you know?"

I shook my head, and now I felt myself shaking.

He took a step toward me. "So you're out here looking for her."

"No."

"What?"

"Right," I said. "Yes, I'm looking for her. I don't—I don't know where she is."

"Okay, okay," he said. "The two of us together, four eyes beats two, you and me will get her."

"I can't." I blew on my hands to try to warm them. "I can't be outside anymore."

He handed me his keys. "Wait in my car," he said.

"Turn on the heat. I'll look." He took a step toward me, and I could've kissed him without moving my head if I wanted.

"Try Bledsoe's," I said. "She hangs there sometimes. I was heading there when I saw you."

He looked puzzled. "That's the opposite direction."

I shrugged. Once he was out of sight, I opened his car door and stepped inside. It felt different knowing I had permission to be there. The car choked three times before the engine turned over. He'd left the heat on, but it took a second for me to feel it on my fingers. I pushed the heat dial up to the right and waited. That was still within my capabilities—I knew how to wait. I wouldn't have really done it, I told myself.

But I had hit her. That much was written in unwashable ink. The heat was beginning to thaw my hands, but it didn't feel like a relief. For less than a second, I heard a cry and I felt a tug at my chest. I was feeling the baby under my shirt, squirming and rolling and cawing out his noises like a baby bird.

I heard a rapping at my window. Thomas the Prophet signaled me to come outside. Beside him was my mother, with Thomas's coat drooped around her. "You get to warm up at all?" Thomas asked. "She was right where you said."

"She recognize you?"

"I can hear you," Mom said. "Don't talk to me like a child."

We walked inside and up into our apartment. Mom shed Thomas the Prophet's coat on our welcome mat and then disappeared into her room. Thomas said he'd make us some dinner while I put Mom to bed.

I draped the covers over her and put my hand on her collarbone. She was sweating but very cold, and her breath sounded like a dust-buster with a faulty battery. She signaled for me to come close to her. "I know," she said. "I know what you are and what I am." A thin stream of snot ran from her left nostril, and she wiped it away before it touched her lip. "And I didn't mean to do this."

"Do what?" I asked.

"You are who you are, and I am sorry for my part."

"That doesn't sound like an apology."

"But I mean it," she said.

"Go to sleep," I said. "You're friendlier when you're asleep."

"You don't scare me," she said. "Do you even know who I am?"

I flipped off the light. She was using my language. She'd learn to talk how I talked. After all, that was how I learned to speak, by repeating her words.

I considered telling her a story, one of her own. The curious child talks to a stranger and has her eyes turned into glue. When the child forgets, a pack of wild monkeys turn her brain into a gumbo.

"Is she asleep?" Thomas asked when I walked back into the living room.

"I don't know," I said. "She's always half asleep."

"If I'd known that, I'd given you the hard job," Thomas said.

Suddenly, I felt very hungry. "Tuna casserole?" I said. "That's pretty much what I get every night I'm home."

"I don't know how to make casserole, so supper's going to be whatever I can boil."

"If you give me money and you let me warm up then I can pick up whatever," I said. "We can get a bottle if you want one."

"We have crackers and noodles," he said. "I'm thinking that's about enough for two assholes who don't care about themselves."

"What'd you come here for?" I said.

"Shea said you had questions for me. Said you're mad at me?"

"I don't know," I said. "It's what I was told."

"So you let some prick boss you around." He threw some salt into the pot and then licked the palm of his hand. "You're a father to your own mother, living as independent as a homeless man's dog, yet you take orders from him?"

"He was Aaron's friend," I said.

"You think he was nice to your brother? Bullshit, nobody was nice to him." He looked down at the pot and nodded his head, acknowledging what he said. "I don't mean nobody. He didn't seem happy. I was okay friends with Aaron. Not thick as thieves or anything, but nod-in-the-halls-type of friends. He's a year or two behind me, but I think he liked me because of my hand."

"Were you friends with Egan?"

He shrugged. "I knew him, and we had this girl in common."

"Nah, you were friends," I said. "The way you hate each other now, you must've loved each other. That's the way it works on TV."

"I don't know why he hates me," Thomas said. "I hate him too, I guess."

"He said you, you know, fucked the kid. Otto." I shrugged. "Not fucked exactly. Fucked with. Otto's mom was there, and she said—or implied, really, if you want to get technical—that you fucked him. Or jerked him off a little."

"It's a lie," Thomas said. "And this kid's mother hated me from the jump. Her getting together with Mr. Rabbit to smear me is perfect. It's like a tropical storm getting together with AIDS, two flavors of shit that taste shitty together."

"Tell me you don't believe it." There was a tremor of strange laughter in his voice. "All I did is let a neighbor boy in my house. This is my fault because why?"

I put my hand up to silence him.

"And you," he said. "I need you on my side for this. You and me and Shea, we're not like the Rabbit people." He waved his arms like a man under attack by mosquitos. "Maybe we don't sing for the tabernacle, but does that mean we're evil? Do we have to beg permission from jackals just to live?" He tried to touch the pot of boiling water with his bad hand and pulled back, burning his fingers. I laughed.

"Are you with me?" he asked, shaking out his hand.

"Sure," I said. "Why not?" As I heard myself say it, I realized I meant it. Why not believe him? He saved my mother. In the endless fog of right and wrong, I could hold onto that if nothing else. Surely, I could spare him a little faith.

That night, he stayed on my couch. Before long, he drifted off to sleep. I brought him a spare pony blanket off my bed and laid it across his chest. It barely stretched from his shoulders to the curve of his waist. I believe you, I said, but I didn't, not exactly. Whatever happened was lost to the dark spots of our brains, and we wouldn't get it back. Even now, in its mystery, this is as clear as we would ever know it. May we never have this clarity again.

If I had to choose sides, then I would choose this one. Thomas and I saved and ruined lives. Whatever happened to the boy, Thomas the Prophet had saved my mother. I was on the side of more life, miserable or not. I was on my own side.

I walked to the window to look at Thomas's car. No one had touched it yet. From inside my head, I heard the hissing of a spray can. Nightwolf was out there, wrapping our building in purple paint, line by line and layer by layer.

I was on my own side, but only when alone. As soon as I speak, I hear my voice slipping away from my body. I was on the side of whoever else was in the room. It was a shallow conversion, but real. I could clear my throat and yell like a circus-caller: Speak once, and watch me become you. As soon as you recognized yourself in me, I'd be gone.

I learned your language to lose it. The only common word we can say to each other as equals was goodbye.

8.

I don't recall my brother's face. Of course, I know what he looks like, but I'm reciting, not remembering. My imagination of him is set, and I can't send it wandering again. He keeps the same open-lipped stare, his eyes stay slightly crossed, and he has a fading bruise diagonally above his chin. That's how he looks on the picture on our refrigerator. He was thirteen then, impossibly tall, and staring at the camera like it fucked his girlfriend.

Night after night, he'd tell me stories. About Gotham and Jebediah, the name he gave to Joker's hitman for whom he'd created an entire character history. Once I asked him if Jebediah was Joker's slave or if he worked as a free man.

"As a free-mason?" he said.

"Nah," I said, dropping my hands and stepping into his range. "As a free—"

He smashed a model helicopter across my face. I cried and tried to fight back, but once he got his body on me, I fought as well as a sack of ground chuck. He grabbed me by the balls and dragged me to the corner of our room.

"You don't say my name," he said. "What's mine is mine."

He stuck his fingers into my mouth, and it tasted like the lavender soap in Mom's bathroom, the type she made me brush with when I cussed. He pinched my front teeth, not to loosen them, but because he knew if he kept in that position, I couldn't stop smiling.

People tell me of Aaron's long fingernails and dog-jaw and crooked neck. But I only think of the lavender soap, the weight of his body crushing mine, the way our laughs blended together. That's what's left of my brother.

That night at my house was peaceful. Mom made us toast and honey in the morning, and Thomas fried the last of our eggs. It was a fragile peace.

Thomas took me outside. For a second, I thought someone had thrown paint on his car, and I scurried across the street to check, but up close I saw it was only mud.

"This paranoia's bordering in delusion," Thomas said. "Even my most dedicated enemies have lives." His voice sounded somewhere between a whisper and a wheeze. "If you're not going to school, and you're not a Rabbit boy anymore, you're going to need something to do all day."

People on motorcycles rode past us, and we stared at them in silence until they turned the corner. Seeing a pack of bikers in the morning felt as out-of-place as seeing one of your teachers at the mall.

"Work for me," he said. "I've got a consulting job in Columbus so my house's empty for ten days, maybe more." He cracked open his car door. "With all this shit, I can't leave my house as an effigy to burn."

"So what am I?" I asked him. "Security on your house? Maintenance?"

"Don't get ahead of yourself," he said. "You still live with your mother, job or not, and you're still a dropout, and, as far as I know you'll always stay stupid."

"If you're firing me, I want unemployment."

"Patience, young Milo," he said. "You will have many opportunities in your life to say that same sentence."

"So am I inside the house, just living in it?"

"Sometimes," he said. "At night, maybe, when you can't take the cold. But the weather's not going to keep like this forever." He leaned on the car door. "Most times, I want you on the porch, out where he can see you."

It wouldn't take Egan long to hate me as much as Thomas. If he wanted to take a bulldozer to the top of Prospect Hill, then me on the porch wouldn't slow him down.

"Make yourself known at my place. When you're inside, turn on the lights, the TV, the music. Your job is to be there. Look like you're part of the neighborhood. You exist in that house—you are that house."

"You're making this up as you go, aren't you?"

He nodded and took out his wallet. "Here's, I don't know, seventy dollars. What did The Rabbit pay you?"

I shrugged.

"Then you're moving up." He offered me the wad of cash, and I pretended to wave it away before taking it. "You need to keep the house in a somewhat standing position. Prospect is changing. I need warm bodies, on the porch and in the front rooms to put a face on where we are."

"These guys, they don't hate your *house*."

"There's a thousand dollars in it for you," he said. "That's for the week. You know what I'm paying you for."

An alliance, I thought. I was a burning bag of shit placed on the Welcome Mat of his tormentors, the signal that he could steal from The Rabbit as surely as they could steal from him. "They're going to kill me," I said. "You have to know that."

"It's a game," he said. "Just like any game, it feels more

important while you're playing than it does five minutes after it's done. He won't like seeing you, but it's going to wake him up. All this *kill you* talk they throw around. If they don't ratchet it down soon, they'll start believing it, and someone will get hurt."

"I fit the description of 'someone.'"

The following Tuesday, Thomas set sail for Ohio, and I took a toothbrush and a plastic bag full of clean shirts and set up my watch at the top of Prospect Hill.

Meander joined me. On the first night, he drank some of Thomas's good scotch and draped a blanket over himself. "I bet he lives around here," Meander said. "That's why this is the one part of the city he never tags."

"Nightwolf?"

"The whole city's bathed in this asshole's name except here." He waved an arm toward the neighborhood. "He won't risk a neighbor catching him."

"The guy loves himself," he said. "He wants to be surrounded by his work, his name."

"His name?" Meander said. "So, in the phonebook it says Wolf-comma-Night?"

Aaron Byers, I thought. That name felt strange in my mouth, like a loose tooth.

"You ever think what you'd do if you caught him?" Meander said. "If you had fifteen minutes in a room so dark God couldn't find you."

I closed my eyes and imagined Aaron as he was now, puzzled and filthy, his bones stretching his skin. There isn't a person alive I don't want to bury at least a little. Why apologize for trying to be the last man standing?

The folks from The Rabbit came the next night. I suspect it was Meander who told them about me. He understood secrets as a concept, but he didn't grasp that he had a role in keeping them. At four in the afternoon, I saw Petey Peyote drive by, slow his car to a stop, and then drive off again.

When Petey rolled by, I was working in Thomas the Prophet's garden. I was digging holes in his front yard and planting bags of frozen vegetables in them, just the sort of joke he pulled on the rest of the city.

I figured I had an hour before the shitstorm hit. I ran inside to prepare the house. But I didn't know what to do. Hide the valuables, I thought, followed by the realization that I had no idea what he valued in this house. I ran upstairs and took a framed picture of a couple with matching long noses, coke-bottle glasses, and bad teeth. Thomas's parents, I figured, or at least they looked almost as off-putting as he did, but knowing Thomas, it might be the couple that came with the frame. I hid it in a pillowcase.

After that, I ran into the dance room. At least I'd always thought of it as the dance room because that's the room where the partiers would dance. Who has a dance-room? I thought. We were ridiculous people, and the thought stopped me cold for just a second. At this point, I wouldn't know how to spot a sensible person out of a lineup—their routines and habitats as exotic and foreign to me as that of the lowland gorilla. Still, now was no time to reconsider my life, not with the Rabbit making its way up the hill. I unplugged his record player and put it at the top of an unused shoe closet.

After about forty-five minutes, I'd turned the house over. I didn't find any money, but I found a box of Christmas ornaments and a purple hummingbird feeder that looked valuable, so I stuffed them in the shoe closet too.

After that, I was tired and in need of a drink. Plus, I'd been inside longer than Thomas wanted me to be, and for all I knew, they'd skinned and hanged a kitten on his front porch in order to scare away the neighbors. I poured myself two-thirds a glass of whiskey and retook my position on the porch.

You backed the wrong pony, I told myself. I didn't even feel regret, just a dawning certainty. I bet on the horse who ran the wrong way.

After an hour, I closed my eyes. Stay awake, I thought. My heart had slowed, and I was falling asleep. You're a target out here. That's all you were ever meant to be—all either side wanted—a target.

I imagined Hallahan's hands on my face. That's who they'd send. He'd be eager for me, and I knew full well what his eagerness felt like. The hits are smaller, sharper, and you feel every knuckle.

If I froze to death on the porch that night, then that would be okay. I could grind their feud to halt. What's the good of moving the pieces on a chessboard when there's a body lying between the players? My mom would miss me for fifteen minutes, and then she'd go back to where she'd been before: waiting for Aaron.

I woke on the couch, tucked neatly under two blankets. As I blinked myself awake, I figured I must have stumbled inside in the middle of half-blackout. But I wouldn't have tucked myself in. Somebody did this for me.

From the kitchen, I heard the teapot whistle. Bonnie Larkin stepped into the living room. "You awake or are you just rolling over?" she said.

I sat up and squeezed my temples. "Hey," I said. "Why are you here?"

"Isn't that the cry of the ingrate?" she said. "Did you stop to ask what you are doing here? It's not where you went to sleep."

"I haven't stopped to ask myself anything."

She walked to the couch, carrying a plate with orange slices on it. "I see I left quite an impression on you." She put the plate on the table halfway between us. "Here I thought we'd connected, but I guess I can't shame boys like y'all."

"Who told you I was here?"

"Boy thinks he's a God now. When He closes His eyes, He becomes invisible."

"You may have God confused with a preschooler," I said.

"You were passed out on a porch, snoring loud as a motorboat."

"I fell asleep," I said. "Saying 'passed out' implies judgment."

"That night at The Rabbit?" she said. "Did you not understand what I said?"

"That's not it," I said. "I listen to everyone. You made your point."

"You didn't believe me?"

I looked down at the blanket pooled around my feet. "I kind of believed you."

"And with all that, you were able to forgive yourself. That's open-minded." She reached out as if to put a hand on my knee and then brought it back to her own lap. Habit, I thought. She was used to comforting people she shamed.

"Ms. Larkin, I don't want to upset you, and I don't mean—"

"It happened on this couch," she said. "Where you're sitting. Where you slept face down in the cushions with your mouth open."

"That's not—that's not fair." I smelled yesterday's cigarettes on my skin. "You put me here."

"That's right."

"What do you want from me? You cut a pretty righteous swath for someone who won't call the cops."

"I don't want from you," she said. "You've made your choice, and now we're where you want to be."

From above me, I heard a toilet flush. I thought I saw her smile until we both caught eyes, and I realized she was angry. "Is that Egan?" I asked.

"He'll be by later."

"Course he will," I said. "For thinking this place is a pit of hell, you all don't mind making house calls. Maybe you and him and Thomas are all—"

Then I heard footsteps coming down the stairs. Somehow, I knew. There was a clumsy gentleness to the step that I'd heard before. Maybe I hadn't heard it, only imagined it. As it grew louder, I looked at Bonnie, and she looked back at me, like she wanted to chew off my eyelids. Otto Larkin walked into the room.

"Oh hey, Milo," he said moving past me. "What's up?"

"Wait in the car," Bonnie said. "I'll get you in a minute."

Otto walked away. I shut my eyes and heard the door close. "You'd bring him here? In front of this couch?"

"What's wrong?" she said. "As far as you're concerned, nothing happened."

My teeth felt fuzzy and it hurt to clasp them together. "That—this—it doesn't seem fair."

"You're going to sit where you're sitting, and talk to me about fair?"

He's not scared, I thought. That must mean something at the very least.

"He's going to school," Bonnie said. "It's what people his age do on a Thursday at seven in the morning. It's what people your age do too. He's going to school like a normal person. Like someone who has a future."

"School's not for everyone," I said. "Did you know Einstein, instead of going to school, often got drunk on his friend's porch?"

"He's going to be a good person," she said. "This? All this? It's not going to control him anymore." She clenched her fist, and it looked like the weight of the room was bending down her head. "You had a choice, you know? Not everyone has a choice."

I knew that speech. It's not true, of course, but it's beautiful. I wish to God we could leave our pasts as easy as we leave our friends.

She stood up to leave. "I understand this isn't your fault directly. Please know that doesn't make it better."

"I know," I said. "You may not think I do, but I do."

"I used to go to church a lot." She looked up toward the lights and made herself squint before refocusing on my face. "Preacher always said, 'You know you're a sinner.' Even then, I'd think, 'Knowing is no excuse.' What do you say to someone whose only case they make for themselves is they know they're sinning? Congratulations?"

When she left, I called Thomas. The first time he didn't answer. The second time, he laughed. "It'll get worse," was all he said to comfort me. It kind of worked.

After noon, I reposted on the porch, this time with a blanket around my shoulders. In my head, I could hear the school bell ring, sending Otto Larkin out into the halls. He was small for his age. It's not just his shoulders or even his voice, but in the way he looked away when people said his name. Loud noises brushed him back. Then I imagined him pounding a chained dog with a rock.

The paint on Thomas's pillars was chipping. Someone was coming for me, but, like always, I was waiting. The waiting felt like a presence, like an insult pulling me down by the elbows.

I was alone in the mid-afternoon until the front door opened and Meander popped out, nursing a beer. He came up on me so quickly that I didn't admit what I saw at first.

"Don't act so scared." His shirt was torn at the side

from his rib to his hip. "You're getting a reputation."

"What?" I said. "Where did you come from?"

He shrugged. "Is that a real question or are you scared of saying nothing?"

"People are threatening my safety here," I said. "You just waltz in?"

"Waltzing," he said. "The thinking man's polka."

"I'm waiting for any number of these jerkoffs, and you sneak up behind me? How do you expect that to make me feel?"

He took a swig of beer and offered me the can.

When I took it from him, I saw his knuckles were purple and misaligned. "Did you punch a horse?"

"More like a rabbit," he said. "Hallahan made me hit The Rabbit wall over and over until he was satisfied." He shook his head. "He meant it kind of like a joke, but him trying to make a joke is like an elk trying to understand the opera."

"I thought you were done with those guys," I said. "They sure as shit seemed done with you."

"Milo, look at me. Look at you. The sun's shining, and we're young. Not too goddamn stupid, at least compared to what people say about us. And with all that, where are we? And what are we talking about?" He tried clinching his hand but he could barely move it. "Walking away's all right for some people, but all it bought me was a seat on the teeter-totter. Are you like a hostage here?"

"I'm here for the same reason you are," I said. "Except I get paid."

"Why am I here?" He snapped the fingers on his unhurt hand. "Yeah, I forgot. Can you hang until like two? I meant to say this earlier, but Egan's coming by. He knows he's not meant to be here, but he says he'll stay on the porch."

"Are you going to be here too?"

Meander sat down. "He told me not to, but I've got to take a stand somewhere."

We sat on the porch for over an hour, him out-drinking me two to one. It didn't help my nerves. Something was changing. Thomas's house was lurking over me. I saw the house Otto saw: a couch with infinite space around it. The fear wouldn't follow him—it'd build a nest at the base of his spine and make a home.

Two p.m. came and went. I couldn't stop staring at Meander's hand, the way it sprang from his wrist like an exploding bag of flour. It didn't look like Thomas's bad hand—it was more gruesome and less permanent. The house was growing on me, working its way into my doubts.

"Enough of this," I said to Meander. "You said he wants to see me, where is he?"

"Mysterious ways," Meander said. When someone gave him orders, he had direction. He usually didn't follow them, but he felt purpose in his defiance. "Man's like a doctor. He says two o'clock, he means two-thirty."

"It's three-fifteen." I stood up and started to walk off the porch. "I got to check on Mom. You see him, tell him to come get me."

I crossed High Street and headed toward Orman. School had let out and the kids were working their way home. Behind me, a car honked. I fished out a cigarette from my pocket and put it between my lips. I started to ask the kids for a light, but the car honked again. When I turned around, I saw Egan in his pickup. He pulled into the middle of the road and kept honking and a slight and uneven pace. I'd asked him about the truck, and he put it in practical terms. It's not an unabated piece of shit, he said. More like an abated one. His theory was that a car thief had to drive something half clunky. It's good for the soul, he said. To show you can take what you want, but you don't need it. It's the sort of logic that makes sense after you're around it too much.

He kept honking his horn and waving me over. Traffic piled up behind him. Other cars were starting to honk now as well. I checked the back to make sure no one else was inside.

"Come on, drama queen, just get in," he said. "I'm not going to beat your ass in public in the middle of the day."

"You've done it many, many times."

"Not true," he said. "I paid people to do it. It's just me now."

A car behind him honked, and it made me nervous. I was holding up traffic. In my panic, I felt myself moving to the car. I got in, unsure exactly why. He didn't start the car immediately, but sat there nodding to me. Egan's hair had grown since I last saw him. He was sucking on his lower lip, so it looked like his bad tooth was acting on its own and attacking the rest of his face. "I wondered when I'd see you again."

"I waited an hour for you," I said, "and I won't wait two hours for the Pope."

"Meander wouldn't leave." He started the car and pulled into traffic, the front left end of his bumper dangling slightly over the yellow line in the middle of the road. "I don't mind that boy every now and then, but he doesn't understand silence. You think you're being a good friend to him, but you're not. You don't even like each other."

"What about you and me?" I put my hand on the glove box and felt it purr. "Are we friends?"

He shook his head. "You have an amazing ability to hear what you want."

"I'm just trying to get home," I said. "What're you doing to me?"

"I do nothing," he said. "A woman talked to you about what happened to her son. Why do you include me in this dialogue?"

He passed my street—now I wasn't sure where we were going.

"I tried bringing you honest shame, but you didn't

take it," he said. "You'd rather get a thumbs up and a pat on the back. If you won't feel shame, you'll never feel joy."

"What you do," I said. "I'm not part of it anymore. If you're mad, fine, but that's the end of our business."

"Business doesn't end," she said. "Conversation is negotiation. Everything we say is business."

"It's ex-business," I said. "I don't work for you."

"No one works for me," he said. "I'm selling The Rabbit. Group buying it just cares about the lot, so the building is dozer-bait. The farewell party's tonight."

"No more Rabbit?" I said. "You leaving town?"

"You missed the important part," he said. "Big send-off tonight. Attendance is mandatory. I got something there you need to see."

"Where are you taking me?"

He pulled to the side of the road and then nodded out his own window across the street. "You understand?"

All I could see was a Chinese restaurant the color of an unwashed undershirt.

"Over there is the office of Gary Stanford, private investigator," Egan said.

"Shea's uncle?"

"No, he's just a big fan of Shea's uncle," he said. "Were you always this stupid?"

"What am I doing here?"

"I don't know what you were thinking, trying to put the screws to Luke Larkin," he said. "I especially didn't know why it never occurred to you to look in your rearview mirror. But I bet you don't have a license or legal reason to approach him on the street."

"He came to me." I tried remembering if that was true, and I was surprised to find it was. "We never mentioned Shea's uncle."

"Maybe," Egan said. "Not how he remembers it, or at least it won't be once we talk to him. Anyway, he can't sue you two as you're broker than a cripple's legs, but he could damn sure cause enough of a panic to play the death knell for that place."

"You wouldn't."

"You don't value yourself, Milo," he said. "I wish I didn't have to go to extremes to get you to listen." He spread his fingers out and touched my wrist. There was so much tenderness in his threat that he didn't know where one began and the other ended. "I thought I showed you that being near Thomas, being on that path, you were standing in front of an ocean of shit. Then you put on your scuba gear and went snorkeling in it."

I swallowed and tried to look at him. "What do you want me to do?"

"We're almost square, Lemur," he said. "I just need your word on this. You're going to come to the bar tonight at six. Then you're going to go home to your mother and stay there. She needs help and love." He rolled his head around and cracked his neck. "But come six tonight, I suggest you get to The Rabbit and enjoy the party."

"You think I want to party with you?"

"I do," he said. "We have a special guest."

"Senor Low-Penis and the Violators? They're good."

"Close," he said. "We got your buddy The Night-wolf." He stared at me until I met his glare. "Believe it. We caught him dead to rights."

"You don't." The engine purred and rattled, I felt sweat break out on my temples. I watched Egan's smile flicker from taunting to nurturing. Aaron smiled like that too, but only when he was in pain. Did he still smile that way with more teeth than lips? "You're lying. Wait—who is he?"

"Ask him," Egan said. "For one time and one time only, you know where he's going to be. Come seven o'clock, though, he's in the wind. You'll never see him again. We'll make sure of that."

"You going to hurt him?"

"Cousin of Christ, we're not those sorts of men," he said. "What do I want to hurt a pussy-curdle like that for?"

I reached in my pocket and fingered my cigarette pack. "You did offer me money to hurt him," I said. "That's eighty percent of what I was basing my statement on."

"Leave what used to be in the used to be," Egan said. "You're forgetting what's changed about right now. I used to own a business. Now I'm the proud owner of some other cunt's cement farm. Purple paint isn't the banshee it once was."

"Tell me who he is."

"Tell me who you are." He reached out and squeezed my cheeks. "I've given up trying to pluck you out of the fire. They teach you that in recovery. Helping the afflicted can function as another sort of addiction."

I looked at him. "Okay, I don't want to sound like a dick here, but I don't think they say that at recovery."

He shrugged. "My aunt worked the program, and she said something like it. It's not that exactly, but that's how I remember it."

He was waiting for me to get out. I opened the door, undid my seatbelt, and stepped outside. I could walk away forever. This is what I'd told myself for months, but only now, in this moment, did I believe it.

Were the men at The Rabbit looking at me now? Surely, I'd feel it. We see and are seen without asking for permission. Had they seen me the night I left my mother?

I've been the fattest and swiftest wrecking ball to my own family, and I had to be the one to piece it back together again. The greatest relief about knowing you can run away right now is knowing that you can run away tomorrow just as easily. You can stack up all of the tomorrows in eternity—the world will never call for a ceasefire. Tonight I would meet the Nightwolf.

9.

Six p.m. From across the street, The Rabbit already looked like an abandoned building. It felt wrong to not see Lemon or Petey Peyote hustling the passersby out front. But this was a new place, no longer The Rabbit. I wasn't a worker anymore, just a customer. Aaron wasn't my brother anymore, but The Nightwolf, and The Nightwolf wasn't some bagman vigilante, but a man at the mercy of the meanest motherfuckers I knew. It looked like the world's worst magic trick: people change.

Inside, The Rabbit smelled different. The polish Egan used to wax down the wood had pickled and spread throughout the place, clinging to the dust bunnies in the air. No women, I thought. The Rabbit had turned into a locker room. They didn't expect women and didn't bother to prepare for them.

Hallahan sat crosslegged on the bar, drinking from a bottle with the shot separator still attached. He looked at me with a glazed scowl. In slower days, in slower times, we could've been allies. I nodded hello, and he took my greeting like a bump on the head.

Lemon pressed his fingers against the back of my neck. "Milo, Milo, a man in time." He pointed to the back wall where, in purple box letters, someone scrawled OLD FASHIONEDS 2 FOR 1, LADIES DRINK FREE, HIGHBALLS, FIVE $ WELL DRINK.

"That your idea?" I asked. "Egan's going to flip when he sees that."

"That was last week's Egan," Lemon said. "Rich Egan is a more agreeable asshole."

It was dark in the bar, but it was definitely Nightwolf's paint color. The handwriting looked off, like reading a *Ziggy* cartoon in Hebrew. The O's and G's and all letters with loops looked too pinched. It was an imitation, but a good one.

"Tonight's the night," Petey said. "Drink until you see God, but stop before you meet Him." He patted me on the shoulder, and I could feel his fingers stick to my collarbone like already-licked peppermint sticks. "Don't you love the sounds of a collision? One of God's great inventions."

Hallahan reached behind the bar and lifted out a boombox and placed it on his lap. It was playing some tear-spattered country waltz, which was Hallahan's go-to music. Goddamn, I'm going to miss this place, I thought. It hurt to let go of that much anger.

"Where's your friend Meander?" Lemon said. "I figured they'd have to pry that kid off the walls like a bumper sticker."

"I was told he shouldn't come around."

"When's he not told that?" Lemon said. "Unless he was born a month overdue, no one's ever been happier to see him than to see something else."

I stared at the graffiti on the wall. It was happening right here, around us, and we weren't talking about it. Nightwolf was close. I was close.

"Is he here?"

Hallahan handed me his bottle. "Enjoy it," he said.

I looked at him, but his face was as expressive as a slab of pork. "Did you see him?" I asked. "Do you know who he is?"

"Listen to him," Petey said, shaking me by the elbow. "Superstitious as an altar boy, afraid to say his name." He had trouble spitting out the word superstitious.

Hallahan tugged the bottle out of my hands, stared at it, brought it up to his lips. "Are you going to kill this guy or what?"

"Kill him?"

Asa Graves, a chubby part-timer who was a year ahead of me at Dunbar and who I'd never seen dress in anything but baby-blue denim from head to toe, stood up. "Is it a kind of blood oath thing?"

"A blood oath?" I said. "Like a videogame?"

"You don't mean a videogame," Hallahan said. "You mean like a comic."

"Stand-up comics?" Asa said. "Those guys are pussies. Blood oaths are like—"

"Kill him?" I said. "What are you talking about?"

Hallahan wrapped his arm around my shoulder and pointed with his free hand to the wall. "Deep down, you know it, right? Is this your brother or is this just some piece of dogshit from the street?"

It's what they wanted from me, to beat my brother to death for their amusement. If it actually happened—if I had that sort of strength—they'd see it looks clumsy, like a slapstick silent movie.

The front door opened and Egan walked in with two boxes of fried chicken. Behind him was Bonnie Larkin, wearing sunglasses big enough to swallow her face. Everybody sucked in their guts when they saw her.

"We got supper," Egan said. Then he looked to me. "I didn't think you'd come."

Bonnie Larkin reached out and grabbed me by the

wrist. To a stranger, it would have looked friendly, but it felt as cold as a dishtowel soaked in milk.

"This is dramatic, I know," Egan said. "But I wanted to see what you'd do with a choice."

"He had one once," Bonnie said.

"He's had a million choices," Egan said. "But those were other-people choices. I'm curious to see what *he* wants. Which way does his blood run?" He clapped his hand on my shoulder. "You don't believe we have Wolfman, right? I didn't ask him for ID, but I hear there's no room for doubt."

"What's he wearing?" I asked. "Does he look like he looks in the papers?"

"He looks like he looks in the paper after I throw the paper away," Egan said. "The apprehension process has not left him looking his prettiest."

"Is it—" I didn't want to, but I could feel in my sudden stream of shivers, a desire to lean closer to Bonnie. "Is he Aaron?"

Bonnie shook her head. "This is pathetic."

"You disappoint me, Lemur." Egan said. "I tried so hard to make you a man. At best, you're a brave preteen, saying prayers to protect yourself against ghosts. You had a chance. Remember, no one walked you down this road but yourself."

I willed myself not to reach out to them for comfort. They waited until you had the resistance squeezed out of you, and then they spoke in riddles. A tired mind is useless against an unanswerable question.

"You're the family man now?" Egan said.

"He's not coming, is he?"

"Your mother's dying in front of you," Egan said. "All we did is figure out what you want. And you, no imagination whatsoever, just follow whatever we say. It was in front of you. The only thing that could have helped your mom is you in the house. But you wanted to go on a snipe hunt and chase this Nightwolf."

"You lied," I said. "You told me he's coming just to get me here."

At that, everybody around me laughed. Lemon was laughing the loudest, and soon they were all laughing at the fact they were laughing. Only Bonnie Larkin kept mum, just pressing her lips together airtight.

"You can see him," Egan said. "He's here."

I felt Hallahan's thick hand on my shoulder, spinning me to the backroom.

"We cut him a deal," Egan said. "Let him be his own folktale, walk away without further physical damage. So long as he knows this is indeed the last time any of us see the words 'Night' and 'Wolf' in his handwriting, then we won't pick him up again."

Hallahan pushed me to the back of the bar. The rest of the crowd followed, like I was a soccer ball and they were two teams of five-year-olds.

Hallahan's hand snapped down on my mouth, snapping my jaw into place so hard that I came within a wisp of chomping my own tongue. His hands smelled familiar, like a dreaded old friend. Egan nodded in the other direction, and Asa went running out of the front of the bar. Lemon grabbed my body and Petey Peyote took my hands. I bucked against them, but it did nothing.

"That guy in there," Egan said. "Do you know him? It's okay, you can look."

They shoved me in front of the door where I could see through the slit of window. At first, they brought me too close and my breath fogged up the glass. But then I looked again, and I saw him—it was a man, eating chicken from a box and slowly licking each finger.

"You told me once that stories don't end," Egan said. "You told me and Bonnie to be okay with not knowing. And I had to think about that. Because am I an asshole for wanting to see something finished? Is there such a thing as finished?"

Hallahan punched me on top of my skull. It rattled my head against his hand holding my chin, and doubled my vision. When I could see clearly again, I thought the man looked like the little man with the crooked nose from my night with the baby.

"Can you see him?" Egan said. "Is that the man you've been chasing?"

I couldn't open my mouth wide enough to speak, so I poked my tongue out and licked Hallahan's fingers. He loosed his grip long enough for me to bleat like a goat.

"You're just making sounds now," Bonnie Larkin said. "Are you listening?"

The back door to the flop room opened, and Asa Graves walked inside. He yanked on the middle button of his shirt, which he did when trying to remember information. Whatever he was saying right now was told to him, and he was repeating it word for word.

Nightwolf—at least their Nightwolf—stood up. The light from the room connected around his head making him hard to see. Hallahan gave me a short jab to the ear, knocking me to the side.

"That him?" Egan said. "Take a second."

They readjusted me in front of the window so I could see. Asa Graves pointed toward us, and the man turned around slowly and stared our way. I know from my time on the other side of the door that the view from the inside gets pretty cloudy.

Their Nightwolf squinted like he was trying to make out our faces. Aaron, I thought. This was Aaron. Hallahan slammed my head into the door, and when I looked again, it wasn't Aaron at all. His hair had an unnatural curl, like it had been held into place by dirt and butter. There was a speck of dried blood between his chin and the edge of his fat lip.

"This is it," Bonnie Larkin said.

"You have anything to say to him, say it now," Egan said.

I tried to speak, but they wouldn't let me move my mouth. The man gnawed on a chicken wing like a Doberman. It wasn't blood on his chin, but sauce.

I kicked out, certain, I'd connect with Lemon's knee but missed by a good eight inches. They laughed but didn't seem surprised. Petey tightened his grip on my head and wrists, and Hallahan moved his hands from my face to my neck.

"Come on, come on," Egan said. "Don't be a dick. I'm doing this for you."

"Not just you," Bonnie said.

"You want a new start, don't you?" Egan said. "Isn't this what people pray for when they're not begging for convenience?"

Their Nightwolf shrugged and turned around. Asa Graves said something and pointed to the outside. The man scratched his neck and raised his hands skyward like he was trying to crack his spine. Then he shuffled out the door.

I tried yelling again, but this time it was Egan who clasped his hand over my lips. All it left was a muffled hum. The man turned around, like he either heard me or he was worried he'd left his wallet behind. He may as well have had a bag on his head.

They dropped me. I fell shoulder first and then my forehead bounced against the floor. Someone put his boot on top of my elbow. Jesus, I thought, they still expect me to fight. How many times can one man admit defeat?

Egan squatted down above me. "It's okay, buddy, it's all behind you now. What you have here, if you want it, is a brand new world. That doesn't happen by accident. It happens by burning your current world piece by piece, the most valuable idols first."

The Rabbit looked huge just then. The ceiling may as well have been the North Star. I wanted to touch it, but I knew I never could.

"The question you have to answer right now—and I mean right now—is do you want this new world?" He laughed, and just then, he reminded me so much of my brother, I could have hugged him. "You said to be okay with not knowing."

"He doesn't get it," Bonnie said.

"No one gets it at first," Egan said. "But if you're ever going to be a new man, you'll have to admit what just happened. Last train's leaving, buddy."

"I don't know," I said, unsure of what I was responding to. "I don't know."

"Yes you do," Egan said. "You've always known."

My sweat chilled me from my hairline to my lower back. "I don't know what you—I don't know right now."

Hallahan put his forearm across my chin and pushed down.

"What was it, Milo?" Egan said. "Because it looked to me like it was your big mystery walking away with all those answers in his back pocket. You can be the man you're meant to be if you accept that the past is behind you. Tell me that was your brother, your mother's best friend, and when he walked away, that's the last time you're ever going to see him. That sound all right to you?"

"It was." I coughed and turned over to my side. "It was."

"It was what?" Egan said. "It was Aaron?"

I felt saliva or blood dribbling from mouth.

"Say it was him."

It was him, I tried to say. The man's face was already fading from my mind. I pictured him staring my way, licking his ring finger. "Was it him?" I said.

Egan stood to his full height. "At least I tried." He shook his head. "Just so you know, as disappointing as you are to all of us, you can still be a new man. But I can't shock you into it. We'll bring you to it the other way." He nodded to Hallahan.

That was the last thing I saw clearly. Afterward, there were shapes and colors, but I could only feel them. They were beating me, I thought. Just that—I thought it. Somewhere, somehow my body was registering this pain and storing it away. When I was a boy, Mom once locked out of the house in the bitter cold for a whole night. It started as a punishment, but then she forgot to let me in. This was as close as I felt to that—only an aching, a reminder of pain. There's no special hurry, I thought, I'll feel all of this soon.

Hallahan grabbed me by the shirt and shook me, so the back of my head knocked against the floor. We can shelve our pain and start again. Wasn't that the promise of those forever-ago preachers? Maybe this was the new world, the one Egan told me about.

"Knock it off," Petey said.

Hallahan flinched as if he'd hit me one more time, but it was just the bully move of making me cower.

"Knock it the fuck off," Petey said. "You'll break something."

Hallahan backed off. I couldn't make out his words. His voice sounded far away. When I wiped off my eyes, I saw that Egan and Bonnie were behind the bar, laughing. Bonnie was pouring a beer from the tap and letting the foam spill over. I tried to twist in that direction, to see it more fully, and as I shifted, my guts piled on top of themselves.

I moaned, and that, somehow, was the signal for everyone to ignore me. My arms shook, and I couldn't see straight. Egan and Bonnie were talking to each other now about some other problem. At least for today, they were done with me.

10.

Iblinked myself to awareness in the shotgun seat of Lemon's Oldsmobile. Lemon had pulled all his remaining hair back into a ponytail, and he wore a moustache as thick as a chinchilla's coat. He used to joke that he looked like a NASCAR champion if NASCAR only hired drunk drivers. Three boney fingers pressed into my each of my cheeks, propping my head up. They belonged to Petey Peyote, sitting directly behind me.

"Are you trying to hurt me?" I mumbled. "If so, you're not trying very hard."

"Just making sure you don't fall asleep," Petey said. "That's how you lose brain."

"I know that was bullshit in there," Lemon said. "Egan's like a high school actor. You know, the way it seems important to them if they can act well or not? Egan thinks it's important someone's scared of him."

"I don't care no more," Petey said. "You want to look for your graffiti man?"

"He's gone," I said.

"Probably two blocks away." Lemon said. "I was

always for giving you the happy end." He took a left turn toward Prospect Hill.

"Sorry you went through that," Petey said in the back seat.

We were near the top of Prospect Hill. With the windows rolled down, I could smell the dogs and rats from the Leckett Ark. The scent rolled into my nose and the back of my mouth.

"Don't worry," Lemon said. "Prophet's house is still standing. We thought about it. Hallahan, subtle as a Cuisinart to the nutsack, wanted to break his windows and scatter raw meat for the Ark animals. Said we should plant guns and porn and enough coke to get the cops interested. But guns, coke, and porn make for Christmas in my house, and I didn't want to do him a favor. Plus it's bad form to get the law involved. Not sporting."

"Plus, he might not have done what they said," Petey said.

Lemon pulled over to the side of the road. We were still a hundred yards from Thomas's. I could see clearly again.

"This is where we leave you," Lemon said. "As far as us, The Rabbit, everything else, we're square. Bonnie Larkin may still want you stuffed and mounted, but that's her dance. You are now free to be whatever sort of man the people around you can stand."

I stepped outside the car, and I felt a hint of a warm breeze that cleared my head. They started to roll off, but I put my hand out and knocked on the driver's side window.

"Did you see him?" I asked. "The Nightwolf?"

He nodded and looked at my feet.

"Do you know if he was my brother?"

Lemon laughed and looked at Petey. "Man, we never met your brother. The rest of us got our own shit to deal with."

And then I was alone. I took four steps down the road before I understood I was walking down Prospect Hill, away from Thomas's house. The dogs were howling from the Ark, and I wanted them closer to me.

I wobbled from side to side of the street like a bear riding a unicycle. My head was clear except for my eyes swelling in my skull, and my teeth, which felt like they had a thin spool of yarn wrapped around them.

I stepped onto the Leckett yard and the strays surrounded me. I noticed two dead squirrels and one lower half of a chipmunk. The smell was horrifying, and it blended into the sound. It moved over me and through me, and I dropped to a knee. The dogs licked my face.

Next thing I knew, Roxy and Monroe Leckett stood over me, Monroe with his oversized Atlanta Braves jersey and Roxy with her scarves and necklaces.

"He's blinking, he's blinking," Monroe said. "He all right."

"No he ain't," Roxy said. "His eyes don't focus."

"That's how he always looks," Monroe said.

They took me inside, laid me on their couch, and gave me a plastic bag full of stuck together ice cubes. This was the first time I'd seen them working together as a team in fifteen years. There was a sweetness wrapped around their root. Maybe there is a small, strong goodness at the heart of crazy people that sends them up the mountains and into the woods.

The backyard chickens squawked like they knew they wouldn't live long. Roxy brought me peanut butter and crackers and Monroe gave me Natural Lite and Merit cigarettes. I tried to explain everything to them. I owed them my story. My brother, my mother, Thomas, Otto, Nightwolf—they all belonged to the Leckett twins.

"Stay," Roxy said. "You're not in no state to be on your own. This's what comes with messing with them up the hill and down it."

I smiled. What was the opposite of importance? It's here, in this place. Wasn't that what Roxy preached for all those years? We have already died, and this is the heaven we have. Long live the conquering now. We are our reward, and we are what's left when the reward is over. I am my injury, and all that's not me is my splint.

I conked out on the Leckett couch, certain I'd sleep until Gabriel's horn, but an hour later I woke, and an hour after that I was ready to prowl again. Through the open window, I smelled the wet fur and dry kibble from the yard, and I wanted to be out with the animals. Monroe was slumped on the opposite couch with a skin-tight blue skull cap pulled down to his eyelids. To thank them, I left my sunglasses. When the animals took over the inside of the house like they'd taken over the yard, those shades would be the last thing they'd eat. So when the Leckett twins turned into bones, there'd still be some evidence that this house held humans once, and they were loved.

In the yard, the dogs, cats, and opossums circled one another in an uneasy detente. A mastiff whose head went up to my breastbone came and licked my hand. It was strict pity. It'd been so long since I ate a proper meal that this dog now eyed me the way a buck hunter looks at a vegan chicken patty. It was time to go home.

One lonesome beagle kept sniffing my shoes until I was halfway down the hill, but then he sensed he was on enemy territory and ran back.

On the way home, I saw a young girl sitting on the corner, biting her own toenails. Newly homeless, if I had to guess. Not a brand new runaway, but her clothes were cleaner than mine. She had a miniature pink hat and a scar running from the fold in her forehead to her right temple. Before long, she'd wind up with Father Compost, and she'd never look the same again.

"Take your boner and point it away from me," she said when I approached.

Behind her was one of Nightwolf's old, purple squiggles. I'd miss him. I tried thinking of him as my brother and then as a stranger. Both felt cold as raw grouper. All that mattered was he was gone. Runaway. I held the word in my mouth, rolling it from cheek to cheek. The girl was older than my brother had been, but that felt impossible.

When I opened the door to our apartment, I saw Mom sitting on our couch, staring at the turned-off TV. Her shirt and the couch had both faded to the color of a coffee stain. "I wasn't expecting you," she said.

"Do you know me?"

"Are you crazy tonight? You're my son."

"Which son?"

"Well." She laughed, high and piercing. "You're about loopy as cursive tonight."

I walked past her to the kitchen. "You eaten today?"

"Oh good, you're hungry," she said.

I filled a pot with water and put it on the stove to boil.

"Where have you been all this time?"

"With some bad motherfuckers," I said. "On the motherfucker side of town."

"There it is again," she said. "Talking like we're friends, not mother and son."

"You weren't in one place that whole time. No one stays still for that long."

"I do," I said. "I'm patient."

"I've missed you," she said. "Milo too."

I ducked my head and closed my eyes. The room was stretching now, reshaping itself around her wheezy breaths. What if I was him? I thought. It made as much sense as anything else, so why not? That way, she wouldn't be crazy, but a seer who catches us hiding under our false skins. If I wanted to solve my own mystery and help her have the one conversation she needed, all I had to do was not be me. The idea had a delicate, counterintuitive beauty like a puddle of gasoline, and I didn't want to let it go.

"How long do you think I've been gone?"

"This isn't my first rodeo either, you know?" Her voice was plump with humor. "I've been places, places the likes of which you can't imagine."

"You think I can't imagine Arizona?"

"They once had me lined up for TV," she said. "Not as an actor, but as a stand-in. It's like an understudy but different."

"You told me this before." I went to the sink and washed my hands.

She smiled and signaled for me to come closer. "What'd you leave me for all this time? No word or nothing. It's practically criminal."

"I'm home now," I said. "What's the point of being here if you're just going to talk about me being gone?"

"You should show me more affection. Not just gratitude, but real affection. All I do is miss you, and when I finally lay eyes on you, you treat me like a stranger."

"You got to eat, Mom. I'll get more medicine for you when Thomas comes back, but for now food's all we've got."

"I'm okay."

"Not what I heard," I said. "Eat and stay quiet, and your mind will get right."

She looked up and—without warning or even a notable change of expression—started crying. "My mind? He talks to me about my mind? About medicine?" She punched the couch cushion beside her. "You did this to me."

"I know."

"You did it to yourself too," she said. "God knows I didn't make you like this."

"It's okay. I know you tried. You just failed."

"All these years alone. It's not easy to be by myself."

"Years?" I said. "And there was no one else here? Not one person?"

"I don't want to fight," she said. "All boys ever want is to fight. And you don't think of me, locked up and stranded, no one around me for miles."

Miles? I thought. Where do you think you are?

"I wish I could give you better news," I said. "None of us are doing great."

"It's not the same," she said. "You being here now's not the same as you being here when it mattered. They're out to get me, I know it."

"Who?"

"They'll find me and eat me," she said. "They'll eat me in bits and pieces."

The coyotes, I thought. She wasn't here with me anymore but lost in her story. I stared at her mouth, her lips quivering around her gums. I expected to see her breath. All those stories, with Aaron and me squirming in terror, she wasn't imagining another world, but seeing into the future.

"I'm cold," she said.

I sat beside her. "It doesn't have to end the way you tell it. What if I was to tell you he's close."

"I'm hungry," she said. "I want to go to bed."

I took her by the wrist and pulled her to me. "I left because I was scared," I said. "The monsters were everywhere. For most of my life, my nightmares began with 'Once upon a time.'"

Her hands shook and she steadied them on my knee.

"Why didn't you look for me?" I said.

"Me?" she said. "You knew exactly where I was. How am I supposed to find you?" She tried to stand but couldn't. "I didn't tell you to get thin. To lose your looks until you're what you are now. I remember when you were handsome."

I waved my hand over my belly. "Do I look thin?"

"And I was handsome too," she said. "I remember the judges told me. Not pretty but handsome." She reached into her mouth and plucked out her top teeth. A strain of spit connected her palate to her mouth, and when she smiled, it snapped away. "I didn't mind that. All the girls were pretty. Handsome stands out."

"Do you remember those stories?" I said. "About the coyotes?" I put my hand on her knee. "That'll stick with me so long as I can hear your voice."

She put her fake teeth onto the back of my hand. Then, with her free hand, she covered her eyes. "They say I'm not right. That I can't remember. But you'll tell them, yes? Now that you're back. I know how things are supposed to be. Sometimes I see it wrong, but I know how it's supposed to be."

I closed my eyes and felt the saliva from her fake teeth pooling around my knuckles. She was trying so hard. Not for me, but for her fear of silence, of the darkness of her mind. "Once upon a time," I said, "the coyotes came to catch us. And you remember how they attack? It's all tongues and bad intentions, and if you're not fast, they'll lick your cheek straight off your face the same way a horse licks an oat."

There were no coyotes. Whenever I ventured this far into her imagination, I had to hold back by telling it to myself over and over—there were no coyotes. But tonight, right then, I had to feel it, their fur between my fingers. I hated both rooms I was standing in, both languages I answered her in—the real one and the imagined. I hated both the man she saw and the man she pretended to see.

"What did the boy do this time?" she asked. "It must've been ugly."

"He didn't listen," I said. "Or he listened to the wrong thing. We're always listening to something, I suppose, but he heard the wrong voice. The other voice that most folk keep stuffed away."

"What's the point of this story? What are we meant to learn?"

Not learn, I thought, forgive. That was the moral, with the tune swiped from the Leckett's hymnal. It didn't matter which collection of voices the boy followed because he was forgiven. That's the nature of following. The coyote was forgiven his hungers, same as the storyteller gets pardoned for his stories and the listener his nightmares.

Coyote, I thought. This was the point of her stories, of all of them. Only the humans can forgive, she was telling me. The other animals exist to destroy.

What could I give her that she didn't have? For the longest time, I thought all I could offer her was a quick death, brutal and painless. But now, in the dim, unending light, I knew she wanted to live. I wanted her to live.

She stared at me, her cheeks looked huge and hollow without her teeth. No one survives her stories, not even the animals. They're stuck in the same freezing cell as the rest of us. The only chance we have is to escape the story. You escape her story by telling a bigger story.

"I can make it hurt less, Mom," I said. "I know how."

"You say that, but you're going to leave again," she said. "Your type leaves."

I pictured the Lecketts taking me in. For whatever evils I've done, I've seen goodness. It confused me, and I ran away, but I could identify it as something apart from me, something bigger than my imagination.

She rested her head on my shoulder. In the pot on the stove, the water boiled to nothing. It warmed us, keeping our stories and memories tucked away for the night.

PART TWO:
FATHER COMPOST

2006 A.D.
LEXINGTON, KENTUCKY

1.

Six years passed. That's neither good nor bad, but it is relatively accurate.

Mom is with God now if you believe God is hiding in a plywood casket in a Lexington cemetery. Her life insurance offered to pay for a funeral, which I found ironic, but I took them up on it on the hope my brother would show up. He didn't, and, coincidence or no, Nightwolf has remained in hibernation.

I got my GED, and while I don't use it every day, I did parlay it into an assistant to the production assistant job at a local talk radio station. It's like being a fluffer for racism. I live in Mom's place, and I'm civilized enough to vacuum once-a-girlfriend.

Corey Casey had a son, and he loves that baby almost as much as he loves the memory of not having a son. When the boy was in utero, Corey wrote children's songs for Senor Low-Penis and the Violators, but they never caught on. So Corey waved goodbye to his punk-rock aspirations and decided he could better serve his child by being unemployed. Meander sang the baby Violators songs as lullabies to taunt his brother. When I asked Corey who the mother was, he said, "No one in particular," which would be quite a trick if true. But Corey, according to everyone except Corey, doesn't matter. It's just another way of showing how we outlive our dreams.

After the dust-up at The Rabbit, I stayed away from Prospect Hill. From what I heard, Thomas came home from that week in Ohio to find his house turned inside out. The boys from The Rabbit had moved all his furniture to his front lawn. Honestly, all of his furniture—from his one pot cooker to his unplugged refrigerator to his claw-footed bathtub—lay in his front yard. They also mowed his grass and moved the clippings to his living room where they sprinkled them over a fresh layer of peat sod spread across his carpet. When Thomas the Prophet came home, he found Curt Lemon, naked except his denim vest and shampoo-flecked reflector sunglasses, half-asleep in his bathtub. Ollie Hallahan was sitting on Thomas's unplugged oven, slurping up a pot of noodles, waiting for his arrival.

By the time a story lays its eggs in my ear, it's been filtered through Meander's double-fisted double-ginned double-vision. Every sentence he says sounds like a Jack-the-Giant-Slayer tale, chock-full of monsters and morals and bullshit.

What I can say for certain about Thomas the Prophet is that he paid me in full for my week-long debacle of house-sitting. According to him, I'd chosen sides, and in our middle school of a battleground, that's all he needed. When he offered me the cash, I shook my head and made at least three 'I can't possibly' noises before taking it, which I felt showed maturity on my end.

The Egan Rabbit shuttered its doors, and Egan Hopper set sail for parts unknown. We crowned him the winner of the Prospect Skirmish. It helped that he never got in touch with anyone back here. If he didn't care about us, how could we beat him? I like to think he's in the flatlands of Missouri or some other place I don't like to think about.

The biggest, saddest change happened to Prospect Hill itself. The university bought all the old row houses, razed them, and then replaced them with cheap student housing. Suddenly, the neighborhood was as full of plastic crap as a kid's Christmas stocking. The heathens stopped calling it Prospect Hill and renamed it Sophomore Mountain, which struck me as an offense to both mountains and decency. I remain nostalgic for a place where kids could go to get high and maybe molested.

The action moved to North Bennett—"NoBee" as the people who thought pronouncing the ends of words took too much time called it—and Thomas the Prophet moved there as well. As part of my ongoing protest against time, I refused to climb up Prospect's summit and stare at the square monstrosities full of ugly children pretending to be adults. It wasn't for Thomas's house or because I hated watching visual proof of my youth receding in the rearview. I couldn't stomach the thought of civilized sunlight shining on the Leckett house. If the city government made them tame the jungle on their yard, then there's no hope for the rest of us.

Ironically, that week in Ohio proved to be a coup for Thomas. He created a commercial for a burger joint, and his tagline, "A Day From Hell Needs A Hell Of A Meal" was precisely the sort of bullshit the public found cute for a month-and-a-half. The commercial spread through the Midwest and then nationwide, with everyone from morning talk show hosts to sports commentators parroting Thomas's line. He returned home a richer and reinvented man, albeit one with his house inverted. But the blood had been spilled. To pretend the mess didn't exist was like walking away mid-face tattoo and expecting it not to be an issue in your upcoming campaign. So he moved.

Thomas's name popped up in the paper about once a month, which in itself wasn't surprising. I always assumed he'd be in the paper for selling drugs or public harassment or touching the kids in *Family Circus*. Instead, Thomas the Prophet bamboozled us all by becoming an actual force in the community. He did one of those things with his money where he turned it into more money that wasn't gambling. Now, he gave enough cash to charities where the gatekeepers wanted to take pictures with their arms snaked around his shoulder. He didn't fool me. If he could have worked his left hand, he wouldn't even be giving the camera the finger—that would be too abstract. Instead he'd hold a sign saying, "Picture Me Giving You The Finger, Motherfuckers!"

As for me, I've been living exactly the life I deserve, which says very little for me or karma. Every morning, when I brush my teeth, I repeat the following catechism to the mirror: Are you scared today? Of course. That's the price of observation. Do you deserve your fear? Without question.

These are my beliefs that I didn't believe as a teenager: if hell exists, then it is close, nipping at our shoelaces, trying to lure us into obeying our gravity and collapsing. That's what we want—to give up the fight. I'm still fighting, at least for now. Be patient, I tell my devils. Hell will always be with us, so long as we can imagine hell.

Six years isn't an eternity, but it's enough to feel the fire in your blood flicker. I saw goodness once. It sticks with me like yesterday's stench. It doesn't shape my day-to-day actions, but I wish it did. Sometimes at night when I'm alone or sober, I hear it calling me to fight for its cause. In the daylight, the spell is broken.

I no longer believe history repeats itself. I'm not certain history exists.

Brody Jenkins—"The Broj" to advertisers and his handful of insomniac listeners—tried to keep Lexington awake by screaming his opinions through their radios from midnight to 3 a.m. This was amateur hour, but on my lucky nights, I got to work "Still Awake With The Broj." I loved how he could whip himself into a sweaty rage-tornado over any conglomeration of words in the news. The man could find an insult in a blowjob, and he seemed convinced that whoever wrote the headlines for the *Lexington Herald Leader* had a personal vendetta against him. "Trade shortage?" he'd say. "Trade shortage? We have an exchange of goods, and now they want to say trade shortage?" He had the sarcasm and self-loathing of a stand-up comic, but with none of the jokes. He declared himself "the last man in town who preferred politics to basketball." As a result, Lexington liberals would call and ask about who should start at power forward and whether the Wildcats would beat Florida just to make him yell.

The Broj didn't like me being in studio with him because he was self-conscious about how his fury-sweat melted his delicately maintained combover to where it looked like he wore a ladle's worth of gravy on the left side of his head. It was not an easy listening experience, but it was a remarkably easy working experience. All he wanted from me was a check-in every hour.

I heard a pebble rattle against my office window. When I opened the back door, I saw Meander, equipped with a shit-eating grin and a case of beer. Whenever The Broj was phlegming up the airwaves, Meander would creep into my office.

Some of the late night DJ's assumed Meander worked at the station. It was, of course, the exact way he found his job at The Rabbit. I would've figured that's what he thought a job was except that Meander was cobbling together a living as a substitute teacher at the very public schools that said thanks-but-no-thanks to him as a student.

That night, Meander was upset. Two of the kids who used to torture him at Orman Park, calling him Squirrel, had moved in next door. They were now eighteen, and they didn't recognize Meander, but he hated them living that close. Most nights, he came home and peed on their front door as a "Hey, fellas, remember me?"

The teenagers were greasy and spotted, wearing oversized concert T-shirts from KISS and Bonnie Raitt handed down from aunts and uncles. "When they look at me, they see their own future," Meander said, sounding far too happy about it.

Except that night, he was as mopey as a puppet without the strings. The boy's aunts had noticed the pee-stain, and Meander was worried they had blamed their beagle and put it to sleep.

"You never killed a dog before," I said. "It'll look good on your resume."

"Don't say that, MB." He shook his head and squeezed his temples between both thumbs. "I just wanted to pee on a door. It was supposed to be innocent."

"Wait, that's not true," I said. "One time, I remember you were about to punch a hole in the Leckett Ark, stray dogs first."

"What?" he said.

"You said you were going to drive up in the yard and squash a couple of those shit-hounds that used to prowl Prospect Hill."

"The biggest Prospect shit-hound I recall is making a name for himself in North Bennett."

That started us on a jag. On these nights, when I was high on beer and squandered work hours, I had a lot of conversations that started with, "There was this one time." We valued our memories—they were another country, our country, and this was our time to lapse into our native tongue.

Over the speaker, I heard The Broj's theme music taking us to the half-hour break. I walked down the hall to check in. In the hallway, there were cutouts from old newspapers from the last fifty years. They weren't the biggest stories of that time, but the quirkiest. So instead of the picture of the Berlin Wall falling, we had pictures of the time The Kentucky Wildcat mascot grabbed his crotch in front of the mayor, or when a coked-up alderman accidentally burned down one of the old courthouses. One of the pictures, said, "Is This The Night-Wolf?", complete with an artist's rendering of me. It made me feel at home—my past was watching over my present, scowling.

"You come to see me, Starling?" It was Brody Jenkins, who'd come out of his radio pit for the commercial. All men were "Starling" to him, and all women were "Darling." It kept him from having to learn names, and it also made him sound gentle—he needed that misdirection when people expected a screaming, stuttering mess.

"You got everything you need?" I said. "Coffee still hot?"

He looked where I was looking and saw Nightwolf. "Jesus, that guy. Didn't they pin it on one of the horse farm workers?"

I shook my head. "Never caught him. Probably some punk runaway."

"No, it was a seasonal worker. That's why he stopped."

I gave him my notes. "My friends teased that was me in that picture."

"You?" he said. "No way."

"It looked more like me back then," I said. "It's been a rough couple of years."

"You're twenty-two, twenty-three?" he said. "If twenty-two's treating you rough, then you'll be on a slab by fifty. Anyway, you're handwriting's too shitty for that." He patted me on the meat of my arm. "I swear, someone told me he was a horse farm worker. That he's likely back in Dublin, shitting all over that city."

"You think your red-eyes remember Nightwolf?"

Red-eyes were what we called our sleepless, perpetually stoned listeners. It wasn't derisive—we hated them for different reasons. "Put it out there. Say you have a source?"

"Fake a source so I can stick my neck out on a story no one cares about?" He nodded his head. "I knew there's a reason I hired you. It's that I'm bad at my job."

When I returned to the back room after a smoke break, Meander was howling. "Memory lane, buddy," he said. "Memory motherfucking lane."

True enough, The Broj was in mid-tilt ramble about Nightwolf. He wasn't angry yet, but his emotions only flowed one way. "Who? Who, seriously, who? Who puts a garbage bag on his head? Is there a quicker way to advertise that he's a pile of trash?" he said. "Now I have a buddy—keep in mind , this is just buddy talk now, not a police report or affidavit—who swears up and down that this was the work of a stable boy. Then again, another person I know swears he saw first-hand it was an art student. This was part of his—I don't know—his thesis."

Perfect, I thought. In fifteen minutes, he'd forget he was lying. He could yell himself away from reality and into his imagination without ever asking directions. From his tone, I could tell he was pumped.

"Memory Lane, indeed," I said. "The amount of time I used to spend on this guy. I'm not sure how either of us made it out alive."

"What guy?"

"Nightwolf?" I said. "Who are you talking about?"

He handed me my notes, with a gigantic highlighted section. These were the daily notes we tried to work into the show. It included the public relations blurbs that the well-to-do crowd sent our way. The highlighted section told me that Tom Mercer was being honored by the Gold Kids Foundation for of his work with homeless youth.

Tom Mercer was Thomas the Prophet, his work involved signing over a good number of checks to the Gold Kids Foundation—in fact, he single-handedly kept them afloat. Gold Kids struck me as an ironic way of referring to poor children.

"You think they know where that money comes from?" Meander said. "It's commercials now, but that money's grandfather is dope and high times on Prospect."

There was a synchronicity here. Both Thomas the Prophet and Nightwolf never left my life, but they skirted around the edges. One couldn't reenter without the other—they were either side of the same mystery.

According to the promo material, Thomas the Prophet was starting an arts scholarship for the Gold Kids called Tomorrow's Sunrise. Although "Tomorrow's Sunrise" sounded like the title you'd get when you put a focus group, a greeting card and early onset dementia in a blender, we Prospect veterans remembered "Tomorrow's Sunrise" as the name of a vicious strain of LSD he used to sell.

"It's open to the public." Meander licked his lips. "Maybe we should say hi?"

"That's a shirt-tucked-in type of party," I said. "They'll sniff us out."

"Open to the public," Meander said. "I've been kicked out of public school. The public library called public security on me to get me out of their public restrooms. The public charity event is all I have left."

When my shift ended, the night had started to relent. This was the peaceful time, before we had to choose sides between yesterday and today. Meander was bleary-eyed and swaying, which made me think he was going to make some Middle School social studies class very happy in a few hours when he fell asleep in front of them, but he was a master of second winds. After a misspent life with him, I could remember only a handful of times when he gave up the ghost before I did. Some joker had tagged Nightwolf on the side of our building with a Sharpie. It looked nothing like the real Nightwolf's handwriting, but it was nice to know we had listeners.

Six years later, this was Nightwolf's legacy. In his wake, up sprung a slew of taggers and vandals, each one more talented than the one before. These people were painting pictures and multicolor animals. Comparing these tags to Nightwolf's block letters and Burma-shave insights was like comparing a greyhound to a Greyhound bus.

Thomas was building something. I didn't know what yet, but it was taking shape. It made me miss him. It gave me a twinge of jealousy too—whatever his plan was, I wanted it to involve me. After all, I did take his side once, almost intentionally.

Meander and I had twenty minutes before it started to feel like tomorrow. We walked down Main and sat on the bench across the street from The Grieving Taco, so nicknamed because it was a Mexican restaurant adjacent to a funeral home, and most of their business came from mourners. The salsa was above average, but it made it hard to enjoy a margarita when the table to the right was muttering hymns and sobbing into their hot sauce. Before it was a Mexican restaurant, it was an especially obnoxious McDonald's, and the new owners never got rid of a Ronald McDonald statue outside. It felt appropriate if a little dark. This was our Playland, full of sugary booze and elegies.

Meander perked up. "You looking at this?" he said. "I don't believe it."

He pointed to a swirl of illegible graffiti around Ronald McDonald's feet.

"How you like that," he said. "Speak of the devil, and yonder he comes."

"Wait, you mean?" I cocked an eyebrow at him, stood up and darted across the street to see. It was happening,

I thought, and I wasn't even surprised. Nightwolf was such a precarious ghost that speaking his name could tip the balance and conjure him into reality. When I reached the other side of the street, I so fully expected to see the purple letters that it took me a few breaths to realize they weren't there.

"Yup," Meander said. "I suppose some shit dies worse than Jesus. You think you put a cleaver to its head, but it keeps popping up."

"Right," I said. But I didn't see it, whatever he was looking at.

"The way they did it, it looks like it's Ronald McDonald talking, but that's too weird. For one, it makes me think of clown penises and for whatever reason…I don't know how to finish that sentence, and I regret starting it."

I swallowed and looked again. Under the Ronald McDonald statue, someone had written in bright scarlet, "Tom Mercer Raped My Son!"

"Of course, if Ronald McDonald's son was raped as a boy, it'd explain why he became a hamburglar," Meander said. "Traumatic childhood experience and all."

One ghost at a time, I thought. Please, one ghost at a time. I already lived through it once. I've been almost happy these six peaceful years, but I missed the struggle. I wanted the fight to come back for me, put my head in the crook of its arm and take me away. But come slowly, I thought. I'll dance to your rhythm and travel where you tell me, but please, one ghost at a time.

2.

I'd been asleep for three hours when the phone rang. I picked up, and before I heard his voice, I knew it was Meander. The man was a demigod of bad timing.

"You got to get down here," he said. "Chop, chop."

"Where are you?"

"Henry Clay," he said. "It's what we talked about."

"Are you calling from class?"

"God no," he said. "Or not exactly. They're watching a movie."

"Are you in the classroom?"

"The doorway," he said. "Trust me, they don't care."

"How can someone be bad at substitute teaching? That's like being unqualified to be a mascot."

"I need you here," he said. "If you're sober, I'll get you in as a guest speaker. If you're high, I'll just sneak you in. Shit, that's probably easier. You should get high."

"What?" I coughed. "Why—why am I even talking to you?"

"Good, you sound high," he said. "First lunch starts in twenty minutes. Second lunch a half-hour after that.

Really got to be here within the hour."

"What for?"

"Missing the bus is not an excuse. If he's sick, he should have a note, and what sort of a father would let—" I heard a shuffling and then Meander came back in his normal voice. "Sorry, another teacher came by. We have to get this kid."

"What kid?" I asked, but it was pointless. He had hung up, and anyway I knew. He was talking about Otto Larkin. Otto must have been sixteen or seventeen now. I tried picturing him aging, his hair turning stringy and matted with sweat, him sprouting a translucent moustache. He's as old as I was when this all started.

Meander prided himself on his plans. They stood up to reality as well as a penny stands up to a vacuum, but that didn't matter. He patched up the holes in one plan with the mortar of another. To him, thinking a way out of his problems was as good as being rid of them. For the most part, I was happy to come to his call, but not that morning. The one giant of the past I absolutely did not want to tangle with was Otto Larkin. Some alleyways stay dark for a reason.

Meander greeted me in the parking lot and took me into his classroom. The lounge freaked him out, he said, because it was full of "real-life" teachers. "Kids have sticky hands, they smell like puberty, and the boys can't even look at the edge of a desk without humping it. Who wants to work with that forever?"

"We don't have to do this," I said. "We can let this kid alone."

Meander sat on his desk. "Why'd he write it for then? If he wanted to be left alone, he wouldn't have written what he wrote."

"It said 'my son.' It's Bonnie Larkin."

Meander pointed to the kids streaming by his door. "You know how many of these fuckers' notes I read? I can tell child handwriting from mom handwriting." He must have read my face. "Well, doubt me if you want, but, palm on a Bible, I can tell when that tag got started, it was going to say, 'Thomas Mercer Raped *Me*.' He got shy— maybe nervous about the gay stuff. Otherwise, you've got pushing-forty Bonnie Larkin out there with the skate punks, tagging her name."

"If it is him, it's not our place to tell him to shut up. Why am I here?"

"Couple reasons," Meander said. "First, the kid always hated me. I used to make him clean Thomas's gutters and then get girls to throw acorns at him when he was on the ladder. Once we put bulbs on his ears and glitter in his hair and made him act as our Christmas tree. So if he gets a chance to tell me to fuck myself now, he'll take full advantage." A bell rang but Meander didn't flinch, even as the din outside in the hall whipped up. "Most importantly, you said you wanted to."

"Wanted to what?"

"Last night," he said. "You said if you could do it over again, you'd let people know where you stand." Students filed in but Meander didn't look at them. "Here's your chance," he said. "Figure out why he's dredging this shit up now."

"Did I say that?"

"Implied it." He turned to his students. "Any of you know Otto Larkin? Maybe sixteen, whatever grade that is? Kind of, I don't know, bug-eyed. His mom's weird."

"I appreciate your help."

"Don't talk to me," he said. "I'm a fucking substitute teacher. I'm not positive I'm in the right room." He gestured to the students. "These piles of shit can be replaced by literal piles of shit, and I wouldn't notice. Talk to your ally. She's here this term."

Shea Stanford, he meant. She'd been teaching drama, rotating from high school to high school, serving at the pleasure of whatever principal needs a teacher they don't have to give health insurance. I still had beer-and-catch-up sessions with Shea once every few months, but we'd almost eliminated the catch-up aspect. She still had dreams and talent, but she'd lost her fastball. Out of that whole jambalaya of friends, Shea Stanford had the most shadowy relationship with Thomas the Prophet. On one hand, she found him obnoxious—his manner of preening and coked-up philosophizing felt tiresome. On top of that, Shea's Episcopalian, and Thomas the Prophet's needling version of atheism struck her as less blasphemous than childish. Still, they listened to each other honestly, in a way the rest of us avoided. Some took them as a squabbling romantic duo, but I never bought it. They were flawed friends—people always mistake that for love.

For the better part of an hour, I tried to find Shea Stanford's drama class. Coming back to high school felt insulting to every fear I ever had. The halls smelled like fish sticks and Tang and looked so small that I felt bloated. Finally, I heard her. She had a ridiculous teaching voice, booming and clearly faked. When she was reading from the board, she took on the odd phrasing of Pennsylvania prep school girls. When she improvised a joke, she sounded like a sitcom Brooklyn smartass.

I stood in her doorway and watched her wave her arms to the class. The students stared at their phones or kept their heads tucked in their arms. I kind of hated them. We had the decency to write on our desks, to leave something for the next person. They couldn't even dick around with their friends face-to-face. That thought made me ashamed because I could see the liver spots on my imagination.

I assumed Shea Stanford was saying something about Shakespeare or the author of Our Town because I couldn't remember another playwright. When she saw me, she stopped. "Okay, and now, as promised, we have a guest speaker. Mr. Byers, you're late, but I am to assume that this is part of your condition?"

"Yes, right," I said. "Because I am here to talk to you about this topic."

"We thought your expertise would be beneficial to the students."

"My expertise," I said. "Yes. As Ms. Stanford might have explained, I am an expert on the man or woman who wrote Our Town."

"Very cute, Mr. Byers." She wagged a piece of chalk at me, like an indulgent babysitter. "But we invited you here to speak about your life experiences. As our liaison to the drug resistance program, we thought you should be the one to share your story."

"Yes, of course," I said. "The things you need to know about drugs is: one, they are almost certainly not healthy. I'll pause here for your questions."

Shea raised her hand. "Tell us what your experience is with the drug force."

"The drug force?" I said. "Drug enforcement, needless to say, means that you have to keep certain drugs in line. Now, it's all about observation. I can look at any of you and instantaneously know how many drugs each of you use. You want to try me?"

She used to wind me up this way all the time. Pound for pound, I couldn't stand my ground against Shea Stanford, but I had fun trying. She looked at me like a dog who shook hands with his left paw—yes, he's doing it wrong, but he's trying.

"Those are the facts, and when it comes to facts, I'm something of a connoisseur." I tried booming and angling my voice like she did. "In fact, I come into contact with over six facts a week." I clapped a fat, sleeping kid in the small of the back, but he didn't stir. "Did you know that cows have regional accents. No joke. If you're the sort of person who studies this, then you can hear the difference between a Boston cow and an Arizona one. Moreover, you'll die alone." I was flailing, trying to remember fun tidbits from the radio. "Also, did you know that Ronald Reagan personally appointed over twenty percent of the nation's perverts to positions of prominence, including scout leaders and lifeguards. In fact, if you think back to your own experiences, pretty much any minute you don't remember, in all likelihood, you were either asleep, looking at a flasher's penis, or other." I shoved my hands in my pockets. "What I was trying to say is that drugs are sabotaging our society. As for perverts, I was being relatively sarcastic. Inasmuch as—"

The bell rang. It was the first time I saw any movement from the students, who went from asleep to skipping out of the classroom in about four seconds. As the class thinned out, Shea patted me on the back. It was a familiar touch, one I've felt after bad dates—the "It's okay, I'm sure you'll have sex some other time" pat.

"Don't worry about it," she said. "Those kids have stopped caring."

"You're just saying that to be nice."

"Your skill for improv is dazzling, but I'd rather you get to the point." She'd cut her hair short, and it made her look young, even as the lines around her eyes were starting to form. "You're here about Otto Larkin?"

"How do you know so much?"

"My detective partner needs a brush-up," she said. "First, Tom Mercer has his reception Friday, so those memories flare up. Second, Meander told me this morning."

"It's just that last night, we saw this—"

"I heard this story," she said. "Or rather, I heard a better, less true version. But I don't get it, and I don't imagine you do either."

"We didn't finish it last time. We almost did, but we stopped short." I leaned forward and put both hands on her desk. "Everybody's made it out okay but him. You're working, I'm presentable, and Meander's life is mediocre. That's better than I expected. But we never got to the bottom of that story for Otto."

She shook her head. "Some stories don't end. That was your position, I recall."

"But not like this," I said. "Stories should not end because that's just the shitty part of being alive, they shouldn't not end because we stop looking."

"We already know what we'll know," Shea said.

"No, listen," I said. "One night, six years ago, Thomas fucked with that kid or he didn't. And if he did it, then nothing in that boy's life will ever be the same."

"You say we're doing better, but you're wrong." She stood and walked around the desk to be next to me. "We have jobs? We're in our twenties, Milo. We're meant to have jobs. That's like putting, 'I never gave my boss AIDS' on your CV. What about everybody who's doing worse?"

"Who?"

"Your mom," Shea said. "Lina. Corey, if he's being honest. Think about Prospect and it's makeover. Never mind Ollie Hallahan, if you believe the gossip. Egan and the Rabbit boys are gone. And you? Please."

"I'm as happy as I need to be."

"I don't know what that means and neither do you," she said. "If you were happy, you'd let this go."

"Either way, we have Otto. If he wants to talk about it, I'll listen. And if not, we've got to shut him the fuck up."

She squeezed my cheeks. It was her friendliest way of telling me to give up. This was how she loved me, by trying to prevent me from losing. The bell rang for the next period. The two of us—not too far removed from high school—tensed, expecting someone to teach us a lesson.

"We have one success," Shea said. "Thomas the

Prophet succeeded, and it damn near killed him. For a time, I thought it'd kill you too."

"But if he did it?"

"Milo, take a look at this." She pointed to a poster on the wall showing a cyclist in the distance going over a mountain, splitting an ice-blue sky. The text read, 'Luck Is A Byproduct of Effort.'

"What does that mean to you?" she said.

"Stop waiting for the world to help, and try to work it out myself."

"You're close, but think harder."

"I know what these words mean, but I can't figure out the mountain bike."

"I'm showing you this to remind you how easy it is to get you off topic," she said. "You need to keep focused on Thomas, on our success. We have to protect each other."

"Do you teach Otto? If he still lives in Prospect, this would be his district."

She handed me a piece of paper. "He dropped out of school."

"What's this?" I said, shaking the paper. "Does he still live on Prospect?"

"There is no Prospect." A kid poked her head in the doorway, but Shea waved her away. "Last address we have on him is that same house, but it's complicated."

"Complicated is what people say when they mean 'go fuck yourself.'"

"In that case, it's complicated."

"Is he dead?"

"That's where your mind goes?" she said. "Before he dropped out, I got the impression he was sleeping somewhere that wasn't a bed. He looked unhuman, like a hyena, but with these puffy, tired horse eyes. Plus, he smelled like a wet rat, and his neck was bendy. Like it wasn't strong enough to hold up his head. And when he breathed, he purred, like he couldn't get his wind past his throat."

Aaron, I thought. "He's a street kid now?"

"Not officially. We could do something about it if he's homeless, but he's just on the sidewalk most nights. Dirk Henson fixed the deck across the street from his mom, said the house looked abandoned. Just speculation, but odds are he's run off."

"With those grubby Christians?" I asked. "Doesn't seem like the type."

"That paper I gave you," she said. "Otto's not popular, but he has one friend—Calvin Mayhew, a kid about as bugfuck crazy as he is. He still shows up once a week." She pointed to the paper. "That's his address and his mom's name. If Calvin doesn't know where he is, he can't be found."

"Don't say he can't be found. Everyone can be found." Only after I heard myself say it, did I think of Aaron. When I looked up, she was staring at me.

"I saw a Nightwolf across the stop sign on Grovesnor. A fake, but it made me think of you."

I put my hands in my pocket and met her gaze.

"You're right about one thing," she said. "Last time, we didn't finish it."

3.

Shea told us to visit Calvin Mayhew, but Meander's first instinct was to tear up any plan he didn't invent himself. He insisted we first try Otto Larkin's house, and see if his mom had any clue where he was. I considered complaining, but Meander was watching a lot of *Court TV* back then, and he met any disagreement by saying "duly noted" and then continuing unabated. It made second-guessing him exhausting, and few of us had the will. So I set aside my six-year silent protest, and returned to the neighborhood that had been decorated with my ghosts.

The animals had abandoned Prospect Hill. They now lived in our imaginations, in our Beefaroni cans and glue bottles. It made the place feel dangerously under-populated. Whatever had taken the animals would come back for us.

"They're gone, you know?" Meander said to me as we walked up the hill. "I don't want you to be alarmed."

"Who's gone?"

"Roxy and Monroe," he said. "They're not here anymore."

"All right," I said. "So?"

"Well, aren't you in love with Roxy Leckett?"

"No," I said. "She was—I liked her. Both of them."

"I thought loving Roxy was what made you act so dumb back then." He tugged at my jacket. "Be honest, admit you were in love with her. If not, I can't trust you."

"How's that?"

"I've known you since you were a medium fucker, and I've seen you happy and I've seen you messy as a shitstain. But if you didn't love Roxy, then I don't think you've loved anybody. That makes you untrustworthy."

"I'm okay with you not trusting me."

"No lies," Meander said. "Have you ever loved someone? Something at least?"

"I'm a little in love with the concept of you changing the subject."

"I've loved two girls, a dog, and a superhero I made up when I was thirteen," he said. "I'll love more things before this time next year. But you don't have the capacity to love. The only time I thought you did was Roxy."

"What happened to her?" I said.

"She's gone," Meander said.

"There's a million ways to be gone."

"I'm telling you all that matters. She's gone, and you can't see her."

"Just because I'm not in love with—" I stopped. We were distracting ourselves. "I guess I loved them both a little. That weirdo religion. All those animals."

"I'm glad it's different now," Meander said. "I don't want it to be like before. But I still wish we could come back to how it was sometime. Time moves too fast."

"Your dad was in the army, right?"

"National Guard," he said. "The Diet Army."

"He saw war, real changes," I said. "A building becomes sawdust. Middle class families cooking supper over trash fires. That's real change. This is an adjustment."

193

We walked past the Leckett yard, what used to be the Ark. The grass was stripped, and a contractor was outside taking measurements. On the porch, a young boy threw a tennis ball against the warped front door and caught it off the bounce.

Maybe it's good. People were reclaiming the land. Instead of the hazy gospel of the already-dead, we have science and math—the measurements of the yard, and the geometry of the boy's game. Except another two people get lost in the exchange. The bargain is relentless, even when you win.

The Larkin house smelled moldy, like the termites were so close to the surface that they were going to come out of the grain and greet us. I banged on the door and rang the bell. "This house is as dangerous as a busted condom," I said.

Meander went to the side of the porch, down and peered through the window. "I'm pretty sure she still lives here."

"Why?"

"Because she's asleep on the floor." He stood up.

I ran to the window. She was lying face down, directly below the window. "Holy Jesus," I said. "Is she okay?"

"Well, my doctorate is in Victorian Literature, so I'm not technically a medical doctor," Meander said. "But no, she's not okay. She's pretty penised up right now."

I tried rattling the window but she didn't move. "Ms. Larkin," I yelled. "Bonnie. Can you hear me?" Dead, I thought. It wasn't a sentence, just a growing certainty gonging in my brain. I looked for a tool to pry open the window. There were a few potted plants and a chair with no back on it. In my panic, I ran out to the yard, and found a garden trowel amongst the small pile of debris by the trash cans. I darted back to the porch and tried jimmying open her window. My experience in opening locked cars didn't help much. A sudden smashing noise stopped me cold. Then Meander walked into the living room from the back, put his toe on Bonnie Larkin's back and shook her awake.

He opened the window, and I climbed in, both of us ignoring that we were five feet away from a door. On the floor, Bonnie Larkin spasmed.

"Can you hear me?" I squatted and put my hand on her chest. Her face was red. "It's a heart attack." I knew from TV to push on her chest, so I tried it.

Bonnie yanked my hand off her chest, causing me to topple onto her. She wriggled out from under me and sat up while I was on the floor. "I don't have money," she said. "I don't have no money."

"Are you okay?"

She looked back and forth between us like we were part of her dream. "I don't have no money."

"Money?" I said. "Fuck your money. It's Milo Byers. That's Meander Casey." I tried catching my breath. "Come on, we don't look that different, do we?"

"I know who you are," she said. "You're the thief, aren't you?"

"No, goddamn it." I stood up and pinched the bridge of my nose. "I used to be a thief, but now I work in radio."

"Then what are you doing in my house?"

"Listen," Meander said. "Let's not get into who is in whose house or who does or doesn't work in radio. We're looking for Otto."

She winced like the name was a valued sweater we were stretching.

I remembered her rage from six years ago. It was soft and quiet, and it looked like a funhouse mirror's reflection of laughter. "You," she said, waving her hand back and forth between the two of us. "You don't have the right to stand here and say his name. You're here, whyever you're here, and I guess I can't make you leave. But so long as you're looking at me, I don't want you to say his name again"

She made us tea. She didn't want tea, nor did we, but it felt like the social drink. I drank from a mug with at least six months of lipstick stains around the rim. It surprised me that she kept wearing lipstick. The house gave me the impression she regarded the outside world as a rumor.

Otto was elsewhere. She said that this time he'd been nesting at the bus station. "He's not a part of me anymore," she said. He slipped away from her. "Slipped" she kept repeating, like her son was an oyster, difficult to grasp.

"How often does he come home?" I asked.

"Some," she said. "Once every couple of weeks. But not since New Years."

"That's almost two months."

"Yes, thank you, my calendar works fine," she said. "Used to be when he came home, he'd say it'd be for good. Not last time."

"You sound more like his wife than his mother," Meander said. "You want him so bad, call the cops, force him home."

"The cops?" she said. "You ignorant semen-sock, do you want him arrested?" She jerked a finger toward me. "At least he knows."

I didn't. It was a proper assumption, but these conversations never happened in my house. Certainly, we didn't talk openly about Aaron like this, letting the words plop between us, fat and lifeless.

"Look, he's threatening Thomas like a moron," I said. "It's probably just dick-swinging talk, but if not, he could bring trouble to himself. You're better off with us fuck-ups finding him than some mean cocksucker who's actually good at his job."

"You and a bunch of other men sang me this same pretty song last time," she said. "It went something along the lines of 'Trust me.' I don't recall how it turned out."

"Fuck you," Meander said. "You talk awful confident for someone who doesn't know dick. All I hear is you doubling down on being certain because it's the only way to distract yourself from the reality that you lost your son."

Meander's voice was cracking. I'd seen him suddenly angry before, but this was different. He sounded like he was about to cry.

"Why are we here?" Meander asked me, his voice still cracking. "We thought she could help us, but she's too fucked up to know her middle name. Why'd we think she even gives a shit about Otto? Why did we think she——"

In one motion, Bonnie Larkin sprung up and hit him in the chin. The precision of the punch was so perfect that it surprised us all, even Bonnie. She reared up to hit him again, but with her hand at the apex, she lost her anger. She laughed. The energy had shifted before anyone knew why or how.

"Both of you," she said. "Let's drink. We don't have to be miserable all the time, do we?"

She sauntered into the other room. When she left, I leaned into Meander and elbowed him. "What's wrong with you?"

"She has a gun," he said, still not looking at me.

"No she doesn't," I whispered.

"I was seeing if she'd use it, but she won't." he said. "Now that I say that out loud, it doesn't sound like a good plan."

"She doesn't have a gun, so stop messing around." But as she walked back to us, a scotch bottle in her left hand and a cluster of three coffee cups in right, I saw a bulge in the hip pocket of her robe.

She poured us each half a coffee cup full of scotch. It smelled like peanut brittle. Meander looked at me and then back at Bonnie: he was ready to fight.

"Back when I knew you," she said, "I thought I'd take Otto to California. Can you think of anyone who'd do worse in California than me?"

In a way, the gun was the least threatening thing about her. Her face looked like a mascara-stained skull. Six years is long enough to move on, to let some new God or monster dam your imagination so it flows a different direction. Not for Bonnie. Those years never left her, just wormed their way deeper into her soul. Maybe I never escaped Prospect Hill either.

"Let me ask you something," Meander said. "You're friend in your pocket, what're your plans for it?"

She coughed out a small laugh. Then she jumped to her feet and reached for the gun. Meander grabbed her wrist, and I grabbed her in an awkward and ineffective bear hug. She slumped against my body where I expected her to squirm. With a ferocious yank, Meander tore Bonnie's hand from her pocket, but on the follow through, he elbowed me in the mouth. The three of us broke up our stance like roughhousing kids who suddenly heard a snap.

"Settle down, settle down," Bonnie said. "I'm trying to show you something."

I sat, rubbing my mouth. Meander backed away slowly.

"It's just this." From her pocket, she took out a brown handgun. "Wow, you'd be easy to kill. All I had to say was let me show you my gun, and you forgot I had one."

Take it, I told myself. Surely, if I got my hands on the muzzle, I could swipe it away from her. But I could see the accident happening, feel the gunmetal heating up in my fingers. "You're forgetting something," I said. "If you do this, you're going to have to tell the cops a hell of a tale. He and I, we're not even supposed to be here."

"That's right." She started laughing, and soon the laugh controlled her. For a second, I thought she was going to lay the gun on the ground. "I could do it. You broke in. Goddamn, I wasn't even going to, but it's within my right. You make it so tempting."

Meander grabbed the bottle of scotch and took a deep swig. Then he wiped his mouth and topped off my cup. Bonnie still sounded young when she laughed—it made me believe we were young as well. Surely, the young wouldn't destroy the young.

"How's your aim?" Meander said. "You've been fermenting longer than most bourbon barrels, and you're probably seeing three of me."

"You'd hate that worse than anything." Bonnie cocked one eye and dramatically took aim at Meander like a kid at the circus trying to BB down a row of plastic ducks. "Any of you tough guy faggots can take one to the skull that turns the lights out, but what if I just chip you? Fuck up the way you talk? Make it so you can't chew your food, and you have to shit in a bag? You going to be brave then?"

"Milo said to come here, that we ought to help you," Meander said. "I told him you were nuttier than an allergic kid's nightmares, and we ought to let you rot in whatever hole you crawled into. You fuck up the way I talk, you're costing me years of gloating. Can't you shoot me in the dick? I use my mouth."

"Relax." She dropped the gun to the ground. Meander and I jumped when we heard it clatter on the linoleum, but Bonnie just shook her head. "Believe it or not, guns don't fire when they hit the ground—that's TV. And I haven't been waiting for you for days on end, gun on my hip. That's TV too, but maybe cable. Accidents happen when nimrods like you do nimrod shit like reach for a gun in a pocket or try to struggle it out of someone's hands."

I could hear Egan in her voice, in her sarcastic, articulated whisper.

"I keep that gun for accidents." She gave us a thin smile. "I'm not suicidal, but not for any reason. I was a Catholic kid, and I'm mostly nothing now, but it scares me."

"Hell?"

"Hell's part of it. Also thinking what if I chose wrong? Like, if the decision mattered, and I chose wrong."

"But accidents?" I said.

"Not much of a loophole, is it?" She resumed her place at the kitchen table. "But it wouldn't be my fault if I roll over it in my sleep. Or if I'm reaching for my lighter. What are you guys now, twenty?"

"Twenty-three," I said.

"No kids? Either of you."

"I have a nephew," Meander said. "But he just sits there."

"I was twenty-two when I had Otto, but you two seem younger. It deepens you, having kids. I'm not even recommending it, but it alters you in a way you can never set right again." She took the mug out of my hands and took a drink. "I don't hate you boys. Not really. It's just after all this time of wanting nothing, and then I hear the name Tom Mercer—I started to feel again. Not good or bad, but warm. Even in my fingers."

"The paint outside the Grieving Taco," I said. "That was you?"

"Of course," she said. "I can't close my eyes without seeing Otto shake in my arms. Other people had to know."

"You think that worked?"

She shook her head. "Nothing ever works for people like us. It works for him, the slimy ones, the ones who survive snakebites. He's a vampire, sucking other people dry, and discarding them. I can take that. But I won't take this city honoring him."

"You're too late on that one," I said.

"You sure?" She smiled at us both. "Might not make his own party."

"Really?" I said. "Seriously? You'll shoot him?"

"I'll shoot at him," she says. "God knows what I'll hit, but I'll pull the trigger."

Meander shook his head. "You bring a gun to Thomas's house, two things will happen," he said. "One, you won't get within two blocks without getting picked up by the police. Two, your life will be worth less than a gallon of monkey cum. Three—I just thought of this, so it's three things—this house will get bought by the college and Otto will be a street rat for the rest of his life. Shit, I just thought of a fourth thing. Four is—"

"Give us five days," I said.

"I won't get within a block?" she said. "How you going to make that happen? He's not the president. And if you think I give a shit about what happens after, then—"

"Nine-eleven was hilarious," I yelled. They stared at me like I was a motorcycle crash on the other side of the highway. It was the only way I could get their attention. "You give us five days, we'll find Otto, make sure he's safe, and bring him here."

"You can do that?" she said. "Liar."

"Hilarious?" Meander said. "There were some funny parts, but hilarious?"

"We can find him. I have leads," I said.

"What happens in five days?"

In truth, I said "five" because it sounded like the sort of number people say when negotiating, but I could improvise. "In five days, it's Prophet's gala. That's the place to make a splash."

"A splash?" she said. "This is about a splash?"

"If we don't get Otto in five days, you go Dirty Harry. Do what you want to him."

"I can do what I want to him now," she said.

"Otto," I said. "Wait and we give you Otto. We'll find him either way, but it's up to you whether we bring him home, or we tell him what happened to you is his fault."

"So you know," Meander said. "If you shoot him, if you shoot at him, I'll kill you. You can have your shot, but if you take it, you'll die."

"Okay then." She stood up and nodded at the front door, signaling for us to leave. "I kill him, or you kill me. Either way."

4.

The bartender who brought us our whiskey sours smelled like curdled Yoo-hoo and strawberry gum. Normally, I stayed away from Marimow's, the ostensibly Irish pour house next to the Gold's Gym that used to be The Egan Rabbit. Jerry Marimow, the owner, openly detested his customers, putting up GOP flags just to antagonize the college kids too alcoholic to be idealistic in a coffee shop. But right now, it felt like the proper panacea to Bonnie Larkin's cold, cramped living room. The bartender's scent made me feel an eon away from the mold and spilt cat food smell of Prospect Hill.

We asked Thomas the Prophet to meet us. We could have told him everything over the phone, but Thomas, ever loyal, agreed to meet us without question.

"Her," Meander said, meaning the woman who brought us our drinks. "I could fall in love just like that." He snapped his fingers. "Somebody like me, I can make myself be in love without hardly trying."

"You're mighty proud of your capacity for unrequited love," I said. "That's like bragging about your skill as a taxi passenger."

Behind us was another party. It sounded like women unconcerned with checking their voices—women with no men around. I tried not to look. Uninhibited women make me jealous in a way that's hard to pin down. It's almost like hunger.

"I'm proving a point." Meander yanked my shirt collar like I was a dog. "You think love is unimportant, so you wait on it. My father said, 'Never trust a man who speaks of love in the passive voice.'"

Someone from the girls' table dropped a glass. "How do we look for Otto?"

"We got time," he said. "We know where the Compost Christians hang out."

"How do we know that?"

"We'll find the fucker," Meander said. "But that mom's not even a horror show. She's a blooper reel."

I took a drink. "So you think it's impossible? Thomas and the boy?"

"Don't try me on this. Not at all. That woman's full of shit, and Thomas the Prophet is a hero."

"A hero?" I said. "Our old dealer?"

"I was on cardboard for a while," he said. "You know what that means?"

"On the street?" I said. "Sleeping on a box?"

"That's right," he said. "For almost six months."

"No you weren't," I said. "Really? No you weren't."

"I confess something that broke up my heart, and you call me a liar?"

"I'm not saying that," he said. "But you weren't really a homeless, right? As in, you didn't live like they did every day."

"For almost a month, I had no house to come back to at night, and I slept in Orman or behind the bread factory on Winchester." He tapped me on the wrist to make sure I paid attention. "This was spring, around March Madness, so people thought I was partying. The rest? I slept at

Mom's maybe twice a week. What do you call that if not homeless?" He shook his head and drummed his fingers on the bar. "I'd be there now, starved to death, except for Thomas."

"His foundation?"

"I am his foundation," Meander said. "I went to Thomas's thinking if he had a party, I could stay, rest my back for a night. There're no parties anymore, but he put me up, gave me—I don't know if it's a job or an allowance. I cleaned his house, wrote letters for him, fed his bunny. That warmth, man, I got addicted to it."

"Being part of a household?"

"No, asshole, warmth," he said. "Being warm. Even if you're just chilly for a week, it freezes your core. It took a whole year to feel regular again."

"But that doesn't mean he's not a pervert."

"Does to me," Meander said. "The idea that he could be this Spiderman-style figure in my life, saving me when I was lower than a potato root, and be a man who'd fuck a little boy? Doesn't seem possible." He took a drink and shrugged. "You could do it. That I can believe. You strike me as untrustworthy."

I felt a soft hand between my shoulders, and I turned to see Lina Darby, former singer of Surrender Dorothy and current UK grad student, studying physiology, a topic which, with practice, I could correctly pronounce one out of every three times. She was glassy-eyed but steady on her feet. Behind her, at a distant table, I saw Shea Stanford, Harmony Dulles, and two other girls. They were the ones laughing and breaking glasses.

"This place is a middle school dance," Lina said. "Girls on one side, boys on the other." Back in the Prospect days, Lina never liked Meander or me. At least that's what I assumed. Since then, she softened her stance. "You guys want to come over and bridge the gap a little?"

"We can't," Meander said. "We're waiting."

"It's a shame they posted that 'No Waiting In This Area' sign over our table."

"We're here on business," Meander said. "You wouldn't understand."

"Well then." She picked up her drink. "I'll leave you to it."

We watched her walk away. "Her," Meander whispered to me. "She's another one I could fall in love with."

"You're close," I said. "Maybe if you tell her to fuck herself just one more time."

"You've got lazy eyes," he said. "Look at her ring finger. Dirk Henson asked her. That's why they're celebrating. I just meant I could fall for her in some other life. " He ran his finger around the rim of his glass. "We're not here to make cooing sounds at someone's ring. You and I are waiting."

We were waiting for Thomas to warn him of Bonnie Larkin's lurking wrath. Thomas, according to Meander, would know exactly what to do. It was the dumbest idea I ever loved. Thomas the Prophet may play the white knight, but I remember him as a cherry-eyed confidence man. But if he wanted to make a down payment on this tire fire of a plan, then tremendous.

I felt a longing for life as it was right then, without rearrangement. This small scoop of the past made me grateful for the present day in the same way a woman who divorces an abusive pyromaniac is grateful her second husband is only an alcoholic. And goddamnit, I felt myself drawn to these people and conversations. You belong here, I thought. This is you and all you'll be.

Thomas looked good in person. Both his eyes and clothes looked sharper than they ever did on Prospect Hill. His hair was still brown and fluffy, but it had crawled back far enough up his head, so we could see it had an expiration date. He bought the first round and closed the tab, which we saw as an act of aggression. We believed the richest person should buy every round. While we both could be cited by the House Un-American Activities Council for our booze communism, I was more of the squishy-hearted campus socialist and Meander was the Joe Stalin of binge drinking. Still, I had work tonight. I pushed my whiskey in front of Meander.

"You full up already?" he whispered to me. "We got business here."

"My shift starts in an hour." I stood and rapped my knuckles on the bar. "It's not a two man operation to recount your day."

"I want to be in touch with you." The hillbilly in Thomas's accent had gone the way of the unionized miner. "Give me a call after work."

"Is everyone crazy?" Meander said. "We have shit on our plate for the first time in forever, and you guys are shrugging it off like a court date?"

"You're not supposed to shrug off court dates," I said.

This was wounding Meander. He figured this would go deep into the night, that we were in it together. No matter what we lost, we still had each other.

But I had work. I shook hands with the boys and nodded goodbye to the girls. As I left, I heard Lina Darby cackling. Her laugh always stayed with me like the outline of a disappearing dream.

Brody Jenkins was wearing a turtleneck and oversized glasses, like a sketch comedy version of an intellectual. He had his legs propped up on his desk and was reading a folded over newspaper and smoking a cigarette. "You're here on time," he said without looking at me. "What's the occasion?"

"What are you talking about today?" I said. "I'll dig up a story if you're thin."

"No more of that Nightwolf shit, I can tell you that

right now," he said. "Did you see what those queers did to our building?"

"Don't say queer," I said. "Definitely not on the air."

"They wallpapered us." He was chewing gum. "There's got to be fifteen, twenty Nightwolfs on there. These people have no respect."

I squinted. "Are you smoking and chewing nicotine gum at the same time?"

He stood and slammed his newspaper on his desk. "I'm supposed to shut up? Shit myself because they have spray paint? Does that sound like me?"

"You said you weren't going to talk about him. Seriously, just now."

"This is a setup." He breathed on his glasses, and then replaced them without wiping them off. "Radio's not what it used to be—fine. But we mention this guy, and these cunts hate me to where they take their limp-dick aggression out on this building?"

"You sound proud of that," I said.

"They want me to shut up about him? I'll put a bounty on his head."

"I knew a guy who tried that once," I said. "Worked out okay for him, I guess."

But he wasn't listening. He was working his way into his pre-show lather, which he needed to power himself through to the morning.

I went back to my office. It was hard for me to focus on the radio show, on Thomas, on Bonnie's gun, or on finding Otto Larkin. Instead, my mind was firmly locked on the engagement of Catalina Darby.

She grew up in Essex, Ohio, two hundred twenty miles from where I met her. Her father was big and clumsy and gentle with her and her stepsister when he was sober. He focused his rage on Lina's brother, a wispy boy with a mousy face and a speech impediment. She never told me her brother's name, saying only that it started with K. The other letters were for her memory, not mine.

"Kyle?" I said. "Kevin?"

"The only reason I'm still here," she said, "is both those guesses are wrong. You guess it right, that's the last you'll see of me. Try again?"

Her brother had a flat nose, pushed slightly to the left. Growing up, Lina thought it was natural, just part of his off-putting package, no different than his baloney smell. Only in the hereafter of retrospect, did she realize that her father set K's nose to the side. It must've happened when they were both very young. Maybe Mr. Darby saw his son dawdling into traffic, and the need to save him felt identical to the need to hurt him. It took one second to wind up, less than that to ball his fist.

K was picked on in school—not much but it never ended. A couple kids called him faggot, and Lina suspected he was gay, but he never told her. He tried lifting weights, wearing a leather jacket, and speaking with a Brooklyn accent. It made him ridiculous. He was two years older than her, but she had more friends his age than he did. Sometimes he'd come to Lina's room and show her the welts on his thighs and forearms.

Lina herself was small and nervous. Her father nicknamed her sparrow because she twitched and danced and hopped on one foot like a bird when her parents fought. She was fragile, and she knew her brother was taking beatings for them both.

Later, years later, long after the father had moved away and began living with his girlfriend and sponsor, he showed up with a hammer in one hand and a red-wrapped box with a white ribbon and a card in the other. The present was for Lina, a week-and-a-half-early birthday present. Their mother wouldn't let him in, saying, "You don't live here." He went around back, and when he saw that door was locked, he used the back of his hammer to claw out the nails holding the ceramic cornucopia on her door. She wouldn't answer his knocking, so he pounded the door with the hammer.

He moved on to the windows and smashed them in. The mother opened the door, but he kept bashing the window. She ran to stop him, but he backhanded her. Then he walked in the house.

He went for K. One of the therapists Lina had to see suggested it was the father's way of educating K, of teaching him how to be a man in a heartless world.

Their father beat K bloody in the middle of their den. He used the hammer but only the wooden part. If he used it properly, he'd have been jailed for attempted murder. The father made him swallow the claw, and when the boy tightened his lips around it, he said if he kept crying, he'd uppercut him in the chin, sending the hammer up through the roof of his mouth into his brain. K put the hammer in his mouth and closed his eyes. The father wound up to hit him but walked away.

The cops caught the father on a tire swing near an elementary school. He said he planned on running into the street and getting dragged by a car, but there was no traffic.

Apparently, he changed his life in prison. I didn't know what that meant since he'd already given up drugs and booze. Lina said he married his sponsor while still behind bars, and he tried to adopt her twins, but the law wouldn't allow it.

The doctors induced a coma on her brother, but he was allergic to the medicine. It got worse, and they brought in a priest to do last rights, but he stabilized. The doctors said he had a bad concussion and had lost oxygen to his brain. Even if they were lucky, he'd already lost some hearing. He didn't wake up the next day, and his blood pressure kept dropping. Right when the doctors were about to give up, he squeezed Lina's hand.

"Did he ever wake up?"

"Sort of," she said. For once, I knew what she meant.

We cause each other so much pain. How do we talk about it? How do talk about anything else? Except now, Lina was getting married. We can change.

By the time I left work, dawn was breaking. My body was aching for a proper bed. When I stepped outside, I saw a familiar Studebaker. Thomas the Prophet was leaning against its hood, his ankles crossed. He had that old familiar smirk again.

"Get in, Milo," he said. "There are a few outstanding issues from our last go-round that we need to discuss."

"What are you doing here?" The morning traffic was starting to whir, and it was waking me up. "Meander told you everything, right?"

"You owe me, kid," he said. "Maybe I owe you too. Now we're going to settle."

5.

The back of Thomas the Prophet's Studebaker was littered with breakfast foods. There were fast food wrappings and bits of children's cereal scattered on the floor. Meander lay across all the garbage, dead-to-the-world asleep. I lit two cigarettes and handed Thomas one. He had a hard time lighting his own due to his dishrag hand.

"Is my life in danger?" he said. "Be honest."

I shook my head, not sure if he could see me in the dark.

"Meander thinks so," Thomas said, knocking on the roof of the car.

"Two years ago, Meander thought putting Ritalin in Cheerwine would make him seem more sophisticated than putting it in Pepsi."

"I've never seen him that scared." The smoke gathered around his face. "Whatever she said rattled him."

"It wasn't so much what she said as the gun she was waving." From behind the Citibank, I could see the first few rays of sunrise litter the sky. Morning comes slowly in Kentucky. "If you knock on her door like we did, it might be trouble, but aside from trips to refill on booze and mouthwash, I doubt she goes out much."

"A middle-aged woman scared to leave the house. Sounds familiar."

"If you want protection, call the cops," I said. "You want someone to take the bullet for you, I nominate Meander. That's as far as we go this time around."

"What about the boy?"

"Fuck the boy." I coughed. "I mean, forget the boy."

"Kendall Irion."

"That supposed to mean something to me?"

"Of course, you don't know who your own boss is," he said. "Kendall could bankrupt your station tomorrow if he woke up feeling like a son of a bitch. He's responsible for half the ads you run. I'm freelance, but I'm in his bullpen. Guy wants to shake stuff up in radio." He looked at me like he was waiting for me to speak. "This could be lucrative for you too. I'll need a producer or whatever you pretend to be."

"A producer for what?" Then it dawned on me. "Wait, you want a show?"

He smiled. "Do you plan on being The Broj's Geisha forever?"

"You in front of a microphone wouldn't last a week."

He shook his head. "Kendall thinks like I do, and the station will put up with a ton of bitchy letters before they cross him. Anyway, these are the last days of radio. About the only way to get an audience is for the host to accidentally burn a cross."

"You want a show, fine," I said. "The world is filled with anus-gerbils like you. I wish you success."

"But I have a particular show in mind," he said. "The one time where radio really matters is on Sunday mornings."

"Do you mean—"

"I want to be a radio preacher," he said. "Hardcore Biblical literalism. I do it all brimstone-like and fuck them nonstop until they realize their buddy in the sky played them for rubes."

"The rivalry's back on?" I said. "You and JC? He's up in the points, so you're going for the knockout?"

"I intend to turn Lexington into the first anti-Christian city," he said. "Not atheist, because that's easy. I'll embrace God word for word, not let them escape what they worship. Once they face it, then everything they've built turns into stardust."

"Seems ambitious for commercial radio with sound effects."

He put his bad hand high on my neck and it felt like a baby bird gnawing at my spinal cord. "Once people get wind of my intentions, it'll get rough. If people hear the shit Egan and Bonnie spread then that's curtains for me and everything I've worked for."

"So if we don't act now, there's a chance Christianity could outlive you?"

"Don't get me wrong," he said. "We're going to find this kid because the kid is lost. I'll let a lot of shit go, but not a Prospect kid. Maybe a kid from Prospect now, but not from when Prospect mattered."

"But if it helps your career, then you'll especially do the right thing?"

"Act like you're above it," he said. "That's been your go-to since you were a boy. You're part of the scene but in the corner taking notes. You're one of Egan's goons, but you're full of second thoughts, so it's okay. The fight's still happening—has been this whole time. We miss you, but we'll get along okay whether you're with us or not."

I got some sleep. That was the one advantage of working with Thomas—he has basic human decency and a sizable car, so when Meander rose, I took his place in the back seat. When I woke, it was two hours later. Meander was sitting over me, eating a breakfast burrito. "Patience," he whispered.

While I was asleep, Thomas and Meander had parked outside of the house of Calvin Mayhew, Otto Larkin's friend, according to Shea Stanford.

"School starts in about ten minutes," Meander said, his mouth full of fast food. "He'll be home in an hour or so."

"That doesn't make sense," I said.

"Follow the process," Meander said. I could hear a video game coming from his phone. "Like all worthwhile things, there is a lot of sitting around involved."

"You sound like retarded Buddha."

He took another bite from his burrito. "The difference between no plan and the perfect plan is patience."

The plan, as Thomas the Prophet explained from the driver's seat, involved relying on probabilities. There were different levels of homelessness, he explained, and Calvin wasn't a chronic case. If the kid wasn't kicked out and the parents worked, the child often came home in the mornings to sleep. It didn't work for the truly homeless, but Calvin was to the real runaways what bowling was to exercise. To get a word with him we simply had to catch him before he reached the front door.

Thomas had so much confidence in his own plan that I wasn't even surprised when, an hour later, we saw a kid in a green poncho wander up to the house. The second he stepped onto his yard, I could see the tension in his shoulders release. He started swinging his arms as he walked, his neck already priming for his pillow.

I heard the door slam before I saw Meander had left the car. Thomas was slapping himself in the face to wake up. I stumbled outside, but my leg cramped, and by the time I shut the door, Meander was already speaking to the boy.

"So you're with the school?" Calvin Mayhew said.

He had a patchy red beard and arched, uneven eyebrows. "And who are you?" he said to me.

"I'm, you know, I'm with the school," I said. "I'm the guy he told you I was."

"We don't give a fuck about you?" Meander said. "We're here for Otto Larkin."

"I don't have to talk to you," he said. "Are you the police or the schools?"

"Otto Larkin, asshole," Meander said. "Tell me where he is."

"Listen," said. "I don't have anything to do with that dog boy."

"Whoa, whoa," I said. "I thought you didn't know him."

Both he and Meander looked at me. "I never said that," Calvin said.

"Well, I'm sorry, but I watch a lot of TV."

Thomas walked up close, crowding him. "What do you mean, you don't have anything to do with that?"

"You want a thesaurus?" he said.

"Maybe you ought to be grateful for a minute," I said. "We know who you are, and we don't care. If I were you, I'd be relieved us three aren't here to bust your head."

"Man, I'm tired," he said. As he said it, I knew it was true. He had a softness on his face and his gut. His extra weight must have set him apart on the street. In school, they called it weakness, but outside, it elevated him. He needed these days to insulate himself against the night. Jesus, he was young.

I grabbed him by the chin. "Tell us where Otto is and you'll be in bed in two minutes. Or we put you in that car and take you away from your blanket and teddy bear."

"I don't do that no more," he said. "He got tied up in that twisted shit, and I stopped it with him." He tried to wrench his face away from my hand but I tightened my grip. "That's not me, I promise." Mayhew reached down and pulled up his shirt. From his hip to his lower rib cage was a zigzagging red scar. It had healed, but it still looked like it would burst if he took too deep a breath.

I let the kid go. "Otto do that?"

"Not exactly," he said. "He talked someone into holding me down and another one into cutting me with the lid of soup can. An *appendectomy*, he called it, to see if I had any guts left."

"Is this the Compost people?" Meander said. "Is he warrioring for him?"

"Worse," he said. "Those guys at least had a point, and they mostly stuck to each other. The stuff now is terror. He thought I was spying. Said he went easy on me because I was a friend."

I didn't know what he meant, but before I could ask more questions, I saw Meander was walking back to the car.

"Did he fuck with one of yours?" Mayhew asked. "He mess with your kid?"

Meander stopped and turned around. "I'm twenty-three," he said. "Go inside, Calvin Mayhew, and stay in bed. You're lucky to escape as well as you did."

Mayhew leaned closer to us and spoke low, like he was sharing a secret with Thomas and me. "What did Otto do to you? What are you going to do to him?"

"Believe it or not, we care about the kid." Thomas's voice was steady and practiced, a trick I guessed he learned from being around professional pitchmen. "We think it'd be wise to save him from the street."

"I cared about him too." Mayhew put his hand on the doorknob. "He cared about me more than anyone else I've seen him with, and he split me open to prove a point. I'd hate to see what he'd do to a stranger." He sounded more in control—this was likely the first time he explained his situation out loud, the first time he heard himself. "Good luck, but you may be better off saving the streets from him."

6.

Father Compost lived in the Lexington streets the way that Bloody Mary lived in children's bathroom mirrors. Kids used his name to scare themselves when their own reflection looked too regular. Sometimes Mr. Compost called himself Colonel Gardenias because his home base was an abandoned flower shop by the reservoir.

When Meander was on the street, he had friends in the Compost crowd. They sermonized, which was obnoxious, but they always looked happy, and happiness was a valuable commodity out there. But sometimes he ran into Compost's "warriors," kids who would "talk like prayer monkeys," but would beat the holy hell out of each other as they did it. Father Compost, it was rumored, took bets on the winners.

"There were specific rules," Meander said. "These kids wailed on each other. If anyone tried to break it up, both fighters beat the interloper until his face looked like Big League Chew. Girls did it too." Anyone who got bloodied in the fight had to preach after the match. Sometimes both fighters preached together, arm in arm, like brothers reunited after a war they both lost. "They said they're showing us the violence in our hearts that we have to face if we want to learn how to love. It sounded like stupid shit Thomas says."

"I'm literally right in front of you," Thomas said.

"A few kids fighting?" I said. "Assholes do asshole things to assholes for asshole reasons. Freaking out about that is like calling 911 because your dog is licking his balls."

Meander shook his head. "They bring weapons— chains and hammers and shit. It gets raw."

"Bullshit," I said.

"I saw it," he said. "Well, not the hammers, but I saw two girls go after each other with garden spades. By the time they were done, I couldn't tell the outside of their face from the inside. And then they started beating dogs." He crossed and uncrossed his legs. "Strays, I thought, but people came around asking about them. Nobody asked about the kids, but they searched for the dogs."

"Hurting dogs is against the law," I said. "Let's get the cops to arrest Compost. They'll pick up Otto, and we can tell Bonnie that her boy is fine. Not fine exactly. But she didn't ask for proof she's a good mother."

"Compost's not doing anything illegal," Meander said. "Kids come to him—he talks to them. Nothing more. Far as I can tell, they didn't need much convincing."

"So he convinces desperate, violent people to do what they want?" I said. "I don't mean to sell this guy short, but it's not like he's convincing the Pope to blow him."

"I was grown when I was out there," Meander said. "When kids leave home, it's a whim, a brutal vacation. Then they see this guy, and a few weeks later, their face is sauced, and they beating on dogs like psychos. I don't want anybody who can talk like that to get near my head."

"But your life is fine," I said. "You're mediocre. Same as me. Mediocre means half of the whole planet is worse than you. Being mediocre is amazing. And you think a

Shaman can talk you out of mediocrity to club a puppy if you sit with him for a minute?"

"I'm not worried about me." Meander looked puzzled, almost annoyed. "I'm worried what I'll do to him."

"How long since you've seen this guy," Thomas the Prophet said.

"I never saw him," Meander said. "Just the kids he sent out."

"We've heard this guy's name for years," Thomas said. "How long can you be on the street and keep selling yourself? I know how to sell a kid medicine he doesn't need. I work in commercials, and I was a pretty good Christian for a couple years. But if he's on the street this long, what's he look like? It gets harder to say, 'follow me' when your teeth are gone and your skin looks like a page of braille. Guy like that tells you anything, the answer is pepper spray. I don't know if he's dangerous, but he's got game."

The next day, Meander and I parked outside of the reservoir on the far north end of town. The flower shop was still there. The sign was riddled with bullet holes, and the paint had chipped away. We waited.

"Do you know what happens at this reservoir?" Meander was on his fourth cigarette of the hour, and he wasn't slowing down. "Any reservoir?"

"Reservoirs?" I said. "Unless Bruce Springsteen's a liar, there's an asshole named Jonny who falls in love a bunch. Aside from that, I don't know, water?"

"It gets dark out here. Real dark." He bit down on his smoke. "This is where they bring the dogs. After they're dead. This isn't even the worst reservoir."

"This place looks like a mold convention," I said. "If you think Otto's in here, can't we just go inside?"

"It doesn't work like that," Meander said. "If we go in

there alone, nobody will talk to us. We have to go in with someone."

"What do you remember about Otto?" I said. "Would you recognize him?"

"He had brown hair," Meander said. "Four out of five white kids have brown hair, but he had a little too much hair, and it didn't fit his head." He spit the cigarette butt out the window. "And his face—honestly, I don't remember a fucking thing about him."

"Yeah, me neither."

Meander laughed and clapped his hands over his eyes. "So we're saving a kid we didn't bother to remember. We're imbeciles, aren't we?"

"You asked me that once before," I said. "About Aaron. Not if I remembered what he looked like, but what he sounded like."

"What did you say?"

"Don't remember, but it's a safe bet it was bullshit." My collar was scratching the back of my neck. "I don't know what he sounds like, and I didn't know then."

"Remember Otto." He tapped his temple. "We're finding Otto because he deserves to be found. Aaron's his own story. Don't look for one kid because you feel guilty not chasing the other."

"I don't feel guilty for not chasing Aaron," I said. "Okay, I do, but I was a kid. But maybe I could've made our home better, our room better, and he wouldn't want to leave. By the time I knew he could run, he was gone. I'm always late, and when it occurs to me to help, I can't even remember what the people I'm helping look like. And Otto—Otto could be anyone. Would it have killed Thomas to molest a more memorable person?" I closed my eyes, but I knew he was staring at me. "Relax."

"Don't joke like that," Meander said. "How many times has he had your back?"

"A lot," I said. "With my mom, with Egan. He's a

good guy in a lot of ways, most ways. But, you know, maybe, there's some half-truth?"

"You can't half-fuck a child," Meander said. "Bonnie accuses Thomas. You can believe her or doubt her. Doubt always pays off. That doesn't mean it's right. People lie, and our counterattack is doubt. Have you ever seen a movie before?"

"What movie?"

"Doesn't matter," he said.

"I've seen approximately four movies."

"You know what happens in a movie?" he said. "Where the actors say all the right things and never seem lost. And people come and go for a specific reason, and everybody who shows up in the first ten minutes boomerangs back in the hero's life?"

"This sounds like a buildup to nothing."

"No, life is a buildup to nothing," he said. "Movies have points. You think we're living a movie. You think we get to understand. But I know every crevice of your stunted imagination, and what you're thinking now is bullshit."

"What am I—"

"Don't make me say it." He clenched his fist. "It's insulting to us both. You hear about a mystery-guru-compost-priest, and you think it's your brother. Like everything will come together and make sense."

"I don't."

"In a movie, it'd make sense," he said. "It'd be Aaron who's been pulling the strings all along. You think he's the God behind the curtain."

"That's not—"

"Let me show you something." He picked up a crumpled receipt off the floor and took a pen from his shirt pocket. He spread the receipt on the console between us and wrote down "Nightwolf." Then he wrote it again in cursive. "Do you see where I'm going with this?"

I shook my head.

"My handwriting," Meander said. "I write thin and small—nobody would ever mistake me for Nightwolf, but you see the common denominator? The G's."

I felt myself nod before I knew why.

"They look like eights," he said. "Twenty percent of people write G's like this. Their handwriting matches Nightwolf even more."

"It's not just the handwriting."

"He thought he was Baby Batman," Meander said. "That's every boy I know."

I remembered that afternoon at The Rabbit, seeing the man through the dirty window. Walk away, Egan told me. With enough discipline, people can be forgotten.

"You have a brother," I said. "You ever picture him disappeared?"

"Of course," Meander said. "I grew up with you, and I prayed he'd vanish, so I'd understand you better. That and he's a prick I wanted gone. You think you're the only one who wishes reality isn't what it is?"

You're wrong, I wanted to say. But he wasn't, not exactly. I knew Father Compost wasn't Aaron, but it wasn't a truth that fit me naturally. I had to keep reminding myself of the fact. Part of me thought every stranger might be my brother.

"This is a real crisis," he said. "A genuine threat facing one of our own. You can't keep living in your head."

A man with a face striped with mud walked past our car. He peered into our windshield and smiled. I thought he was looking at us, but he ran his hand through his hair, and I realized he was staring at himself in the reflection of the glass. On second glance, he was a kid, prematurely aged by the sun. He walked toward the flower shop.

"Come on," Meander said. "We have one chance to get in the shop. This kid's going to help us get in there or he'll wind up on a milk carton."

"Isn't he already on a milk carton if he's a runaway?"

"Okay, then *in* a milk carton," he said. "I'll chop him up and feed him to a cow."

"One day, someone is going to explain the lactation process to you, and it's absolutely going to blow your mind."

"Its difficult to express my gratitude for how helpful you're being right now."

We stepped out of the car and slammed the door.

7.

The kid walked slowly, without rhythm, like he was stomping on a pair of very persistent bugs. According to Meander, playing the kid just right meant the difference between getting inside or not. If the shop was locked, we'd be reduced to banging on the door and begging the people inside to come out, like we were cops from the least entertaining episode of *Law and Order*. When the government wanted to get someone to leave a building, they played heavy metal or burned the place down; if those were the plans of smart people, then we had no chance.

"Hang up a second," Meander said, running to him. "Let me get at you."

The kid was hunched over, and he didn't respond. For a second, I thought he'd run. Instead he brought his hands up and cupped his ears. "Do I know you?"

"I don't think so," Meander said. "We want to—shit, are you all right?"

The kid turned to us, and it looked like he didn't have the strength to smile. His face was splotched and twisted, and when he opened his mouth, he showed black and bloody gums. Meander took out a pack out cigarettes.

"Can I get one?" the kid said.

I offered one of mine, but the kid waved me off and took one of Meander's.

"You looking to score?" he said. "If you're cops, you have to tell me."

"Brilliant, I said. "They must've taught you realistic law enforcement rules on the same day they taught you how to floss."

"You know a kid named Otto?" Meander said. "Say yes and get another smoke. Take us to him, and you walk away with the pack."

"I don't know." The kid's voice sounded rusty and faraway, like a screen door in a windstorm. "You think people go by their real name out here?"

"Don't they?" I said. "What's your name?"

"We don't need your name," Meander said. "All we want's to get in there."

The kid reached out and took the pack from Meander's hand. "You come to see the Father? Most of you fuckers offer money in place of nicotine."

"Come on," I said. "You got our smokes, and you convinced me to never talk to you again, so just tell us how to get inside. Is there like a password?"

"A password?" The kid stood still, motionless except for drumming his very long fingernails on his hipbone. "Password's a twenty-dollar bill."

Meander shook his head.

The kid smiled, again showing his twisted teeth and scarred gums. "The password is you go to the fucking door and turn the knob. It's street kids who want to be inside. No one's hiding nothing."

Meander had his back arched, the sign he was nervous. "You come with us."

"Shit, man, you expecting an ambush?" the kid said. "You newspaper fags ain't the first people to find us. No one writes nothing because there's nothing to write."

Meander and I followed the kid inside the house. There were space heaters in each corner. Someone paid an electric bill here. Beside one of the space heaters lay a conked out boy with one cheek so swollen it looked like he was smuggling a cueball in his mouth, and by another sat a bone-thin girl, cross-legged who looked to be praying into the vent. Aside from them, the room was empty, except for a fat red-bearded man hunched over a side table, muttering to himself.

"Well assholes, what's the password?" the kid said. "Your guy's over there." He pointed to the sleeping boy.

"Compost?" I asked.

"Him?" The kid laughed. "That kid couldn't convince a fourteen-year-old to beat off. Compost's not here."

"Who's he?" Meander asked, pointing to the sleeping boy.

"Otto," the kid said. "Ain't that who you looking for?"

Otto wouldn't wake up when we shook him. With his eyes closed, he looked like he'd grown delicate, with smooth skin and a rat's nest of hair. But I was afraid to see him awake, his yellow- and red-speckled eyes reminding us precisely what those nights at Thomas The Prophet's cost. Nothing could wake him. Meander grabbed his knees and I grabbed under his shoulders. We carried him out of Father Compost's headquarters and into the back of my car.

"So is this it?" I asked Meander in the car. "We're going to be done?"

Meander stared at Otto. "He looks fucked."

"Done with everything. All that. Mom's gone. Your dad's gone. We made it right." I shook my head. "Not right, but better. Even with the old ghosts working against us, we're the ones who made it better."

"Not better for him," Meander said. "You've seen his

mom's place. The room we took him from at least had heaters."

"Better for us then," I said. "And better for Bonnie. He sleeps on concrete, so she sleeps on the rug—it's sympathy pain. Maybe she took too much sympathy codeine, but this is how she gets better."

"We can't take him to Prospect," Meander said. "He needs a hospital."

"For being asleep?" I said. "No way. I've let too much go in my life. I didn't get to have my own reunions, but I at least want to see his. I've done at least one good thing in my life, and I couldn't have said that this morning. This is how we heal."

We stopped at a light and I looked at him. As soon as I did, he jolted upright. His eyes flitted back and forth between us.

"You know who we are?" Meander said, as I turned left into Hambrick Place, a suburb we nicknamed "Little Indianapolis" because we thought it had to be the most boring neighborhood in America.

"You're not in trouble," I said. "I knew you as a kid."

"Where're you taking me?" His voice sounded like it was wavering between defiance and collapse, a line he must have skirted for so long that it had frozen on his face. "I'm not going to do nothing with you two."

"Take it easy," I said. "Your mother wants to see you."

From the mirror, I could see him mouth the word "Mom" over and over.

"You remember us at all?" I said. "Milo Byers and Meander Casey, used to work at The Rabbit. You ran with Avery Comstock."

Otto nodded his head slowly, like if he moved too fast, he'd shake the tears out of his eyes. "Mom asked for me?"

"Asked for you like you wouldn't believe," Meander said. "Asked the shit out of you. Got a pretty emphatic means of asking."

"The last time you saw her, she felt bad about how you left things," I said. "She regrets it, and maybe you do too."

Otto doubled over and wept into both fists. I've always secretly believed I'd be a great unethical therapist because I have an acute skill at accidentally making people cry.

"It's almost over," Meander said. "A lot of shit happened, but it's almost over."

We parked in front of Otto's house. His face was dry, but he trembled softly.

"She's in there?" he asked. "And there's food?"

"There's pills at least," I said. "I bet she has the types you can chew, so food."

Otto didn't want to leave the car at first. We assured him she didn't care what he looked like. Only when we bracketed him on either side, did he agree to walk with us to his house. This kid was beyond curing. As a boy, he'd been curious. I could still see it in him, but it'd hardened into fear. Fear can shrink, but it can never be unfelt.

Bonnie's living room floor was still covered with scattered bags and magazines, and the air held the same tinge of molded sweet potatoes. With a dull fear, I remembered her gun. I pictured the tragedy. Bonnie Larkin bursts out of the bathroom unloading the chamber into her prodigal's chest.

But life tended to go slower. When we walked into the kitchen, we heard a toilet flush. "Sit down," I said to Otto, nodding to the kitchen table.

"Is that her?" His voice was stronger. "How did you find her?"

"Bonnie," I called out. "We're in your kitchen, so don't be scared. You'll want to come out here."

Meander stared at Otto, eyebrow raised. It looked like he saw something I didn't, which happens to those around me from time to time. "Do you know who we are?"

"Yeah," he said. "You told me."

Bonnie walked into the kitchen. She'd been crying too. Even now, they were connected. Was it always this way between mothers and sons? When I forgot simple things, was that simply my mother signing her name in my brain again?

"They told me you were dead," Otto said. "Uncle Eli and them said."

Bonnie casually pushed past me and walked into the kitchen, where she sat at the opposite end of the table. They stared at each other like rival gamblers. "Someone told you I died?" The reality of the situation was slowly worming its way into her face. "One of these two, Tweedle Dick and Tweedle Dickless?"

"Uncle Eli and them," he said.

Bonnie turned to look at Meander and me and nodded us over. I stepped forward despite feeling Meander's hand on my shirttail. "Are you trying to get your friend killed?" she whispered.

"We found him." I put my hand on her shoulder. "We found him for you."

"Don't cry," the boy said, trying to sound sweet. "They found him. They found him, and it's going to be okay."

"Yes," I said. "What?" I took my hand off the back of her shoulder. "He said he was Otto. You said you were Otto."

"No, I didn't," the boy said. "Otto's kind of a stupid name, no offense."

"None taken," I said. "But you remembered Avery and Prospect. Why did you think we were taking you here?"

"I woke up in your car." He looked back and forth. "So is she my mother?"

"Honey, what's your name?" Bonnie said. "It's okay, you can tell me."

He thought for a second. "Otto?"

She stood and turned to us. "You thought you could

do this?" she said. "You two unholy sphincters tried to switch out my son like he was a goldfish?"

"He said he was Otto."

"He didn't," Meander said. "This guy did." He pointed to a picture he'd scooped up from a bookshelf. The boy in the picture looked cleaner and slightly fatter, but there was no doubt it was the kid from outside Compost's place, the kid who led us to fake Otto.

I snatched it from Meander's hands and brought it close to my eyes as if the right angle would make the picture reconsider. "When did you take this?"

"That's Otto?" The kid looked at the picture. "I know that guy. He's a dick."

Our fake Otto's name was Griff Delmar, and he had a vague memory of an Avery Comstock from third grade. We were going to drop him back at Father Compost's, but he begged us to take him anywhere else.

We took him to Thomas the Prophet's new house, a comfortable and forgiving place where our good intentions could replace results. Griff told us about Otto, and every sentence shifted and hardened his story into an accusation. Compost was a voice to preach to the homeless—Otto was all knuckles and spit. When Otto went home to rest, he said, the streets were safe. Sure, there'd be a predator or a bully, but those were simple struggles of strength. Otto was different.

"Think about a kid on the street." Griff held a thick slice of banana bread in his hand, but didn't eat, a hat-tip to middle-class manners that neither he nor we believed in—never show your hunger. "They've all been bullied in one way or another. The street becomes your safe spot. People mess with you, but you're on the same team."

"But Otto was different?" Thomas asked.

He dunked the bread into a container of margarine and stuffed it inside his mouth. "You seen his teeth?"

"He's got a possum mouth," I said. "Just fangs and

scar tissue."

Griff showed me his own teeth. I could see thick strings of saliva latching his lower and upper molars. "Mine aren't like that," he said. "I been out there longer than him. He drank rat poison."

"He what?"

"Generic over-the-counter rat poison," he said. "Swallowed it and all."

"Trying to kill himself?" I asked.

Griff shrugged. "Said he wanted to get close as possible to dying without crossing over. Folks told me his eyes fell out and his skin turned Magic Marker yellow. His kidneys popped. I hoped it was true, but when I saw him, he looked normal except his teeth. He can do what he wants to hisself," Griff said. "But he collects people. He poisons dogs and cats, cuts off their tails and rubs them in people's faces while they sleep."

"What do you mean he collects people?" I asked.

"He talks to you, and you feel like you need an exorcism. Then he'll say he's collected you." Griff shook his head. "I don't want to go back out there."

"You have anywhere to be?" I asked.

He shook his head again. "I don't want this anymore. Living like this's cored me. I could spend the rest of my life on a featherbed, and I won't make it five years."

Those parties at Prospect had treated Otto like Agent Orange treats a forest. It turned him into a derringer. And now this other kid, as much as a victim of our youth as anyone, had nowhere to be. It fell to us, loyal soldiers in the war of pointless struggles, to take him there.

8.

The three of us dropped Griff Delmar off at his cousin's condo in Little Indianapolis. I was in the backseat, sitting close enough to Griff to see the sweat form down his sideburn.

It was his cousin's boyfriend's house—or at least where he used to live. The shelters were likely out of beds, and he'd be easy prey. Some of the Compost Warriors hung out by the shelter to pick on the kids who were turned away.

The house had ceramic birds strung throughout the yard. Griff tensed up. "Did he have this shit in the yard when you knew him?" I asked.

The boy nodded, but he didn't mean it. He was walking to a stranger's house and told us not to wait. We drove off like he asked. Nobody wanted to see him fail.

"Look," I said, as we cleared the neighborhood, "if you want to be done with this, we can be done with it. I'll bring Bonnie Larkin a couple of bottles, which'll keep her indoors for a few days. Then maybe whatever caused this shitstorm in her brain will pass. You two can be clear of it all."

"And you?" Meander asked.

"I want to poke around," I said. "At least talk to Otto."

"A couple bottles buy you a week with Bonnie," Thomas said. "I plan to live in this town."

"It passed once before," I said. "When we were kids, that woman hated me more than crib death. Now she lets me into her house."

"You broke into her house, and she pointed a gun at your dick," Meander said.

"This doesn't have anything to do with me or Bonnie Larkin or any shootout," Thomas said. "Otto may be barreling toward suicide."

"Best you don't say that," Meander said.

"Tell me another reason to drink rat poison." Thomas said.

"I met a guy who drank it once to get high," Meander said. "Only drank a thimble of it, but his mouth looked like he tried to eat a bowl of glass and raspberry jam."

"Griff said Otto's a bully." Thomas slowed the car to where we may as well been walking. "Does that sound like Otto to you?"

"When we knew Otto, he was ten," Meander said. "And he wasn't a hophead neither. Circumstances change people."

"Not like that," Thomas said. "Otto's begging people to shove a knife in his side, and if we don't help, someone will oblige him. Bonnie won't recover from that. None of us will." His limp hand rested at the top of the steering wheel. "The first time around when I had money, I helped people. It's not going to get me thanked by the neighborhood association, but people needed good times and a place to crash."

When Thomas spoke of Otto, his voice rose almost imperceptibly and he clipped the ends of his words. He was performing relaxation. Even now, he didn't know if we trusted him about Otto. Meander certainly believed him—his doubts melted as his hands thawed on the first night Thomas took him in. As for me, I thought he was being honest as he knew how, but I didn't exactly believe him. My only faith was in the dark. I believe the dark spots of our imagination are more real and more powerful than our ability to know what happened. Otto and Thomas were both lost in that darkness. Their beliefs had calcified, but the chestnut of their memories is that deep unending nothing where all stories are born.

"I saw those nights on Prospect nights as a contract, one I still honor," Thomas said. "To make good on it, we need to find him. Y'all found him once. We know he can be found."

The three of us drove back to the flower shop. It was sunset now, and about half a dozen people milled around outside. They didn't look like hardcore homeless people, just kids making a point to their parents through absence. One girl laid flat on her back while another stood over her, stretching her leg over her head. Father Compost must have offered protection. Otherwise, no woman would be out here when they had shelter, no matter how broken the home.

This time, the inside of the flower shop smelled like fire. The sawdust, mildew, and melted rubber scent from the early afternoon had been chased out by a plumper roasted oak. They had turned the heaters up, and it had changed the chemistry of the room. That must be part of the appeal, feeling your body adjust to the elements, sensing that you will be okay, even as the outside world tries to kill you.

Eight people sat in a semicircle. All but two had token dirty clothes—clean except a sweat stain or sauce on their collars. They were the ones who could leave with the rising of the moon. The other two looked like sarcastic skeletons with thin skin painted on as an afterthought. The gatherers had their hands folded on their laps, and when we got within a foot of them, we could hear them humming softly, almost like a cat's purr.

"What're you guys up to?" Meander said. "Praying and shit?"

Nobody moved to even open their eyes except a woman in the back, one of the clean-clothes people with orange hair and a fresh face. "Are you the people from before?" she asked. "The ones looking for that fleabag? He said you'd be back."

"Who did?" I asked.

She closed her eyes and re-folded her hands. "He's in the delivery room."

The three of us walked down a thin hallway, adjacent to the back heater, until we came to a spartan, rickety room, empty except for a mattress and two folding chairs. The back door opened and a man stumbled inside, looking like he was pulling each foot out of a tar pit.

I so fully expected to see Otto walk inside that, for an instant, I did see him. Not him as he was that afternoon but six years ago. In that moment, this man was the boy who was terrified at every step that the ground would fade away. But that was ridiculous. This was a man, older than Thomas, with wispy, thinned hair. He had scars on the side of his face, running from his eye socket to his chin. This was intentional; he had turned his face into a Tic-Tac-Toe board. "You come by the shop before?" he said. "Should've talked to me then, and I'd have saved you some time." His teeth were straight, but the color of dead grass. "You know who I am?"

"Father Compost," Thomas said.

"The name was a joke." He laughed as an invitation for us to join, but no one did. "It's got a new meaning now, but I didn't want to be Father anything. I'm no priest."

Thomas gestured to Meander and me. "These two

call me Prophet, and I don't have a prayer circle in my living room."

"Prophet," he said. "Why have I heard of you before?"

"Maybe I just resemble a holy man or somebody else who's full of shit." Thomas stepped closer. "Fathers, parables, prayers: it's fine, and I believed it until I was seven, but I'm a little out of practice."

"Prayer?" Father Compost spoke so sharply, that Thomas leaned back. "No one here has time for prayer. We spend all day asking people for nickels, people who see us as puddles of vomit, and you think after that we ask God for spare miracles? Fuck you." His voice sounded flat and frog-gish, like an old man confronting an impossibly hot bowl of soup. "Stay with us a little and let the weather work into your bones, then see what prayer will do for you."

"You're doing the opposite of preaching to the choir." Thomas was angry—I could hear it, but a stranger would mistake it for kindness. "Me and God are like oil and some mythological water that doesn't exist. But I know church, and I know worship. Them out there are worshipping."

"We are neither believers nor disbelievers," Compost said. "We are experience. What they're doing is called recovery."

"This doesn't have to be a long process," Meander said. He had no patience for bullshit other than his own. "Feel free to tell your *experiencers* you blew our mind and left us astounded. But tell us where Otto is, and get back to writing *Tao And the Art of Bum-Fights* or whatever it is you do for fun."

"Otto," he said. "I knew someone would come for that boy. He told us he was special. Most want to get looked over, but he thought he was the golden child. They're the ones people come for."

"We've given you the wrong impression," Meander said. "We don't mean to imply we're interested; we're just trying to find the fucker."

Compost smiled and began punching his hand, like he was counting off a game of Rock, Paper, Scissors. "If I don't explain this boy's nature to you, then you won't understand what you find. If you're unprepared to meet him, it will be destructive."

Compost looked nervous, and that frightened me. His movements made no sense. We weren't safe here. I could sense it before I could say why. "We care about the kid." I imitated the tone of our station's radio psychiatrist. "We want to make sure he's okay."

"He's not," Compost snapped. "Why the fuck would anybody be okay? Okay's for people who don't care. He cares a lot, just the wrong way. The boy is dangerous."

"Dangerous how?" I was the only one who could talk to him without confrontation. Meander was too angry—this was close to his memories. Thomas had too much to lose. I had the ability to act curious. "Dangerous-crazy or dangerous-mean?"

Compost shuffled to a cabinet in the back. His movements reminded me of a drunken crab, but it might be an act. He could switch his voice between shambling and sharp, so why not his body as well? After a second's pause, he took out a jug of cheap port. "Most kids want hooch," he said. "Plastic bottle vodka. Used to be, I'd want that too, but I aged out of it." He offered the bottle to Thomas who took a quick sip and handed it to Meander.

"Look," Thomas said. "You want us to understand the kid, and believe me, we're trying. Except I think you're stalling. The longer we sit here understanding this poor bastard, the longer he's got to run off in the shadows."

"You think I want to help him?" Compost said. "No one wants to help him. I want to help you." He patted the top of his stomach like he'd just finished Thanksgiving supper. "You have no idea what you're looking for: he's not high, he's evil. I knew you'd come for him because it's the worst who get claimed." He snatched his wine bottle back from Meander's hands and started chugging. When he came up for air the sides of his mouth were red. "The girls call him Fang. Say he's more tooth than man."

Compost took a step to the right, and I noticed a small pile of shoes at the foot of the bed. They looked like sneakers mostly, but of all different sizes and styles. Some had molded through, and at least one was torn in half. When I looked at Compost's feet, I saw he wore an intact pair of snow boots. These weren't for him. As I looked up again, he met my gaze and smiled.

"You heard my name before," Thomas said. "That means he told you about me. Those nights on Prospect Hill."

"Those nights, he felt alive," Compost said. "He talked about the dance room, the fiddler's circle downstairs. Said someone played with him on your couch. Sometimes it was you, sometimes it was a stranger. Sometimes he said it happened to someone else."

"Played with?" Thomas said. "Those were his words?"

"I don't imagine he meant checkers. Sometimes he told me it was true, and sometimes it was just make-like or a joke. But he kept bringing it up, like he wanted to see my reaction."

"It's not real," Thomas said, but he sounded desperate. "It's a story that's been repeated back to him so many times that he has to keep saying it."

"Real?" Compost shrugged. "Real is slippery out here. In your world too. I wondered if you'd come by. Figured if I met you, I'd be able to find some foothold into the kid. All I know for sure is he loved those nights, and he felt alive. For a boy like him, that's not a good thing. He tries to kill whatever he comes in contact with."

For a second, I understood. Any boy who took a rake to a wasp's nest or threw a pebble at a pretty girl tried to destroy what he loved. Love and destruction aren't even two separate wrinkles in the brain. Those Prospect nights, through exhilaration or pain, taught Otto to love himself, which allowed him to destroy. I looked to Thomas, his bad hand grazing his belt. Impossible, I thought, but in my mind it sounded like a question.

"Look, the kid needs help," Thomas said. "Whatever he's told you, whatever he's done, he's still a kid. Do you know where he is?"

"Please." Compost made a wet hissing noise that might have passed for laughter. "I'm not part of this anymore. I pay the bills as a public service. Could you imagine it with no heat, no electric, no place for shelter? I live in Hartland, drive a Dodge Dart."

"Right," Meander said. "So you just wear that beard to scare off opportunity?"

Compost took a long drink from his wine and held the jug in front of his face after he finished. His body slumped. "I'm sorry I'm not as mysterious as you need me to be. Turns out, I'm less impressive than the man you've been dreaming about."

"Have we been dreaming about this, boys?" I said. "I might be a little less invested than you think."

"You're not." He pointed to Thomas. "Him, he's worried about the gossip." He pointed to Meander. "He's mad. You, I can't tell, but I don't think you like this. A lot of people come down here, and when I tell them what I'm telling you, they get that little flicker across their mouth. Not like they're about to cry, but like they know they're going to wake out of a good dream. Their world's about to crumble."

"You're stalling, telling me what you're going to tell me instead of saying it."

"What I'm telling you is nothing more than what you already figured out," Compost said. "This, what you see, this is all there is. There's no mystery. The only crazy thing I did is never say no to anyone. People aren't coming here to pray. They're here because we have heat. And nowhere else will take them."

"That's going to break my dreams?"

"It's easier if I'm a wizard, right?" he said. "There's food here and warmth. And if a kid ties off, that's his business." He took another sip and handed it to me. I recognized the gesture as one of my own. When I wanted someone to understand, I'd let them taste whatever I was tasting. "I never said no to anybody. And there were some rough boys. But put a rough boy in the system, pissing dirty, you wind up with a neutron bomb of a man. I say yes to everyone."

"What about the warriors, fighting in your name?" Meander said. "Or do I have you confused with a different Father Compost."

"I'm the man who keeps the lights on," Compost said, his hands shaking. "What money I have goes to pay the bills. Everywhere else, they charge you something. May not be cash, but it's something. You have to stare at a picture of Christ to eat their beef stew. You have to toss your weed. I let them stay fucked as they want."

"If a serial rapist comes here, would you turn him away?" Thomas said. "What happens when someone waltzes in with a gun?"

"Then they come in with a gun." Compost offered me the wine, but he reconsidered and took another drink. "You think we haven't got stuck up before? Each day, we lose a little of what we have, and we don't stay safe. I teach that from the start."

"You're talking like a father, Father," Meander said. "I like you better when you talk like a landlord. And I fucking hate landlords."

"You ever teach anybody anything?" Compost said, sizing up Meander. "People teach themselves. Someone plays grab ass with the girls, no one will talk to him, and he usually leaves on his own."

"Usually?" Thomas asked. "Otto was the unusual one."

Compost nodded.

"It must've been bad," Meander said. "He hasn't been here since this afternoon."

"Tell one person no, this becomes a soup kitchen, something smaller than a place of wisdom," Compost said. "Anyway, with him, his only weapon is his talk. He finds people's weaknesses like electricity finds the ground, and his goal is always the same."

"What's that?"

Father Compost cocked his finger like it was a pistol, put it in his mouth, then bucked his head back.

"Talking doesn't lead to suicide," I said. "We heard something about poison."

"He drinks it with people," Compost said. "Says he's immune. People survive, but it takes a bitch of a toll. One girl went blind. A boy bit off half his tongue." He smiled and looked at Meander. "You ever heard of Overtoun Bridge?"

We heard a crash behind us and then a prolonged rattle, like the sound of a top of a trashcan smacking against the floor. "Hey," a woman shouted. "We need help here."

"You're a landlord," Meander said. "Check on your investment."

As soon as he was clear of the room, Meander signaled for us to come closer. "We're not safe here," he whispered. His eyes were red, and for a second I thought he would cry. "I know where Otto is, but can we please go now please."

When Meander Casey and I were eight years old, I ran into him whipping sticks at old gravestones in Lexington Cemetery. A vicious thunderstorm had uprooted small poplars and tilted big oaks, leaving the graveyard littered with branches of all sizes. He'd been crying, and his sleeve was full of snot, but he wouldn't stop to explain. Instead, he'd pick up a stick and snap it over a headstone. Because he was my friend, I joined him, and by sunset, our hands were so full of splinters, we couldn't make fists.

All he told me was his granny took him to church. A few days later, his mom moved out and was gone until the early spring before changing her mind. I've re-tuned the strings on that memory many times, trying to understand his pain. As I grew older, I no longer thought it was about his mother, but about his granny's church. She taught him about a peace beyond understanding, of mysterious ways, fates, unknowable plans, of destructions, and resurrections, and inevitabilities. That was heresy to Meander. He believed actions had reactions, and he didn't trust what he couldn't control. When he whipped the sticks against the headstones that day, he was channeling pain, but also rebellion. He stood against anything that could destroy a person. Against God. Against rain. Against time.

9.

Meander's hands were shaking, so we stopped to have a beer. He wouldn't look at us, only at his glass. Almost below our hearing, he muttered how it all made sense to him. "I promise you this is true," he said. "What am I saying? The fact that I'm talking means it's not true." He brought his head up. "Let me just say this, and don't call me a liar. You're not going to believe it, but believe anyway. Call it a fable if it helps."

No one has figured out Overtoun Bridge in Scotland, he said. It's a Gothic stone structure overrun with vines and fog. Altogether, it looks the way that cartoons taught Kentuckians to picture Europe. The way he described the bridge, I saw knights jousting, young couples walking arm and elbow in the shade of the shrubs, maybe even a monster beneath it, trying to climb one of the piers.

What separates Overtoun Bridge in Scotland from all other places on earth is that, for no reason, the scientific world has identified, hundreds of dogs commit suicide there every year. It's a fifty-foot drop onto a shallow river covering a bed of rocks. A few dogs survive, and when their bones have healed, almost all of them run back to the bridge and try again. No other bridge in the world has had more than two dogs jump off within a five-year period.

These are the tall tales you sometimes hear around the radio station. This is the same neighborhood where the stories of shroomed-up babysitters putting toddlers in the oven and plunking the turkey in front of the TV live.

The Overtoun Bridge story was legend among the Lexington street rats. What sounded to me like middle-school swap talk was uncontested gospel to them. No one knew for sure how it started, but Meander pinned it to the death of Kyle Reese. Kyle was a dedicated runaway, a little quicker to punch his way out of a conversation than most street people. Whenever he got high, he entertained himself by sprinting back and forth over the Shadowtown Reservoir. Shadowtown was a two-block stretch of abandoned factories that used to manufacture mason jars, but now manufactures shadows.

Kyle Reese took a header into the reservoir. At the edge of Shadowtown, there was a rusted footbridge, overlooking a rocky stretch of water, and Kyle hopped over the guardrail and dropped face-first, without even putting his hands up to shield his fall. This was back when the factory was still working at half capacity, and so was the newspaper. That, Meander said, is the only reason we know Kyle Reese's name. The paper called it a suicide, but the street kids who knew him called it something closer to mania. He'd heard some inaudible song, got the scripture from an invisible Bible, and fulfilled his prophecy forehead first.

That's when the Overtoun story started spreading. Kyle Reese—Lexington's mad stray—chases an unseen rabbit over the bridge. The kids on the street spread it until it became a code. If you knew what Overtoun Bridge meant, then you spoke the language. That's how it passed from year to year, the slang sticking like a virus.

The story would have died except, according to Meander, Kyle Reese wasn't the only one. It happened almost yearly, he said, sometimes more. By that time, the factory closed and the paper practically became a leaflet, so it largely went unnoticed, but homeless kids were killing themselves. Worse, as far as anyone could tell, they leapt from the same spot. A quick hop off Shadowtown Reservoir, and then they became slaves to the water.

"There're three-and-a-half kinds of homeless," Meander said. "Runaways you know about. Then the hardcore winos who get behind on the bills, and then the soldiers back from war. Half is the overlap—the runaway winos who can't make it home."

A girl in the corner slipped and fell into the jukebox. I expected it to change the song, but instead she slid down slowly, almost gracefully. It felt like the perfect dance for the background of our conversation—there's probably one for every story.

"People die all over," Meander said. "But back then, the only ones who die at the reservoir are the runaways. When I was outdoors, I wouldn't go near Shadowtown. They heard something. Maybe staying away kept me safe from the dog whistle."

I reached for my beer and saw that my hand shook just as much as his. We were sharing emotions again like we'd done when we were teenagers.

"There were stories," Meander said. "Most thought the simplest explanation's the best one. Reservoir's the most convenient place to kill yourself. But I heard stories about some—I don't know—*helper*. A helper who pushed people. He didn't kill them exactly—I shouldn't have said 'pushed.' But he talked them over. They said in one hour, he could break a man. After that, a gentle breeze could put them over the ledge."

"And you think that's Otto?" Thomas said.

"I didn't think it's anybody," Meander said. "It's a story. Most who believed it, figured it's Compost." He put his palm over the top of his pint glass. "But it's more and more of them. There's been four jumpers last year. Two runaways, a wino, and a soldier. It's growing."

"So what's new?" I asked. "Back in style?"

"I still talk to people," Meander said. "Paper's gone, but I read the police report when I'm at the radio with you. Something's changed in the last year, the year that Otto's on the street." He coughed and wiped his eyes. "We've seen this kid around stories. What if he heard the story and wanted to make it true? Make it about him?"

"That's an awful lot of presumption," I said.

"Remember Mayhew?" he said. "He said 'Dog-boy.' Said Otto thought he was spying. Doing what? Didn't mean anything to me at the time. The prayer people in the front said he had fleas, and girls call him 'Fang.' That's all part of the story. They said it has to be a dog—half-dog who can embody the Overtoun Bridge secret."

"You're stretching," I said.

Meander shrugged. "Something's happening. Four dead in the last eight months, all in the same spot. That's not counting the people who survive with a busted leg. Someone's whispering to these people. What do you think it is?"

"This is what Compost meant." Thomas threw a twenty-dollar bill to the bartender and drained his glass. "The thing that's going to break our hearts. We're scared of simple answers. You get sold on the mystery of what's causing the kids to jump like Scottish dogs? It's a curse, the work of a half-dog Grim Reaper. It can't be that kids in danger don't all make it home. What magic words is Father Compost whispering to these kids to lure him into his cult? It can't be the magic of heat when it's cold outside."

I admired Thomas. He always turned people into

latches and keys. They were tools, answers, and nothing else. It was an efficient worldview, and I wanted very much to share it. But I live in the in-between, the nonsense world, the part where people are charmed and discarded for no reason at all. I see the dogs and the runaways and the preachers naming themselves for garbage peopling the same nothing-world as the Cyclops and the Elves and the Werewolves of my childhood goodnight stories. I have as much faith in imagination as I do in the vegetable world. Why are we so quick to throw away the impossible?

"There's something you should know," Meander said, leaning in and gathering us both together in his arms. "They said it was minks. I looked up what it was at Overtoun, and the closest anyone can guess is it smells like minks. Dogs see with their nose, and in this one spot, the stench of minks makes them leap."

"What's that mean?" I asked.

"Either that Scottish people make up dumb shit when they don't understand something, or we've been following the wrong animal all along."

The Shadowtown Reservoir was made with concrete slabs that didn't fit together. Yellow patches of grass stuck up between the edges as if the earth gave up halfway through its attempt to retake the neighborhood. I could see the future here—we all could. Money would overrun Shadowtown and turn it into a mini-mall. This was an empty space, a forgotten chunk of land, but nothing stays hidden from money. It might not be plastic houses like on Prospect, but maybe chain restaurants and well-lit bars.

Otto was sitting splay-legged, his back to the water, so he could see us approach. If he wanted to hide, then there's no way we could find him, but he wasn't scared of us.

I sat across from him, nodded, lit a cigarette and offered him one as well. He took one from me and kept it in his fingers. He wasn't looking at me, but behind me. At Thomas, I realized, a beat too late.

"This all you got?" he said. "You're handing out cigarettes this morning and now again. That your answer for everything?"

"We talked to your mom," I said.

"Lucky you." He kept his eyes fixed on Thomas, but he leaned in to light his smoke off my flame. "She's a sick person, and she'll remember everything that ever happened to her." He chewed on his upper lip. "Me too. On both counts."

"That means you remember us?" I said.

He shrugged and ducked his head. The second he took his eyes off Thomas, he looked young again—not like a boy, but like a painting of a boy. "Compost says it happened to somebody else. If you believe we're built up by molecules the way most people do, then you have to accept that people change. Not like spiritual change, but actually become a different person."

"Just goes to show," Meander said. "If you're smart enough, you don't even have to go to high school to sound like a high school philosophy major."

"When he explained it, it sounded true, but I don't know." Otto looked like he would keel over from weariness. "Molecules travel, hopping from person to person. It happens in skin and mind both, so we become the same person just by standing beside each other. Every three years, you've gone through an entire new body."

"I preferred you as an eleven-year-old," Meander said.

"So did he," Otto said, nodding to Thomas. He wiped his eyes with his free hand and laughed. "Christ, I don't even know if I'm kidding or not. Maybe I prefer me as an eleven-year-old too. But that theory makes me happy. Out here, there's nothing true or false, only what makes you happy."

"We saw the Father," Meander said. "Heard about you from him."

"Which one are you?" he asked Meander. "Hallahan? Vargas?"

"Hallahan is eight inches taller than me and Irish," Meander said. "And Vargas doesn't exist."

"I remember you," Otto said, pointing a half-bent finger at me. "You'd do whip-its and talk about Nightwolf until you passed out in the corner." To Thomas, he said, "And you. I believe we've met."

"You've met a lot of people," Meander said. "In the last week, we heard you called every adjective that could conceivably end in 'fucker', but nobody said you weren't sociable."

Thomas put his hands up, and his voice was pure reconciliation. "We don't want to fight. Tomorrow night, you can post up here again. But tonight, get in the car, and let us take you to your mother because right now, she's very sick."

Otto laughed, tinny and pathetic at first, but then loud, cracked and dry, a hysterical wheeze. "You see it now, right? 'You need to get in my car. I'm friends with your mother.' Now, after all this time, you approach me like proper child molesters."

"Is that really what you think happened?" I said. "I never heard it from you."

"Oh no, Mr. Nightwolf," Otto said. "Nothing happened to me at all, no sir. Maybe something happened to those molecules six years ago, but I'm a whole new man."

"Overtoun Bridge," Meander said. "Did you talk people into jumping?"

"I saw some jump," Otto said. "I didn't talk them out of it apparently."

"People are scared of you," Thomas said. "Is that what you want to be? Even Father Compost, who's probably seen more shit than a sewage plant, he's terrified."

"You're friends with Compost?" Otto licked the side of his lips. "Men like you build up children in their own image. Because I knew you, I was ready for him."

"Men like me?" Thomas said.

Otto laughed, and when his voice broke form, he sounded happy. "To be honest, I always wanted to kill Compost. Not kill him, but be there when he dies. All you teachers are Pied Pipers, recruiting a new children's crusade."

"Pied Piper used a flute," I said. "They say you use rat poison. All things being equal, I'd rather face off against a flute."

"Please." Otto reached into his waistband, pulled out a small bottle, and waggled it in front of us. "It doesn't just work on rats."

"You made people drink that shit," I said. "And you talked them off that bridge."

I saw a drop of blood on the edge of his lips. "How do I do that? People have been coming here since Jesus times, doing whatever they want. Do I look like a fighter? Some days I can't stand up without a blinding headache, and you think I'm going to shove somebody off a bridge."

"So they come here, meet you, and poison themselves?"

"I talk," he said. "If truth is scary, then I'm sorry, but I don't have to comfort you. Once upon a time, I was the kid in your game. Now I'm the one who shelters you."

For the first time, I noticed a couple sleeping about a hundred yards from me in the dark. I saw another shadow in the scraggly trees and stumps on the edge of the lot. I'd thought we were alone. Thomas and Meander already had their arms clinched around their chests.

"I listen to people," Otto said. "I tell them what they want, what they've always known about themselves. No one should be scared of me." He unscrewed the top of his bottle. "This is just a tool, same as a hammer or a hoe."

"All right," Thomas said. "But you're not operating on gardens or wooden boards. It's people who drink this."

"It won't kill you," he said. "Not if you're strong." He caressed the plastic bottle and held it up to his eyes. "This shows you there's another side, a place that's irreversible. Once you've seen it, you can't pretend it doesn't exist."

I saw another person in the shadows, except this time he was walking toward us. He just wants my cigarettes, I told myself.

"I'm dead, you know," Otto said. "My stomach is dissolving. I taste it when I swallow. There's no cure for me. What I have left is what I always had—the endgame. It makes me aliver than I have a right to be."

"Alive as the other people you run up against?" I said. "Why do they jump?"

"Some see it as a rite of passage. You're never sure if you're part of the street or just visiting. One trip out here, and you're no tourist. Almost everyone survives if they want to—that's the point. I help them see the other side. Most don't cross, but they live close to the line."

"This is simple," I said. "We want to take you home and show you to your mother. We'll pay you for your time."

"I'm okay on money," Otto said. "Maybe some of these guys will take a little off your hands if you're giving it away."

Two of the lurkers were almost to the edge of the light. I didn't know how many of them were coming.

"Do you remember Roxy and Monroe Leckett?" I asked. "The wild kids who stayed at the Ark."

"I remember the Ark."

"They talked a lot of the same stuff you're talking." My fingers were aching cold, and I had a hard time grasping my cigarette. "But it's not the same. They had this idea of us all being dead, of it all being behind us." I gestured around the parking lot. "This was our reward.

There's freedom in having died, they told me." I took a long puff. "What you preach is pretty much the opposite. Get as close to the line as possible. Life is for the leaving. It's a colder philosophy."

"Look at me," he said. "I'm a bucket of disease. You think anyone wants my philosophies? They come to me to feel something, usually what they fear most about themselves. You did too."

"I did what?"

"I remember the Ark kids," Otto said. "And it's a pretty enough story, but did you ever do anything about it? Did you ever alter your behavior in any way? You're trying not to change, trying not to feel. That's not me."

"That's not what Father Compost told us," Thomas said.

"Compost is a pussy," Otto said. "Just a lot of talk, and at the end of the night, nothing changes. We're still sleeping on his floor, eating his leftovers, shining up his dick. Y'all come to scoop me up, but how do I know you're anything more than him? Prove to me you're something better."

"How do we do that?"

He held up his rat poison. "Price of admission."

"No," I said.

"It doesn't have to be all of you," he said. "Just one. Down the hatch, one time, and I'll go wherever you want."

I looked back at Thomas and Meander. We were all so cold just then, desperate to get indoors. These kids must be feeling it every waking hour. It doesn't end, this time on the street. It's one endless drop.

"Your mother pointed a gun at us," Meander said. "You want us to drink poison. Give me one reason why we shouldn't run in the opposite direction."

"Is my life better for meeting you?" Otto said. "You're not here to help me—you're here because you shit your pants. You want to be safe, and I'm telling you that will never happen. You want me in your car, then I've told you what it costs. It won't bother me if you three disappear from my life forever. Not at all."

"I'll do it," Thomas said. "I'll drink."

"Now why would you do that?" Otto asked. "Feeling guilty, neighbor?"

Thomas shook his head. "I don't feel anything. Haven't for a long time."

This was his confession. He wasn't confessing to molesting Otto—he didn't think he'd done that. But he hadn't cared enough, not when it mattered. He let people blend together, and didn't care enough to see who they were. After years of pumping in more noise, chasing more highs, it became impossible to see a child who needs help. Now Thomas couldn't feel, and Otto felt too much. Only pain can bridge that gap.

Otto Larkin passed the rat poison to Thomas. Without thinking, I stepped up and snatched it from his hand. "I'll do it," I said. "You don't need anyone else."

I had made a choice. Bonnie Larkin hated me worse than Thomas because I made a conscious sin, a daylight sin. I heard the warnings, weighed the options, and followed him anyway. Bonnie would want me to drink it. We all ignored Otto, but I did it by choice.

"It won't kill you," Otto said. "Not if you're strong."

I nodded and put the bottle to my lips. Otto put his hand gently on the back of mine and tilted it up. The poison streamed into my mouth. I held it in my cheeks for as long as I could, but he clamped my head in place, not letting me turn and spit.

"Rookie mistake," he said, and his voice sounded like it did on Prospect Hill. "Holding it's worse for you than swallowing."

I could feel myself starting to heave. It tasted like ammonia and razorblades and it crept from the back of my throat into my nose. My vision blurred. Do it quickly, I thought, do it now, and it'll be over forever. The bridge was never an option for me, but I could understand. The world demands speed and courage—not my consent. I closed my eyes and swallowed.

10.

Most kids survive the bridge. The fall's not worse than a ladder and a half, and unless Kentucky's in a dry month, there's a buffer between you and the stones below. There's also danger when it rains too much. Those nights, kids see the reservoir as a swimming pool and dive in headfirst. At that point, they're at the mercy of the water. It can spit them back to the surface or drag them down to the God-knows and hold them until their ghost escapes.

Most kids survive the bridge, though not all the way. Arms are broken; heads are busted. One boy jarred his kneecap loose and it hung in his leg like a softball in pantyhose. That doesn't count the concussions and busted teeth and ruptured kidneys. Wild children prune their lives to the stumps simply because nobody can stop them.

And, of course, some do not survive. Other vagrants fish the bodies out and go through their pockets. When the cops find them, they write it up as drugs or robbery.

Otto Larkin told us this from the back of Thomas the Prophet's Studebaker. I rode shotgun, dry-heaving into an empty KFC bucket that smelled like salt and coleslaw.

The poison lingered in my mouth, coating my tongue.

"I thought about asking you to do the bridge," Otto said. "Might've talked you into it, but that ain't me. These tools, they're only there for those who want them."

The dark outside felt like a presence—a wet, warm washcloth. It was reaching into my mouth and down my throat. "Pull over," I said. "I can't make it."

"Go in the bucket," Meander said. "We'll throw it in a fraternity yard when we get up Prospect."

I shook my head, making it worse. "No, I need to put my feet on the ground. Pull over for a second. I need it to be still."

I puked in the KFC bucket the second I got outside. For a long second, I tasted the poison all over again. When it was over, I could barely stand.

"I told you it wouldn't kill you," Otto said, placing his hand on the back of my shoulder. It felt soothing, even more than the fresh air. "You been drinking tonight. The drinkers yak that shit right up, usually before they swallow." Otto laughed. "I can't throw up no more even if I stick my whole hand down my throat."

"You don't eat enough," Thomas said.

"Just the sort of neighborly advice I wanted," Otto said to Thomas. "I knew you'd circle back into my life because you didn't ruin it enough last time. Human nature hates an unfinished rhyme, and you hadn't finished me."

"I didn't touch you," Thomas said. "I've never touched a boy like that."

"Do you remember?" Otto said. "Do I? Neither of us can be certain, but that's the point. That's why I say it different every time. Sometimes it happened, sometimes it didn't. It feels more truthful than what you say. If we're being honest, you and I both have to live in that doubt for the rest of our lives. It'll never get comfortable."

I tried throwing up again, but I was dry. It was progress.

"Division is the easiest ways to deal with trauma," Otto said to Thomas. "Say you don't remember, say it wasn't you. That's not a luxury your friend here has. Once you drink that shit, there's no division, no doubt who you are. There's no starting over, just one painful purge."

"What's this gotten you?" Thomas said. "What's it gotten any of us?"

"Let me save you some worry," Otto said. "You're not the villain in my life. We were pre-determined to meet here, exactly as we are today."

"I wouldn't have guessed you're one of those assholes," Meander said. "Pre-determinism, I mean. Obviously, I knew you were an asshole."

"You would always find me because you think I have answers," he said. "And I do have some. I know the Night-wolf."

I stood up.

"Now he's listening," Otto said. "Every night back then, you got babbling drunk and say you were going to catch him."

"I didn't talk about him that much."

The other three looked at me.

"What took you so long?" Otto said. "When those fake Nightwolf tags came up a couple days ago, I knew you'd be around. Did you even ask him?"

"Ask who?"

"Father Compost," he said, laughing. "You had to ask. He knows everything."

"I don't understand."

"I used to think you meant it," he said. "That you'd find Nightwolf, hell or high water. It was your brother, you said, or a friend of your brother."

But it's not him, I thought. Compost is too old, and his head's the wrong shape.

"He knew him," Otto said. "That's what he told us anyway. But he'll tell you a different story every day so long as he's in the shop. If you want to pin him to the truth, you have to follow him home."

"That's not my brother," I said. "Aaron was taller, his eyes rounder."

"No one's your brother," Otto said. "Compost could've answered all your questions years ago. But you didn't want them answered, did you?"

Thomas the Prophet stepped between us and put his hand on my shoulder.

"Outside of the shop, The Father is a different person," Otto said. "Guy's more full of bullshit than a bull, but if you surprise him, he'll tell you the truth. He knows everyone who's ever been on cardboard." He pointed to me. "Does that sound like the sort of man who could help you?"

It felt pathetic: my unsolved mystery, his dime store philosophizing, our scramble to protect Thomas. We sounded like kids who refused to put away our toys. Except it wasn't make-believe. I did have a brother as real to me as Santa Claus, a woman who threatened to lodge a bullet in my brain, and a tongue numb with rat poison. Maybe this was the adult world—the same games, except now the toys can kill you.

"Compost's just another preacher," Otto said. "He surrounds himself with miserable people and demands they give him 'glory.' I don't know what glory is, but con artists have a heavy appetite for it." He held up the tin of rat poison. "My goal was to make him drink. I wanted to talk him off the bridge, see if I could convince him to fly. He tells so many stories that I wanted him to feel something honest, unexplainable."

"I can explain it." I spit on the ground. "It tastes like shit."

We drove to Bonnie's house and parked on the far side

of the street. I expected Otto to shrink in the shadow of the yard, but he seemed composed. Thomas, on the other hand, looked as terrified as if he'd run into his parents at an orgy. "This neighborhood," he whispered. "This whole place has gone to hell."

"How do you want to do this?" I said to Otto. "You want to go by yourself, or you want us to come?"

"All things being equal," Thomas said, "I might wait outside for this one."

Otto looked around the car. "I don't want to go alone," he said. "Without you all to back up my story, she won't believe me."

I knew that fear, maybe better than he did. "She won't believe me," he said, but he meant, "She won't recognize me." Every night I came home to my mother, I came home to that. I wanted others around, so when she stared at me blankly, I'd at least know who I was. The difference is that he stopped going home. Maybe that was the humane choice, the one my brother made.

"You'll tell her I'm happy, right?" Otto said. "Because I am happy, happy as I ever was."

The door was unlocked, and after nobody answered our knocks, Otto, Meander, and I walked inside. Otto sat in a rickety chair just inside the door that was littered with junk mail. He looked at his own pictures and his old jackets hanging on the hooks. The house was growing, and he was shrinking. "It's okay," Meander said. "We'll find her."

None of us called her name. It may have woken her, but it felt rude to bust the silence. If she was dreaming, I thought, let's give her a dollop more of time.

The kitchen table was covered in takeout menus. There were blankets on the floor that had recently been Fabreezed, but she wasn't there.

"Fuck," Meander said, pointing to the ajar back door. "Did we pick the one night she decided to go out?"

"Do you think she's looking for us?" I cocked my

finger like a gun. "We have a couple days."

He shook his head and wiped his brow with the back of his sleeve. "Maybe I ought to tell Thomas to drive around the block a few times."

It'd be too much, I thought as I heard Meander slam the front door behind him. She coughs herself awake, figures out which way is outside, and despite having no earthly clue where to find her prey, she sees him in front of her house. That would be quite a turnaround on God's part to suddenly love her. Still, bad luck felt close.

I noticed a small door to the side with a rainbow-colored bedsheet strung across the top ledge. I opened it up, expecting to find a closet, but instead saw a thin carpeted stairway leading up. It looked like it belonged to a different house entirely, but such was the charm of these evaporating old buildings of Prospect. They were built like a Jenga set, somehow staying upright. You could often find an unfinished staircase or a door that led to nowhere.

I walked upstairs. This was either a bedroom or an attic space. It smelled like what would happen if baby powder could rot. I flipped on the light. The window was cracked into a spiderweb of glass, showing a million different Prospect Hills, all of them empty. I tried to open it, thinking maybe I could see The Ark, but it was jammed.

I turned around and saw Bonnie crumpled in the corner. Really, I just saw the curve of her ankle, the only part of her visible under a linen sheet, but I knew she was dead. I flung the sheet off of her, and she rolled over. A flash of hope sparked and then fizzled when I saw it was the momentum of the sheet that moved her body. Her shirt was off, and there was bile coming out of her mouth.

I checked her pulse before realizing I wasn't sure how to check a pulse. I'd seen it on TV, and they can tell within a nanosecond, but to me, it just felt like a turkey neck. Her eyes were cracked open, but as lifeless as green marbles. A note fell to the ground.

I was the one who found my mother. It was the Monday after a weekend I hadn't come home. I'd just bought her a one-button radio, and I planned to make a presentation of it. Even at her sickest, she got excited at gifts. She was on her chair, her eyes open but rolled back. She had thrown up, and it had crusted on her neck and breastbone. Later, they told me it was a peaceful death, like I was a child and still believed in such things. While I waited for the ambulance, I stared at her, face to face, our noses no more than an inch apart. I could only smell her medicine and her medicine's failure.

I set Bonnie Larkin back on the ground. Her hair was stuck to the side of her face and onto the corners of her mouth. I unfolded the note. In clunky block letters, it said, "It was so nice to meet most of you." There was more, but I heard a noise and shoved the note in the front of my pants.

"Are you okay?" Meander said. "You yelled."

No I didn't, I thought, but I must have.

"Did you wake her?"

"I can't."

"What is she—?" He put a hand on his head and made a noise like he was spitting up sandpaper. "Is it over?"

I stood and tried to block his view. "Where's Otto?"

Before he could answer, I heard a noise coming from the downstairs. I yelled, I thought. It must have signaled everybody. Meander put his body in front of the door.

"Let me get a shirt on her," I said.

"Why'd you take her shirt off?"

I threw the blanket on top of her and went to Meander. Neither of us wanted to tell Otto, but we couldn't let him see for himself. When I stood in the doorway, I saw him at the bottom of the stairs. It wasn't the young Otto, not the one on the pictures on the wall or the one slowly being yanked from our imagination, but he still had curiosity in his face. That wouldn't last. Once he saw, that would be over.

"Stay put," Meander shouted.

Otto walked up the stairs. With every step, his face darkened. We were the last buffers between Otto and the rest of his life. Because I blocked his view, I was the only shape in this world keeping him happy.

11.

We stayed with Bonnie until the first responders came. It looked like a makeshift séance, us speaking around the dead, looking at her without looking at her. This is how the homeless gather as well. They can't afford the challenge of staring into one another's face straight on. No wonder so many of them believe in ghosts. It's what takes the place of people.

Thomas first told us not to drink. He said it would seem profane to treat her body like a coaster. Just then, he heard himself sound like the country preachers of his youth, and he changed his mind. It's hard to stay within a yard of the dead and not think they'll sit up, lick their teeth, and say hello. Thomas went downstairs and opened Bonnie's last bottle of gin. We passed it to each other, drinking in silence. The dead demanded our scheming. No one has ever lived a life so meaningless they don't deserve someone to lie about them and show them respect.

In the end, we told everything. When the police asked us what happened, we kept yammering and yammering until the story was complete. None of us planned on it, but we couldn't stop talking.

Meander told about our quest to save Thomas. I told about Bonnie pointing a gun in our faces. Both of us told about me drinking Otto's poison concoction. They looked at us with a sincere, pleading expression that said, "Dear God, we don't care." But we repeated it and repeated it until the words became simple sounds, as articulate as a gong.

And that was the end. When we walked outside, we thought we could shake off the night like a dog shakes off water. But the press picked up the story. Meander and I weren't named. Otto was only called "her son." Thomas, on the other hand, paid for his newfound good name. They focused on the gin. Tom Mercer drank gin on top of a woman's cadaver. It wasn't a crime, they implied, only a sin.

That Friday, I clipped on my tie and dragged myself to Thomas the Prophet's reception. It was a small crowd, well-dressed and embarrassed to speak above a whisper. No one mentioned Bonnie Larkin or our sad toast, but it was on the partygoers' minds. I heard it in the way they strained for another topic, any polite conversation.

Thomas was coated in three layers of sweat. People approached him and shook his hand, and he accepted their well-wishes with the ease of a hostage. At every opportunity, he looked for a corner. I finally had a chance to say hello, and he grabbed me by the elbow like a middle-schooler impersonating a politician. "Hey, thanks for coming," he said. It didn't seem like he fully recognized me.

I went outside to search for my friends. But it was dark, and I was cold, so I started to leave. Just then, someone tugged at my shirt. It was Shea Stanford with a fresh cigarette in her mouth. I gave her a light and stood beside her.

"I don't want to jinx you," she said. "But I think you may have topped yourself."

"What do you think we did?"

"Don't know," she said. "But what it looks like from here is you acted as grand marshal for yet another feces parade."

"We drank her gin." I plucked the cigarette from her mouth and took a puff. "We didn't smash it on her body and lift her around on a chair like a Jewish wedding."

"I don't think they do that at Jewish weddings," Shea said. "There's pretty much no role for a corpse."

Another two partygoers walked past, staring at me all the way.

"I thought this was different," I said. "I really thought we could do good this time. Now we have nothing. Just wall-to-wall emptiness."

"How can emptiness fill a wall?"

I lit a smoke of my own. "I drank poison for him," I said. "It tore up my stomach as bad as if I swallowed a live porcupine, but I did it. Do you see what I'm saying?"

"I want to."

"I think about Prospect, our time up there," I said. "It felt crucial, like it would stick with me forever, and now it's like last night's dream."

"You mean Aaron?"

"I mean everyone," I said. "None of us are as good as we used to be. But I still would put my body in front of a truck for any Prospect kid. It's not even that I love them, but I love my own memories, and I need to save them." I could feel her disappointment creeping on my skin. "You're right, it's not noble—all I did was interfere and make it worse. The only way I know how to be good ruins everyone's life."

"Grow up, Milo," she said. "Love is interference. It's the act of not letting go. It's why you didn't jump ship on Thomas back then. He could've let you go, but he didn't."

"Thomas?" I said. "They're going to kick his ass over this, aren't they?"

"Depends," she said. "It comes down to what the kid says."

"Otto." Just by speaking his name, I felt his mom's note in my back pocket. I wanted to ask Shea, but I didn't know how to phrase the question. Is it easier to believe that the dead died unwillingly? I held a secret, and I had no clue if I should keep it.

Otto talked. It fell short of an accusation, but he said why Bonnie Larkin hated Tom Mercer. The news kept it shadowy, only talking about "impropriety" and "wanton endangerment" but people filled in the blanks.

Nobody picketed his house or went full Egan Hopper on him, but whatever deal he had with my radio station dried up. His charities drifted away from him too. The few times I saw him in the weeks after Bonnie, he looked shell-shocked. This was him dying, I thought.

At night, I kept myself awake by reciting Otto's mother's note. "It was so nice to meet most of you. But right now, I...." It devolved into scribbles at that point, with only the word 'medicine' legible. At the very end, the note read, 'My ghost will not haunt you. I'll be as I am—BBL."

She didn't mention Otto. I studied the unreadable parts for any trace of his name, but the best I could do was one loop in the middle of a word that might pass as an O.

Otto disappeared again. Here's where the road split for me. On one hand, I wanted to find him to say that his mother didn't leave the world terrified, clinging to life. Instead she went bravely, with a fullness of heart. But bravery and a full heart are pointless when you're not here to use them.

A suicide is sadder. It shouldn't be, but it is. The fact that she didn't fear her death only means she no longer loved her life. Twice I had a chance to help.

I found myself parked outside Compost's flower shop, waiting for Otto. If I could see him and feel him out, I'd know what to do. A secret won't save the lost, but it was what I had.

But Otto never showed up. Maybe he made himself one poison cocktail too many. That bridge might have looked tempting, maybe irresistible. Otto knew the university would bulldoze Shadowtown. If he wanted to jump, he was running out of time.

On my day off, I decided to stay all night. I bought a six-pack and waited. Hours passed. The regulars came and went. Finally, I saw the back light flip off and a man walk into the parking lot. It was Father Compost, except that his hair had been cut to just below his ear and his beard was gone.

He got into a red Dodge Dart and drove off. I started my car and rolled down the road, trailing him by a headlight's length. Hartland, he told us in the backroom. I thought it was part of his con, but he hadn't lied about the Dart. Everyone I'd ever loved had lied to me—it was how they showed love. My mother died from the lies she told herself. Wouldn't it blow a hole in my mind if this was the guy who told me the truth?

Sure enough, he drove to Hartland, parked on the street, and walked to the end of a cul-de-sac. I chased after him and reached his yard right as he stepped into the glow of his porchlight. He stopped and put his hands on his hips. Without turning around, he said, "I know you're following me. You tailed me this whole way."

I tried to catch my breath. "I have to ask you something."

"If you want money, you'll be disappointed," he said. "If you want to hurt me, go ahead."

"Do you remember me?"

"I haven't looked at you yet." His voice sounded bigger, more expansive than in the room. Out here, stripped of all the people around him, I could understand his power. "Tell me why you're here before I look at you. It'll keep us both unharmed."

"I want to talk a second," I said. "We already met once."

He turned and looked at me the way a hawk looks at his supper. "Oh yeah, you," he said, his voice softening. "I'm sorry what happened. The second you left, I knew I should've said it more directly. That boy brings pain to all around him."

"His mom wasn't his fault."

"And I'm sure he'll tell himself that for a long, long time."

"Has he been back since then?"

Compost shook his head. "He's gone. And if you want to keep talking, you're going to have to do it inside."

The front room of his house was almost entirely empty and lit as brightly as a refrigerator with nothing but bare bulbs. Electricity was his art. In the light, I saw his hair was cut unevenly, his bangs curved up and down and up like an EKG reading. I expected the stale waft of cigarette smoke and jug wine, but it smelled like mothballs.

"Who found her?" he said. "You or your friends? Not the kid, right?"

"Me," I said. "I tried to keep Otto away, but he blew right past me."

"Better to see than imagine." He shook his head. "You know how many I've seen? It doesn't get easy, but it's still better to see it."

"What's that, just from being in the store, preaching your Fatherly transcendishness? I thought you offered heat."

"No one's died inside." It came out flat, like he'd lost enthusiasm for his best selling point. "I've watched when they fished out a runaway. A couple OD's, one hypothermia, years ago. Plus, in another life, I worked in a hospital."

"You were a doctor?"

He shook his head. "Accidental OD's are the easiest to look at, so long as their eyes don't bulge."

"Otto's mom's wasn't an accident," I said. "No one knows but me."

Compost pursed his lips. "That does complicate things," he said. "I try to be sympathetic, but this feels inevitable."

"What's that mean?" I said. "Saying suicide's inevitable is like saying there's no cure for Autoerotic Asphyxiation. It's a choice—maybe a series of choices."

"Maybe," he said. "But if this is the endpoint, why do we argue about the road?"

"You have a way of talking sometimes," I said. "It makes you sound like a cross between a fortune cookie and an asshole impersonating a fortune cookie."

"You followed me home," he said. "So tell me what you're here for or go."

I looked back to the door and caught my reflection in the glass. Part of me expected to see Prospect outside, to hear the Ark screaming, but all I saw was my red, un-angled face.

"I can't grant you spiritual power or forgiveness," he said. "That's yours to take or leave. And I'm not a nihilist who pretends this life is all atoms and assholes. I tell you that boy is intertwined with death simply because I understand cause and effect."

"Say his name. You haven't said it once. You don't say your name or mine."

"You don't listen," he said. "Cause and effect. Names are an artifact of the past, useless in what I do."

"I once knew a woman who had no use for the past," I said. "She tried to let it go. I discovered her body as well."

"Life's bruised you," he said. "When you speak, you wince with pain."

"It's a condition," I said. "A condition of being over ten years old."

"You came to me for advice."

"I want to help Otto," I said. "Is it better for him to think his mother made a mistake or killed herself?"

"Neither of those will help him. He'll never be well and neither will you—leave it at that and enjoy yourself."

I balled my fists. "That's—I'm sorry, that's a bullshit answer."

He tilted his head to tell me to follow him. The rest of his house wasn't a complete blank space like his front room, but it was oddly underused. It felt like a showroom, as though a slightly demented real estate agent set it up for an open house. There was a living room table, but it was stacked high with toothpaste tubes, contact lens solution and soap. There were pictures on the wall, but they were in the corners, one on top of another. One was a frame with nothing in it. His life was in the shop, and this was an imitation of the suburbs.

We walked through a kitchen that smelled like anchovies and garlic and moldy potatoes. I thought he was going to take me to his backyard, but he stopped short in front of a pantry. "I reckon you've seen your fair share of tragedy," he said. "More than most, you'd say?"

"I'm in the upper fifty percent."

"Do you know the first second when you see horror? Quicker than that, the first nanosecond? They say at that point, your mind splits. It can't take the reality of what it sees, so half the mind scatters, leaving the other half on the ground. Do you know that sort of tragedy? The type that leaves you aching, unable to form words?"

I nodded.

"When the mind splits, it instantly seeks unification," he said. "We say we want love, but really we want symmetry."

"Otto mentioned something about that," I said. "I think he did at least. He heard it from you?"

"In my office, you looked at my sneaker pile. Your

buddies didn't notice, but you did." He opened the pantry and another, smaller pile of shoes tumbled out of a tight space. "They were brought to me, taken off street kids who didn't make it. The ones who hopped off the bridge or who froze themselves into icicles. Seven years out here, I have eleven pairs and some unmatched. Doesn't represent half the people who died."

I squatted down and picked up a gray Adidas with yellow trim, the sole worn down to where I could pop it like bubble wrap with my fingernail. "You took all these?" The one in my hand was a woman's shoe. "You lie."

"They were brought to me," he said. "And I mourn for every one."

"I'd have heard about this," I said. "If bodies show up at the morgue shoeless, they'll think it's a serial killer or something."

He smiled at me like I was his infant grandson. "But you haven't heard of them, have you? Half didn't have shirts or belts either. The most sentimental street kid will remember your name as he's lifting your wallet."

I saw a blue Chuck Taylor with white laces and something handwritten in marker on the side. The words had faded to illegibility, but I could still see the curve of the tops of the letters. I brought the shoe close to my eyes and tried to blink the words into coherence. This was Aaron's size, I thought, unsure if it was true.

"I split them apart intentionally," he said. "As a reminder not to seek symmetry."

It was his handwriting. The curve was there, the wavy, block letters. "Do you remember Nightwolf?" I asked. "Crazy-ass tagger who hit town a few years ago?"

Father Compost smiled. "Otto told me about you. Said you had a theory on The Nightwolf. I'd love to hear it."

"That mean you don't know?"

"I don't," he said. "If he was one of ours, I'd know.

Kids brag when they get to the shop, and no one took credit. Some of the follow-up taggers, sure, but I figured Nightwolf had a home, a place to hide."

"You really don't know?"

"I wish I had better news," he said.

"I wanted it to be you," I said. "But you're too old." I pinched the shoe in my fingertips. "Do you know Aaron Byers? Has he ever been in your place? Even once?"

Father Compost shook his head. "I never heard the name. Doesn't mean he's not been in, but I don't know him. How long's he been homeless?"

"I don't know," I said. "He could be married by now or have hitchhiked to the Pacific Ocean." If it was his shoe, then I was older now than he'd ever been.

"You thought he was me?"

"It'd make sense," I said. "But you don't look like him, not really. And I know he never worked in a hospital."

"You say it would make sense. It doesn't sound like it."

"I know," I said. "But it does make sense. Aaron Byers, come on."

"Who's that?" he said. "Your friend? Brother? Your boyfriend?"

"Brother," I said. "I thought this was his." I let the shoe drop to the floor. "I guess it's better it's not."

"It may be," he said. "I don't know who this belonged to. What's he look like?"

"He was thin, I guess. I don't even remember. There was a time when I thought about him every day. And Mom couldn't remember, so I remembered twice as hard. I swore I'd think about him every hour, but now he's just a chin and eyebrows to me."

"The greatest lesson in life is forgetting," he said. "People think it's easy."

"I knew about the Compost Christians," I said. "I figured if he was anywhere, he'd be with you, but I never went to find out. I'm hearing myself say it, and I know why. I didn't want to have this conversation. If you don't know him, nobody does."

I heard the jarred open refrigerator buzz, and the bulb above us flicker on and off. We were not in a place that sold desperation

"Who's Otto to you?" he said. "If you wouldn't look for your brother, then who's Otto to drag you to my door?"

"A friend," I said. "Not really. But he's another one who got hurt."

"Be all right with that," Compost said. "That's about all I can tell you. Be okay with the mystery."

Just then, I wanted to stand beside my sadness, to pat it on the back like a friend. The point of searching is forgetting what you had. The point of finding is forgetting the search. One can't exist without the other.

"You asked me a lot of questions," he said. "The Nightwolf, your brother, your friend. Have I told you anything you didn't already know?"

I shook my head.

"But you're still here." A bare light bulb buzzed and then went silent. "You're still in this world where the night drips from the sky to the ground, where women and men call to you in different voices promising different adventures. This is the world of sex and weather and music and silence all together."

"Wait, there's sex and weather?"

"You're in the middle of a great storm, same as me. It'll pass no matter how hard we hold it. Don't waste this life looking for answers. Answers create a closed loop. You have a question, you find an answer. New question, new answer. That way, you only see what you're curious about, what you want to see. Instead of answers, find meaning. Answers are the trivia of life. You already know what you're meant to know."

I know my brother is out among the coyotes. If this is life, so be it. I pressed my fingertips together and sealed my eyes. Let my mysteries be quicker than me. Let me see them only from the corner of my eye when I'm unprepared. Let me live in the meantime, in the neutral ground where consciousness dissolves into sleep, reality into imagination. In place of knowing, let me feel the joy and nonsense of destruction, the joy and nonsense of creation.

The thaw continued, and within a week, we were back to jacket weather. I rededicated myself to my job, and after a night of that, I rededicated myself to drinking in public. Thomas, Meander, and I were the three stooges of the apocalypse, so I figured we'd be as welcome as a naked man at a Twister game, but no one recognized me.

Lexington is crowded in springtime, and it's easy to blend and heal. There's basketball on TV, and the wind cuts the heat before you can feel yourself sweat. There's noise from the campus, and the flowers smell sweet enough to break your concentration.

One night in Marimow's, I felt a familiar hand clap on my shoulder. "I thought we'd have to send an APB on you," Meander said. "I didn't think you were coming."

"Coming where?"

"Here," he said. "Dirk and Lina's thing. They'll be here any minute."

"Thing? They're still getting married, right?"

"Next week," he said. "They signed the certificate today. This is their dual bachelor/bachelorette party."

"At Marimow's?" I said. "Weddings don't make any sense."

"You don't have to understand," he said. "Even if you're here by accident, they'll be glad you're poking your head out of the ground a little."

And one by one, our friends filed in, surprised, but pleased to see me. First came Shea Stanford, then Harmony Dulles, staring at her ankles as always. The inside of Marimow's had changed. I only noticed it when my friends began filling up the place—it turned the familiar strange again. Jerry Marimow had taken out the old pictures of Kentucky history, of Republican Presidents, of pretty much everything. It had the charm of a post office, yet it felt like home. Next came Thomas the Prophet, looking like the losing prizefighter emerging from the locker room to meet the press. All he wanted to say was "I tried my best" and disappear. The remnants of Surrender Dorothy came in with Corey Casey tagging along. Up next were the bride and groom. Clearly, they waited outside for the bulk of the friends to arrive, so they could make an appearance, and it worked. The bar erupted into a roar.

I danced. It wasn't proper dancing—I've never been able to dance, and Jerry Marimow had removed the jukebox to drive away customers—but I rotated in my seat, bobbing to an imagined rhythm. This was happiness? I thought. Even glee came to me with a question mark.

Dirk Henson hailed from Texas, but he assimilated into my city better than I had. Lina was small and fast as an electric shock. She sang loud and sharp, and she gnawed her lips when she was confused. Dirk was quiet, softer. He grew his sideburns out to cut into his baby face, so I always thought of him as wearing a convincing costume. This was the fight against decay—these were the first of us to join it.

Later, well into the night, the bar became blurry. People kept stepping out for cigarettes, and when they came back, they brought new people inside until the bar seemed impossibly full.

Shea Stanford took my glass out of my hand and replaced it with a full beer. "This whole thing," she said, with a wave of her hand. "I'm glad it's over."

"That was a mess," I said. "That was a swastika made out of dicks."

She looked at me.

"As in, something bad crafted into something worse," I said. "Right, I get that dicks aren't inherently bad, and you're right. But I'm imagining them bending into a swastika, and it seems painful. A lot of sharp angles."

"I didn't actually ask for an explanation," she said.

Thomas walked by en route to the bathroom, barely noticing us. He'd kept an unconvincing smile welded to his face all night and nodded at his friends rather than speaking to them.

"Bless his heart," Shea said.

"I always thought 'bless his heart' was Appalachian for 'Fuck you.'"

"Bless your heart." Her gaze was fixed on Thomas. "Bless him too. All those sermons or anti-sermons he gave, and now he just looks stunned."

"How much of his life do you think stemmed from that one snakebite?" I worried about the poison, dormant for all those years, spreading up his arm and into the rest of him. If he didn't shake it off soon, he'd be more palsy than man. "What was he planning to do with all that good will?"

She shrugged. "Good will is fickle. Doesn't mean it's not worth pursuing."

In the crowd, I saw a stranger, moving toward the door: the thin man with the crooked nose who I gave the baby to that night six years ago. I swore it was him.

People file in and out of our lives. The man who took the baby—who appeared exactly when I needed him and vanished when I needed him gone—he would come before me again. They all would. We have one plane of vision and limited space.

The stranger walked by, and I reached for him. I tried to grab him by the shoulder, but at the last second held back and only my fingernails grazed him. He looked at me like a frog looks at a flashlight. He blinked twice, waiting for me to speak, and then walked away.

"Thomas's been singing from that same hymnal now for a long time." Shea took the beer from my hand and took a sip. "He thinks faith is all miracles and magic tricks."

"Miracles," I said. "What is a miracle, but a poorly told story? It's all setup and no punch line. How did the girl survive after falling down a well? How did the fortune-teller know you have a granny named Eulys who cooked pies with crabapples? If it's a miracle, we don't need to know."

"When you get drunk, you make everything seem small," she said. "And that's when you're in a good mood."

"It's not small," I said. "It's real. All these miracles have to come from somewhere, so why not us? I've seen it. I've seen it, and I can prove it."

She put her hand on my chest, on the opposite side of my heart.

"But it's real," I said. "Once I saved a baby from freezing to death in the back of a car. A boy, I think, but I don't remember. I was looking for Nightwolf when I saw him, and he'd have frozen if I hadn't saved him." I could feel the beer having its way with my tongue, but I powered on. "But that's not even the most miraculous. After I brought him to a fire station, he disappeared. Not like a filing error, I mean he actually vanished. No police report, nothing in the news. I forget about him about every day but this one, but I swear it happened right here, just like it happens every day everywhere, and we let it slip away. We let it slip away."

There's always a trapdoor under each finish line, spitting you into another darkened corner, another endless adventure. And we were not final. We could give thanks for that if nothing else. So long as we can recover, we remain as incomplete and hopeful as prayers.

Later, Shea and I split apart from the rest of the group.

We were both sleepy and sloppy, but we didn't want to let go of the night. We walked until we hit the small creek on the east side of Orman Park. The light poles are still there, but the bulbs burnt out years ago. Sometimes the high school kids went there to get high or dunk their feet in the water, but outside of their lighters, it stayed black except for the fireflies. The darker the night, the louder the water sounded.

When we were children, Shea and I would come there in the early nighttime, back when the night held meaning for us. We both had curfews—hers an hour later than mine—but when the trees were thick, this dock could lull us into believing we were in the darkest corner of Kentucky. Is there a black that goes beyond pitch? We don't imagine darkness coming in degrees, but there must be a shade of black that outpaces what we see when we close our eyes. There's cold comfort in that. When this world is taken from us, we still go on, maybe to something as familiar as the lack of light.

Shea sat down on the creek side. I wanted to reach for her, to press the back of my fingernails against the side of her neck and feel her slink away. When I remember it now, I imagine touching her is the way to halving the distance between where we were then and where we are now.

Grant me one more miracle. I didn't say it to her then, but I say it now to her absence almost every night. The unreal is always with us, in our muscles and our irises, so can't you indulge me one more miracle? Maybe one day we'll have to say goodbye to each other, maybe even say goodbye to the dark, but not yet.

One more miracle, please. I've torn through life, paying less attention to people than I have the shape people make when they leave. I've not been careful with who I love, who I trust, even who I remember, but I need you to stay with me. Take me back, in time or in space, and let's both be who we are not. It's ridiculous, but if miracles exist, it can happen. First, you must believe what you don't believe.

The two of us looked up at the sky. Between us, even the moonlight is an intruder.

I tell myself this story, any story, to prove we're still alive.

Acknowledgments

The character "Nightwolf" bears a glancing resemblance to the tagger "Borf" who stalked the greater Washington D.C. area in the mid-aughts. This book is fiction. The only intended similarity between Nightwolf and Borf is that both are taggers who gained a small amount of fame and notoriety through the volume of their work. Nevertheless, I found Libby Copeland's article "The Mark Of Borf" in *The Washington Post* to be intriguing, and at least tangentially helpful to fleshing out the character in my mind.

Thank you Leland Cheuk for your insight and the tremendous amount of work you did in improving this book. Thank you for your faith and your edits. You've made the story quicker, smarter, and at least 17% less mopey.

Semi-recognizable forms of these characters first appeared in stories published in *At Length*, *Hidden City Quarterly*, *Cleaver*, *Bridge Eight*, and *Pine Mountain Sand And Gravel*. Thank you to the editors and supporters of those magazines.

Thank you Kermit Moyer and the Creative Writing faculty at American University. Thank you Harvey Grossinger and the Creative Writing faculty at Johns Hopkins University. Thank you Maud Casey and the Creative Writing faculty at The University of Maryland.

Thank you to my colleagues and students at Kentucky State University.

Thank you to the Bread Loaf Writers Conference, particularly the 2010 Waiter class.

Thank you Tamara Coffey and the Kentucky Arts Council. Being named an Al Smith Fellow gave me the confidence to wrangle these characters into a book. The money that accompanied the fellowship allowed me to afford health insurance. Which also helped.

Thank you Gurney Norman for your work as both a writer and mentor. Your stories were the first that showed me that writing about Kentucky could be as complex and entertaining as work about anywhere else. In that way, it taught me to value my voice and my life.

Thank you Tony and Lavenia Baxter. Thank you to the Bell Court Kids, particularly Natalie Baxter, Josh Simpson, Cody and Jennifer Averbeck.

Thank you to my Godmother, Judi Jennings, who taught me how to dance and never apologized to all the people I danced with. Thank you to my Godfather, Nick Stump, who provided the soundtrack of my childhood.

Thank you Uncle Jimmy, Aunt Peggy, and anyone who's ever been a member of the Virginia Vultures, Tennessee Trash, Kentucky Feelers, or the Altered States.

The germ of this book started in a conversation over afternoon beers in a sunless bar with David Schankula. Thank you, David, for our occasional creative beer drinking sessions and our more common uncreative beer drinking sessions. (Also, for what it's worth, thanks for the decades of friendship). Thank you to Becky and Cardinal Schankula as well.

Thank you Liz, Nick, Steve, Steph, Michelle, Katie, Chris, Suzanne and all my friends from DC. Thank you to Noah, David, Jonas, and all my friends from Baltimore. Thank you to Deuce, Joe, Eryn, Jonathan, Eli, Seth, Marcie, Gary, The Trillbillies, Pilar, Leandra and all my friends from Kentucky. If you judge a man by his friends, then you're judgmental and should probably stop doing that. If you persist in judging a man by his friends, then you'd conclude I'm a far better person than I am.

I'm fortunate to come from a family that uses storytelling for entertainment, moral guidance, weaponry, self-defense, slander, lore, and as a simple spice when the truth needs more flavor. I can't imagine any other way to live. Thank you to my mother and stepfather. Thank you to my father and stepmother. Thank you to Clair, Keven, and Jack Widener. Thank you to all my family originally from Hazard, from Pittsburgh, from Palo Alto, and from Louisville who have now spread throughout the country.

Thank you to my brother Isaac Boone Davis, a brilliant writer who told me "Don't let the lick get in the way of the groove" before taking a blowtorch to an early draft of this book. He told me to work with the remains, and I'm so happy he did.

Rest well, Rob O'Neill. Rest well, David Otolara. It's been a decade since you've moved from our outer lives to our inner lives. We miss you, but I hope you've at least found a home there.

While I often roll my eyes at fiction with clear-cut heroes, I'd be dishonest if I didn't acknowledge that my life has two such characters: Bethany Baxter and Eliot Baxter Davis. Life means more when you two are close. Thank you both. I love you both. I love you all.

About the Author

Willie Davis's work has appeared in *The Guardian*, *Salon*, *The Kenyon Review*, *The Berkeley Fiction Review*, and *storySouth*. He is the winner of The Willesden Herald Short Story Prize (judged by Zadie Smith) and The Katherine Anne Porter Prize (judged by Amy Hempel). He received a Waiter Scholarship from The Bread Loaf Writers Conference and a fellowship from the Kentucky Arts Council. He teaches English at Kentucky State University.